Left   Right
Door   Door?

Left Right Door Door?

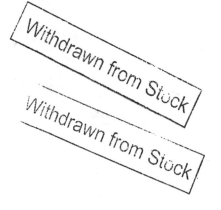

JESS C.

Matador
9 Priory Business Park,
Wistow Road, Kibworth Beauchamp,
Leicestershire. LE8 0RX
Tel: 0116 279 2299
Email: books@troubador.co.uk
Web: www.troubador.co.uk/matador
Twitter: @matadorbooks

ISBN 978 1 8004 6458 2

British Library Cataloguing in Publication Data.
A catalogue record for this book is available from the British Library.

Printed and bound in Great Britain by 4edge Limited
Typeset in 11pt Minion Pro by Troubador Publishing Ltd, Leicester, UK

Matador is an imprint of Troubador Publishing Ltd

To Rob, the singer
Thank you

One

Sophie swung her black 4x4 left off the busy main road, leaving the bright lights of the town, and drove up the long dark uneven narrow drive, and into the wide car park, parking under the security lights, avoiding the dark shadows where other cars were parked. She turned off the engine, sat in the semi-darkness and looked around. The car park was already almost full.

Sophie took her phone from her bag again to look at the advert that her son, Tom, had seen online and had sent her by email. She could remember it by heart. A list of all of September's evening events held at the local Maple Leaf Club.

Tonight the Maple Leaf was advertising:

THURSDAY
OPEN MIC CLUB or LATIN DANCE CLUB

She closed her phone and sat for a while, watching people get out of their cars, kissing hello and couples holding hands, laughing together, swinging their dance shoes as they happily made their way to the entrance of the club.

A few minutes later, a black Volvo was driven fast into the car park. It screeched to a halt, and three men jumped out. They took their guitars and amplifiers from the boot and disappeared quickly into the club.

The car park became quiet and still, with just the occasional coloured leaf being blown onto Sophie's windscreen by the autumn breeze.

In the corner of the car park, which was made darker by the dense overhanging trees, a tall lone figure dressed in black opened the door of his Saab. He stepped out and, leaning on his car, made a quick phone call. He looked towards Sophie as he walked past her 4x4 and strode away into the building, carrying his guitar over his shoulder.

Ummm, Sophie thought.

Sophie had recently divorced after being married for twenty-five years. She had been young and in love when she married Dave and blissfully happy, but in the last few years they had started to have intense arguments and, when they weren't arguing, Dave had barely spoken to her. Sophie and Dave didn't even have any interests which they could have shared at the weekends on the rare occasions when they were together, and Sophie was beginning to feel alone. She was always busy working long hours at her art shop, and although she spoke to customers during the day, she still found it difficult to find time to make many friends.

Sophie accepted that Dave had worked hard throughout their married life, often working through the night, and sometimes spending nights away from home, trying to keep his carpet cleaning company successful. She had suggested that she could work for him occasionally, even though it would have meant more pressure for her but, for some reason, he always rejected her offer.

Sophie thought that she had worked just as hard as Dave. She had had to give up her friends, social life and her job when they married. She had kept in touch with some of her friends for a while, but gradually they all moved on. Sophie had loved working at the Parade Art Gallery, meeting people and taking them around, explaining each painting, and she was devastated when she had to leave Shertsbourne and live in Timberry on Sea with Dave all those years ago.

So, after many discussions and arguments, they eventually sadly agreed to divorce.

Their only child, Tom, had left for Nottingham University at the same time as they had parted and it came as no surprise to him that they were planning to divorce, as Sophie and Dave were making life very difficult and unhappy for him as well. He never took any sides in the arguments; he just left them to it. Sophie thought how he had grown up over the past few years, so non-judgmental.

Tom phoned her frequently from university, trying to encourage her to go out socially again. She looked forward to speaking to him, and they messaged often, went on Skype and WhatsApp, but Sophie knew she shouldn't keep relying on him for company. Tom didn't really understand how difficult it would be for her to move on, but she did realise that it wasn't fair that he should always be worried about her.

But where could she go by herself? Most of the people she knew were quite content to stay at home at night with takeaways and bottles of wine after a busy day at work. Others went to the local gym in the morning or before they went home, but after a long busy day standing up, the gym was the last place she wanted to go.

She didn't have any very close friends who she could confide in, so Sophie wasn't surprised when Tom had sent her the article about the club, but she was worried that she had promised him she would go and report back to him when she had been.

Sophie was slightly upset when she heard that it hadn't taken Dave long to join the social scene, playing pool and darts at his local pub. Tom had told her that Dave had even joined the gym.

After the divorce Dave had moved into a large fourth-floor flat overlooking the sea, in a modern recently built complex in Bilberry on Sea, three miles away. He had no interest in gardening, so the flat was a good choice for him. Tom also informed Sophie that Dave had even cut down on his evening workload. She wondered why they hadn't gone out just once on those long, lonely winter evenings when Dave was at home, instead of shutting himself away in the office on his computer or starting an argument. Even to the local pub for a meal or drink would have been okay. It was probably her fault; she should have insisted. Sophie was slightly jealous he was carrying on with his life so soon and so easily.

Dave had moved into his flat quickly, without any problems. He hadn't invited her to see it, but he had described it to her in great detail. Three bedrooms, three bathrooms, large lounge. He didn't know that Sophie had found herself purposely driving past. Stopping momentarily to look. A large white building overlooking the sea, with balconies on which there were chairs, tables, and flowering window boxes. The second time she found herself in the area she saw his blonde cleaner open the balcony doors and stand looking out at the sea, and then afterwards pick up a glass and a bottle of wine left on the table and disappear inside.

Why would he want such a large flat and a cleaner when he was the only one living there, and why had he started drinking wine?

Another car drove into the car park, its lights interrupting her thoughts.

Car interior light on, Sophie checked herself in the mirror – *not bad for forty-five*, she thought, although she didn't look like this most of the time. Green eyes carefully made up. She sprayed another mist of perfume. Combed her dark, naturally wavy, auburn hair, which earlier had taken her ages to straighten. She couldn't do anything about the freckles sprinkled on her face, but then over the years she had grown to like them.

Opening the car door, she picked up her large red clutch bag, locked the car, and headed with uncertainty towards the entrance of the club, trying to tell herself that she was doing this for Tom. She would stay for just a little while and then leave. He wouldn't know.

Sophie walked through the wide welcoming entrance with its light-brown patterned tiled floor, dark cream walls, and off-white statues, taking a leaflet from the nearby table.

Ahead of her were just two closed doors.

| One on the left marked | One on the right marked |
| OPEN MIC | LATIN DANCE |

Which one?

Sophie hesitated, took a deep breath, pushed open one of the doors and walked in.

Two

The sound of Elton John's "Rocket Man", together with loud mingled conversations, filled the small, crowded, darkly lit room. Sophie stood for a moment just inside the door, nervously looking around, but was soon manoeuvred further into the room by people coming in. She eventually found a seat at the back, after weaving through the groups of club members who were standing talking. Sophie sat down and looked around. Ed Sheeran's song "Photograph" was now being played, before the open mic night started.

Musicians were strumming together in a corner and the drummer was setting up his drums and tuning them in the centre of the small stage. The stage was in an alcove at the end of the room, lit up with coloured lights which glowed softly and changed colour.

Small groups of friends were talking over the round tables, and a few people were smoking outside in the cold autumn evening. Some were sitting on the metal seats or standing huddled just outside the door which was open at the side of the room. Inside a man was leaning against the wall talking on his mobile, smoking his e-cigarette. The sickly-sweet-smelling cloud drifted towards Sophie and she wafted it away, thankful for the cold air that was blowing through the doors and sending some of it in the opposite direction.

Five minutes later she was standing at the small bar, ordering a glass of house red. The barmaid put down the glass of wine and wiped the bar counter.

'Your first night here?' The barmaid smiled, closing the till and giving Sophie her change. Sophie knew her slightly from seeing her around the town, and she told her that she had decided to find out what it was like, as she had an evening free. Sophie didn't want anyone knowing that this was her first venture out by herself for years. She did feel like a teenager on her first night out, although not quite, as she lacked the friends who would have been with her; not forgetting the confidence she would have had then.

'Everyone here's friendly, most have been coming for years,' continued the barmaid. 'The open mic and bar close at 11.30. It's a great night and I'm sure you'll enjoy it.'

Sophie thanked her and picked up her drink and made her way through the group of people now waiting to be served.

While she was standing at the bar, her seat had been taken by someone else – the man in black – who she had seen in the car park. He slowly moved further along the bench seat, making room for her, and she sat next to him. Sophie couldn't help noticing his dark hair and swarthy good looks. She stopped herself staring and, placing her bag and glass on the round table, took off her jacket and put it on the ledge at the back of her seat. The man in black was tuning his guitar whilst talking to the keyboard player, who was looking through some papers, making notes. They didn't talk or seem to notice her, for which she was thankful. She wouldn't have known what to say.

At 9.30pm the group eventually walked onto the stage; a drummer, carrying his beer in one hand and sticks in the other, keyboard player, who was now wearing a grey flat cap, a bass player and the man in black carrying his guitar. Sophie was soon enjoying the evening, talking to two women who were sitting by her. They worked in a charity shop in the high street, and she had often spoken to them when she had looked around their shop.

The group played most of the current songs that she knew, and songs that went right back to the '60s. Sophie looked around. Everyone was singing, listening or dancing on the small dance floor at the back of the room, except for a party group of six men, sitting at the front, who were swaying and singing "Delilah" loudly and shouting, now oblivious to everyone else.

During the short interval, Sophie talked to a young girl called Gina, the singer of the group, who was drinking beer and examining her guitar. She was very slim with dyed black and purple hair tied in a high ponytail. Sophie noticed that one of her tattoos was a large purple and black bird on the back of her right hand. Gina saw Sophie looking at it and told her that it meant freedom as she loved being free. Gina then unzipped the bottom of her tight black denim trouser leg and showed Sophie another design, also in purple and black, on her ankle; a guitar, with two small "D"s entwined.

Sophie admired the artistic design and asked what it represented.

Gina quickly zipped up the trouser leg, saying that it was a new tattoo she had had done recently, and it had a personal meaning. Sophie didn't ask about the purple and black theme and didn't continue the conversation. She drank her wine, while Gina ordered another beer at the bar and walked back to Sophie's table.

Gina was talking in a raspy whisper and told Sophie that she had lost her voice from shouting instructions at her Zumba class earlier that afternoon. She had started the day with a sore throat, and it was now getting worse.

'Could I sing with you?' Sophie heard herself volunteering – where did that come from? She was always singing in her art shop and had played the guitar years ago in a local band, and she even used to dance, but that was in her social era, over twenty-five years ago.

'That's a good idea,' Pete, the keyboard player, interrupted, overhearing. Gina hesitated and looked uncertain, but said, 'Okay. We're on next.'

Sophie followed Gina on stage, legs shaking.

'Just one song, that's all, Gina,' Sophie managed to gasp. Gina started strumming and Sophie joined in, singing "It's a heartache". Halfway through the song she felt someone standing by her side, singing, leaning over her, sharing her mic. It was the man in black. Sophie's legs started to shake again. They finished singing to enthusiastic applause, so they sang two more songs, "Make You Feel My Love" and "Shotgun". The man in black thanked them.

'I thought you said you couldn't sing,' Gina croaked, pushing in front of Sophie, elbowing her almost into a table. Surprised, Sophie wondered why Gina had suddenly turned on her.

Evening over, most of the club members just sat talking. Others who had taken part in the open mic talked about their bookings or were quietly singing between themselves, trying out new songs. The party table had been asked to leave, earlier, when they had started arguing and insisting on singing on stage. The bar manager, together with a club member, had managed to move them out onto the street, where the party group stood for a while, shouting, and then made their way, stumbling and singing, down to The Tavern further along the road.

Kerry walked around collecting the empty glasses, empty crisp bags and unlucky raffle tickets and began spraying and cleaning the tables, telling everyone it was 11.45pm and time to go home. At 12pm everyone reluctantly drifted out slowly.

Sophie said her goodbyes to Tess and Jane, who she had made friends with. It was also their first night at the club, and they had really enjoyed the evening. They had worked together at the animal charity shop in Timberry for a long time, and on Thursday nights, after work, they usually went for a carvery and then walked home. Tess and Jane had often heard the music when walking past, and tonight they came in to see what the club was like. Sophie said she would probably see them next week if they decided to go again. She put on her warm jacket, scarf and gloves, picked up her bag and left the club.

The car park was now in total darkness and Sophie carefully made her way to the car, stopping to take her car keys out of her bag. They caught on her woollen gloves and dropped on the ground. Sophie, wishing she had put them in her pocket when she was inside the club, stooped to pick them up and continued to walk over to her car, looking down so that she wouldn't catch her foot in the potholes. She looked up, startled. The man in black was leaning on her car. Should she be concerned? He pushed back his unruly black hair with his fingers and introduced himself.

'Hi, Sophie, I'm Ben,' holding out his large welcoming hand. She shook it nervously.

She already knew his name. (She had made a point of asking Gina.) He asked if she had enjoyed the night. She said she had.

'See you next week then?'

'Maybe.' She closed the car door and drove off quickly down the drive, bumping over the potholes, watching Ben go back into the club to help dismantle the equipment. She saw him take his phone from his pocket to answer it.

What was it about him?

Sophie lay in bed trying desperately to get to sleep, but the evening kept whirling around in her head. It was the first late social night she had had in years. Certainly since before she was married, and she was surprised by how much she had enjoyed herself. Sophie looked again at her phone; it was now 3.34am. She had another drink from the bottle of water that was on the bedside table and tried to remember the names of the group members, perhaps that would help. Mark, the bass player – glasses, overweight, tall, greying black hair. Pete, keyboard player, not too tall, bronzed, shaved head and hazel eyes. Deano, the drummer, tall, hair braids and his lovely soft Afro-Caribbean voice. Then there was Ben, of course. Ben, tall, black hair, dark chocolate-brown eyes, black leather jacket, the lead guitarist. How could she forget him? And Gina. Sophie wasn't too sure about her. Eventually at 4.20am she dozed and then fell into a deep sleep.

Three

The next day Sophie went to work as usual. Although, not quite as usual, as she had forgotten to set her alarm. The doorbell, being rung by the 8am online grocery delivery man, woke her. She struggled into her leggings and threw on a top and ran downstairs to open the door.

'Someone have a late night?' the cheery man greeted her, bringing in her groceries and helping Sophie empty the containers onto the kitchen counter.

She thanked him and closed the door quickly, looking in the large hall mirror as she passed. Hair sticking up, make-up smudged, and top inside out.

Sophie pushed the frozen items into the freezer, chilled items in the empty fridge and left the piles of other groceries on the counter to put away when she got home that evening. She must remember to phone Tom.

Arriving at work late, Sophie was tired, had a headache and struggled to focus. She opened her art shop, pulled up the blinds and the bright autumn sunshine shone through. She picked up the post from the floor, put the kettle on and arranged new paintings on the wall. She then drank the first of the many cups of coffee she would have that day, sitting at the table in the window. Sophie hoped that she wouldn't have many customers, at least until after lunchtime.

Her thoughts turn to Dave and then to her father.

When her father had died, he left Sophie money specifically to buy an art studio, which was something that she had always dreamed of having since leaving art college.

Her shop had been vacant for two years, and she had often looked through the window, wishing she could afford to buy it and visualising her paintings on the walls. Her father had also given Megan, her sister, a cheque, and Tom, money to buy music equipment. Dave received a small legacy.

How she missed her father. He was always interested in her life, and ready to help her. She wished her mother and sister were the same. She did think that Dave could have also made more of an effort to find out what was going on in her life. She always asked about his. At least she had inherited her father's kindness and that pleased her.

Sophie had left her job working in the art gallery in Bilberry to set up her shop in Timberry. On the first day the shop opened, and when she had sold her first paintings, she knew that her father would be happy with what she had achieved.

At 10am the shop doorbell clanged, and Dave strolled in. They had been divorced for a few months, but it was still strangely good to see him, even after all their problems. She didn't see him very often now; only when he called in to look at her accounts. Sophie thought he had changed since their divorce. Dave had become even less interested in her and seemed much happier. Had she caused him to be unhappy? She doubted it, as they were hardly together the last few months of their marriage, except sometimes over the weekends, and that was mainly for Tom's sake when he was home from university. It was good that there were no arguments between her and Dave now, for Tom's sake.

Sophie told him about going out last night. He admitted that she did look a bit rough. But there was no interest or jealousy in his reaction, and she was surprised how that annoyed her slightly.

'Do you still want my help with the books?' Dave asked, dipping his digestive in his coffee. She watched as the biscuit fell into the cup and disappeared. How that had irritated her on the rare occasions when they had been together. Sophie told him she would be pleased if he could, as she wouldn't be able to trust or afford anyone else.

When they had agreed the divorce settlement, the house was all she had wanted. Sophie had thought of moving to a smaller place, but she would have missed her house so much, with its large garden, surrounded by trees. It was quiet and she could be there without being overlooked. Sophie also loved her relaxing long walks to the beach. She hadn't asked for any part of Dave's carpet cleaning company.

It was hard work having a house and studio to run. Sophie had never been too bothered about keeping the house tidy, especially when Dave and Tom were there, as it was impossible. Although, somehow she seemed to have had more time then. Now that Tom was at university and Dave had left, Sophie felt as though there was a lot more work to do, as the shop was doing well, and she still had to do gardening and general house maintenance. She barely had time to do the washing or cook a decent meal. And now she was thinking about having a social life; how would she manage with the late nights?

And, of course, she still had to look after Kenny. Dave had given him to her as a kitten, ten years ago. One of his regular customers had found Kenny frightened and in a sealed cardboard box in her porch, on the day that he was cleaning her carpets. The customer already had two dogs and couldn't keep him, so Dave brought Kenny home to Sophie. Ginger, frightened and timid when she first had him, but now fluffy, playful and very loving.

Dave returned the account books and papers to the office at the back of the shop. Sophie shouted to him, 'How would you feel if I started dating again?'

He put down the books and papers on her desk, walked back into the empty shop, flicked through the local newspaper that was left on the counter, and without looking up said, 'That would be great.'

He then walked out into the autumn sunshine. He showed no jealousy or interest, which really annoyed her again.

Sophie thought that Dave was still good-looking. Blond, blue eyes, not too tall, slim, although she had noticed recently that he seemed to have more muscles. Had he changed? Perhaps she just hadn't taken much notice of him or appreciated him over the past few years.

Sophie thought about the night that she had first met Dave.

She had been invited to her friend Ally's office Christmas party in Birmingham and although they knew it would be expensive, they had wanted to stay at the hotel venue as transport would have been a problem. Sophie had phoned the hotel two days before and a room had just become available. A guest had cancelled an hour before. It meant that they would have to share, but that wasn't a problem as they would probably spend most of the night talking. Sophie's father offered to pay for the room as a Christmas present.

Sophie and Ally had enjoyed the Christmas meal. Ally ordered nut roast instead of turkey, as she had decided to become vegetarian the month before, but she couldn't resist the turkey and she took a slice from the serving dish, saying you've just got to eat turkey at Christmas. Sophie thought it was strange how she could remember certain silly things that had happened a long time ago, and wondered if Ally still didn't eat meat.

The comedy show afterwards had been excellent, and they had stayed up quite late at the bar, drinking wine and catching up on the time they had worked together waitressing two years before, at the Knife and Fork restaurant in New Street. They also talked about the people who had worked there and the carefree times they had had.

It was after midnight when they went back to their room.

At 3.20 in the morning Sophie threw on the hotel's white dressing gown and closed the door quietly, although she knew that nothing would wake Ally, as she was sleeping face down in the duvet.

Sophie walked downstairs to reception to see if she could get some bottled water, as last night's meal and wine had left her thirsty. She had already drunk the bottle that had been left in her room, the tap water tasted strange, and she didn't want tea.

It was then she saw Dave. He was busy cleaning the carpets in the reception area, trying to get them done by 6am. He was wearing green overalls with a Johnson's Cleaning Company logo on the back. He noticed Sophie standing by the reception desk and told her that he hadn't seen anyone in the reception since he had arrived. Sophie said she only wanted some water and was about to leave when Dave gave her a bottle from his bag. She drank from it thirstily. They talked for a while and discovered they lived only forty miles away from each other and Sophie gave him her phone number.

The following morning, he had gone. It was as though he had never been there. The reception area was busy with people leaving or waiting for taxis.

Dave phoned two weeks later and that's how it began.

Soon after they got married, Dave took over running his father's firm himself, as his father found it too much to organise and reluctantly retired when the company expanded. During their marriage Dave's firm had grown even more, and he now had fifty-five employees and also offered carpet laying, laminate flooring and a suite cleaning service. Last year he had opened another office in Birmingham.

Four

At the art shop the week went by quickly, Sophie trying to source materials, either ordering online or shopping for them, and dealing with customers; some who just wasted Sophie's time, or a few who came in sheltering from the rain, pretending to look around. Sophie always offered them tea and coffee at the small tables in the window, where customers could think about their purchase. On other days she had clients quite often wanting her to design canvases for special occasions in too short a time, but she always tried to help if she could. She sold quite a few paintings and was pleased with the amount of money she earned. She transferred Tom money occasionally when she had had a good week. She promised herself that one day, when she had some money to spare, she would spend some on herself.

Sophie enjoyed working on the high street in Timberry, as everyone in the small shops knew each other, and there was a good community atmosphere. If shoplifters were about, the news would spread down the street and the other shop owners would be ready for them, and if anyone needed help, they could rely on each other.

Timberry on Sea was a beautiful small town which hardly ever became very crowded in summer. It had a lovely sandy beach and sand dunes. It also had a hidden beach which only the locals knew about unless holidaymakers wandered down to it by mistake.

Most people went to the beach in Bilberry, the next town, where there was a lot more going on. There was a small pier with day and night entertainment which attracted a lot of holidaymakers. There were also donkey rides on the beach for children.

At Easter time shops on the high street would hide Easter bunnies in their shop windows for children to find and the child that had seen the most was given an Easter egg.

In September, before the cold weather began, Timberry was the venue for a funfair, with rides and stalls which attracted families in the afternoon and older visitors at night. Many of the local people went there to meet up and enjoy the atmosphere. The music from the fair filled the streets and Timberry had a carnival atmosphere with clowns and men on stilts.

At Christmas time shops had small stalls outside selling Christmas items. Sophie helped with the hot drinks and made dozens of home-made mince pies, whilst Christmas music played down the street.

Although twenty-five years before, the move from Shertsbourne to Timberry had been difficult for Sophie to get used to, she now felt that she belonged in Timberry and it was her home town. She wouldn't want to live anywhere else.

Five

Four years previously, Sophie had run her own art club in the nearby small village of Cornberry. She had started with enthusiasm, taking the club members down to the beach for painting evenings with picnics and wine or they went into the village for "people watching". It was so simple then – the few members happy and relaxed and everyone enjoyed themselves. Sophie had spent money setting it up, but she didn't mind as she received a yearly payment from the members.

As the club attracted more members, she started to display their artwork in the shop for a fee, until one day, when one of the club member's canvas paintings went missing.

The canvas disappeared when Sophie had left the shop for five minutes. She had gone out to buy her midday sandwich from the sandwich bar around the corner, leaving the door open as usual, and when she returned there was a space on the wall and the canvas had disappeared.

Sophie realised that Sandra, the artist, had taken the canvas off the wall herself, when Sophie was out, because she was hoping for compensation for the theft. Sophie had phoned Sandra the day before to tell her that she had changed her mind about displaying her canvas because it just wasn't suitable for the studio. A lot of customers had criticised the painting, so Sophie felt obliged to tell Sandra. Sophie did ask her if she had another one that she could hang in its place, but Sandra was upset and felt insulted. She didn't get compensation and she never spoke to Sophie again, and afterwards she tried to ruin Sophie's name at the art club.

After a while Sophie handed the responsibility of the club over to Phil Thompson, who had recently retired from his job as head of the local library. He had an extraordinarily strong personality and thought he could force his ideas through at the club. Phil was always trying to get her to change the way it was run, and he wanted to change the art night to a Friday instead of a Wednesday, as Wednesday afternoon he went bowling and he found it difficult to get to the art club on time. One night, when Sophie couldn't be there, Phil asked the club to vote for the change without her permission, but no club member wanted to change the night. He had suddenly become in charge without her noticing.

Sophie decided to leave when newcomers to the club became committee members and they wouldn't consider the existing members' opinions. At the art exhibitions that they organised twice a year the committee members would have first choice as to where they wanted to display their artwork, which annoyed the rest of the club. Phil had welcomed the challenge when Sophie offered it to him. And it was a challenge trying to please everyone. Organising different types of art demonstrations and art sales. Not to mention the members' arguments.

Sophie still exhibited and sold artwork for people she used to be friendly with, when she had space in the studio, but she was relieved and pleased to hand all paperwork over to Phil and finish with it. There were too many in the club and it was out of her control.

Six

On Sunday morning Sophie drove to Nottingham to see Tom at university. He was studying business studies and music and had settled in quickly. He had always wanted to study music since he was at junior school and Sophie had always encouraged him. Dave had suggested that he should do business studies as well.

Sophie didn't intend to stay long, just to take food and washing and see how he was getting on, as she missed him dreadfully.

Tom was waiting for her. He was very much like his father, blond, blue eyes, although his hair was slightly curlier than Dave's and Tom was taller.

Tom was eager to introduce Zoe, his new girlfriend, whom he had recently met in the students' bar. Sophie didn't know anything about Zoe and was anxious to get to know her, so she took them for a meal at a local pub, which was next to a café and a bric-a-brac shop up a cobblestone alleyway in the high street.

The bar was crowded with students, talking excitedly or on their phones. Sophie bought sandwiches, chips, coffee and cake and they sat on the high seats by the window. Zoe was a quiet Afro-Caribbean girl. She wore red glasses and had ringlets down to her shoulders and a London accent. Sophie asked Zoe what she was studying, and she told her she was studying music, the same as Tom. Sophie admired her hair and asked her how she styled it and Zoe explained that it took her ages to put it in ringlets, but it would last a long time. If she had gone to a hairdresser, it would be expensive and would take even longer for them to style. Occasionally Zoe's mum treated her to having it done. Sophie didn't like to ask her too many questions, although she would have loved to, but she would ask Tom when she spoke to him next on the phone.

Sophie liked Zoe. She was pleased that he had made a good friend in his first year.

After lunch Sophie and Zoe went around the bric-a-brac shop next door while Tom spoke to three friends who were standing outside. Sophie looked at a red and black rug which was hanging on the wall while Zoe picked up a grey retro lampshade. Sophie saw Zoe check the money in her purse, put the lampshade back on the stand and continue to look around. Zoe asked the shopkeeper, who was carefully watching them, whether she would keep the lampshade until tomorrow, when she would have more money from her bar job. The shopkeeper apologised, saying that all the students say that and never come back for things. Zoe looked embarrassed, walked around the shop again and left. Sophie followed five minutes later. She kissed them both goodbye, gave Tom £20 and Zoe a paper carrier bag with the lampshade inside.

Even Tom was moving on. She felt a huge pang of sadness.

Sophie headed home, appreciating the long drive from Nottingham, as it cleared her head and allowed her time to think as the road trailed behind her.

When she turned into her drive, she realised then that her life needed to change. And soon.

Seven

Thursday night came around quickly again. Should Sophie go back to the club and could she cope with another late night?

She had already made up her mind. Sophie showered slowly, using her expensive foam, dressed in tight black jeans, green jumper, black biker jacket and boots and found herself sitting in the club car park at 9pm.

She locked her car and followed everyone inside. Sophie walked over to the bar, bought a large glass of wine and sat down in the same place as last week. Gina was sitting near the front, tuning her guitar and talking to Deano the drummer, who was hungrily eating prepacked sandwiches from the local shop. He always tried to get there early, giving himself time to set up his drums before the others in the group arrived. Mark, the guitarist, was fixing the mic, while Ben was talking to someone on his mobile. Sophie couldn't hear what he was saying but she saw him abruptly turn off his phone, annoyed.

After ten minutes of feeling slightly awkward, sitting there drinking by herself, Mark came over and asked her if she would sing tonight, and she gave him some Adele and Justin Bieber songs that she had been practising during the week, which she would be able to sing. He continued round the room, speaking to other people, making notes and shaking hands.

Tess and Jane made their way over to Sophie, took off their coats and sat down. Sophie was pleased to see them and to have someone to talk to. They discussed their week, bought themselves a drink and settled to listen to the music. Tess asked Sophie if she wanted to help occasionally on Sundays in her charity shop, as she was short of staff and she thought Sophie might like to support an animal charity.

Tess had been the manager for five years, since the shop opened. The shop was usually busy in the summer months with holidaymakers looking around. In the winter it was quieter, but there was always sorting or gift aiding she could do. Jane also worked there on the till when she had free time from her mobile hairdressing job.

Sophie told Tess she would pop in one Sunday morning after ten o'clock to see her, although she wondered when she would have time to help. Tess put on her coat and then disappeared, following two others outside to smoke a cigarette.

Gina walked around with raffle tickets later in the evening, collecting the money in a beer glass. Sophie gave her £2, and Gina dropped the raffle tickets on the table, sending the £1 coin change spinning onto the floor. They never made any eye contact.

Sophie began to feel part of the club. There were more people this week, including another small group celebrating a birthday, which made the club noisier. She sang again and was getting more confident with the applause and whistles and it was great that the audience went quieter and listened when she sang. One couple was dancing.

Sophie watched Gina counting the raffle money and saw her put a £5 note into the pocket of her jeans. Gina looked across at her and looked away quickly. Sophie knew then that she was fast making an enemy and decided to keep quiet about what she had seen.

As she was leaving the club at the end of the night, Mark asked if she wanted to go to the local jazz club on Saturday. He wasn't playing but he was meeting a lot of people he knew there.

Sophie thanked him but lied, saying she couldn't go as she was already going out. It was too soon after Dave, and Sophie didn't want to get involved with anyone yet. Mark wasn't pleased as it was unusual for someone to turn him down.

Kerry, the barmaid, had warned Sophie last week, when she heard Mark ask Sophie if he could buy her a drink, that Mark was always asking women at the club out.

Mark told her he wouldn't give up asking.

'Dream on,' Sophie thought out loud. 'You're not my type.'

He tightened his belt and strolled back to his seat by the bar.

Sophie said goodbye to Tess and Jane in the club entrance. They walked away down the drive and Sophie made her way across the dark car park. She had a sinister feeling that someone was watching her; or was she just tired?

When she reached her car, she saw that one of her front tyres was flat. Thinking that she must have driven over something sharp, she looked in her boot for the tyre inflator. A car screeched out of the dark shadows, headed towards her and then quickly swerved. Shocked, Sophie looked up but was too late; the car had already disappeared down the drive. It was then she found that her car door was unlocked. Worried, Sophie looked inside. She couldn't see anything missing but she was sure she had locked it.

Eight

Showering early, Sophie wanted to arrive at the shop before eight o'clock as a new client was coming in at 9am. He had phoned her last week to make an appointment and she really wanted to make a special effort.

Getting home late last night hadn't affected Sophie as much as it had the week before, but she still couldn't understand why she had left the car door unlocked. She had checked again when she had arrived home, and had found nothing missing.

Sophie had breakfast, fed Kenny the cat and drove into work, changing the closed sign to open. She checked herself in the cloakroom mirror, liking the orange jumper, one of many items of clothing she had bought cheap online. She was getting more daring with her clothes now, trying different colours from the ones that she had worn for years. Orange went well with her auburn hair. She went into the shop and waited nervously, squinting through the blinds.

Adam James was the interior designer for the new large Fendrix Hotel which had been built in Brecknam. He had seen her new canvas designs displayed on the walls in a solicitor's reception area, where he had attended a meeting last month, and was interested to meet the artist, so he tracked her down. Sophie was excited and apprehensive as these were her latest designs in faux leather and, although she thought they were great because they were very unusual, they really had been just an experiment.

Sophie had positioned all twenty canvases carefully on the plain white wall. She admitted to herself that they really did look good. Different colours, sizes and different designs. She really hoped he would like them.

At exactly 9am Adam James arrived, black jeans, blue casual shirt, briefcase, and a toothpaste smile.

'Adam?'

'Sophie?' his sunglasses reflecting different colours.

Sophie shook his well-manicured hand, changed the open sign to closed and poured him a coffee.

Adam James took off his sunglasses, to reveal hazel eyes, and studied her artwork for a while, walking past them, then looking at the canvases from the back of the shop. He read the quickly-put-together leaflets that Sophie had designed describing her artwork. His face told her nothing, except that he was concentrating. He took his mobile from his shirt pocket, took photos together with a video, and asked where he could make a phone call. Sophie showed him into her office and closed the door. She stopped outside, trying to listen to his conversation.

The shop door rattled, interrupting her listening. Annoyed, she made the sign that she was closed and would open in an hour to the man hunched outside. He shrugged his shoulders, said something unpleasant that she couldn't hear but understood, and walked away, moaning.

After what seemed like an hour Adam James emerged from the office, still tapping away on his phone. He told her he would like to buy all twenty paintings and they would like a further thirty to place around the hotel. They must be all different designs and sizes. He would like the complete set in four months – and they all must be signed. Acting as casually as she could, trying not to show her over-excitement, and also trying to calculate how much she would earn, Sophie agreed, but added that unfortunately there would be no discount available. She bit her lip, realising how unprofessional that sounded; why would Adam James or the hotel be interested in getting them cheaper?

Adam smiled and told her that wouldn't be a problem. They then sat down and discussed basic artwork and sizes. Sophie asked the colours of the walls, so that she could produce different samples. Adam explained that the walls were all magnolia. He would leave her to choose the colours and designs, as he liked the canvases she had done already and was confident that she could produce fantastic artwork.

Two hours later Adam put on his sunglasses, left the shop, and disappeared into the bright sunshine.

Sophie closed the blinds, locked the shop, and opened the fridge in the office. She took out one of the bottles of expensive red wine that a customer had given her, which she had been saving for a special occasion, and poured herself a large glass. Even though it was only 11.30am, she didn't care. This was that extra-special occasion.

One bottle of wine later, and still wondering if she was in a dream, Sophie checked his order again, washed her glass and threw the empty bottle in the bin.

She called a taxi and closed the shop, leaving the car in the car park, and returned home to think about what had happened that morning and to start the artwork. £25,000! She still couldn't believe it.

She called Dave excitedly to tell him. He was pleased for her but said he couldn't stay on the phone as he had to go out to a meeting.

'Who's that?' asked Sophie, hearing a woman's voice in the background. 'Oh, Dianne the cleaner,' Dave replied quickly.

Strange, thought Sophie, *the cleaner didn't usually work on a Friday, she worked on a Monday. She must have changed her day.*

Nine

On Sunday morning Sophie set off to the Two Tails charity shop, carrying a heavy carrier bag of books which she hadn't had time to read, and two bags of clothes. She had sorted through her wardrobe the previous week, throwing out dresses, trousers and tops she considered didn't fit her new lifestyle. Sophie hoped that she would be able to afford new clothes when she had been paid by Adam James for the canvases which she had been commissioned to design for the Fendrix Hotel.

She should have taken the car, but Sophie enjoyed the walk. The air was cold, and Sophie walked down the long, deserted promenade between trees that had now completely lost their leaves. The sun was shining through them welcomingly. She stopped, putting her bags down on a wooden bench, resting her arms and then continued along the row of shops. The door to the charity shop was already open, welcoming customers, and Sophie walked in.

Tess greeted her. After serving a customer with a large pile of books, they went through to the back of the shop. Sophie took off her coat and hung it on the hook under the stairs.

'There's only the two of us this morning as Sheila, who works here normally, has her family coming down from Derby. I like to have two people in the shop usually, but sometimes it doesn't work out like that,' Tess told Sophie, whilst finishing steaming a red wool dress on a hanger. Sophie offered to make tea on the cluttered fridge.

Tess then looked through the clothes and books that Sophie had brought in and showed her how to label and tag them.

Sophie was also shown how to sort the bags and do gift aiding. After a while Tess decided that that would be enough to learn that day. They talked for most of the morning except when there were customers. Sophie also went on the till, which she enjoyed. She talked to the people that came in; some, who she knew, asked her why she wasn't at her art shop.

A middle-aged woman walked in, smiled at Sophie and looked around. After five minutes of browsing, she asked to try on some clothes that she had taken from the rail. Sophie pointed to the changing room, remembering to make a note of what she had taken in, as Tess had advised her.

Eventually the woman came out, smiled at Sophie again, and hung clothes on the rail. Sophie quickly noticed that the clothes she was hanging up were what the woman had been wearing when she came in. She rang the bell on the counter and Tess took over.

The woman was just about to leave the shop.

'Hello, Rosie. Are you going to pay for those clothes? If not, put them back.'

Rosie huffed.

Sophie listened as Tess explained that she was a regular. Quite harmless, but she came in often, tried on clothes, kept them on and put her old clothes on the rails and walked out. Sometimes she got away with it, if helpers were busy in the back of the shop or were distracted. Some shoplifters would go into the changing room and put the clothes that they were stealing over the clothes they were already wearing and walk out of the shop looking twice their size. Tess was fully aware of their tricks. Not many got away with stealing from her shop.

On her first day, Sophie was being initiated into what went on in charity shops.

Sophie watched as her black pleated skirt was sold. She'd

bought it last month, but had decided she would never wear it as it was too long. She could have sold it online, but it would have been too much hassle. A woman who was much taller than her tried it on and bought it, together with a matching top. Sophie had felt guilty about not having worn it, but was now happy that someone had bought it, and the shop had made £10.

Sophie looked around. The shop only sold clothes and books, as Tess had learned after years of running the shop that they were the items customers most wanted, although sometimes in the school holidays she would put out a basket of toys for the children to play with or buy. After trying on and buying a green jumper and black jacket that were brand new, Sophie browsed the bookshelves and looked for any she could buy for presents. Although it was some time before Christmas, Tess's handmade Christmas cards had sold well, as there were just a few left on the shelf.

Sophie and Tess sat in the back of the shop and ate their sandwiches, discussing how they could raise more money. It was a small private animal charity, set up by Tess, so they didn't have much funding. Sophie suggested a Saturday night when perhaps the open mic group could play at the club. Perhaps they could ask the group if they would play when they saw them on Thursday night. Tess wasn't too sure that they would agree to the idea.

The afternoon went quickly, and they became more excited talking about the different ideas of what they could do. Not many people brought in donations, so they were able to restock the shop for Monday. At four o'clock, they cashed up and closed the shop. Sophie had enjoyed her first day.

Before she headed home Sophie decided to call in at her art shop, to pick up an order for three paintings which she wanted to check over. She then strolled back in the dark afternoon, past the small shops in the high street, looking through the windows, something she didn't have time for during the week. The promenade lights had replaced the earlier sun. She was happy with her purchases that she could wear one Thursday night.

Was that Ben and Gina standing in the alleyway at the end of the street? Sophie turned to look again, but they had gone. The darkness was probably playing tricks with her eyes. She walked quickly home, the sound of her boots on the pavement the only noise interrupting the quiet.

Ten

The next Thursday Sophie and Tess were still talking about how to raise money when Deano overheard them mentioning the group. He told them he would put it to the others and see what they thought of the band playing at the Maple Leaf.

By the end of the night, they had arranged to have a reggae night on a Wednesday evening. Alan, the manager, had told them Saturday was always busy, but Wednesday he didn't have any bookings. The group were worried that Wednesday night wouldn't attract many people because of working the next day, but they decided that was the best they could do.

They were all eager to play for nothing and the proceeds would go to the charity and on hiring the room. Gina said she didn't like animals, so she wouldn't be singing. But by the end of the evening, after hearing everyone talking enthusiastically about it, she had agreed to play. She couldn't resist performing. They would advertise it as a Reggae Rave, and it was arranged for the following Wednesday. They would charge a £5 entrance fee.

Sophie and Tess made the posters and put them in their shop windows. Tess handed out leaflets with every purchase and also took some to the local vets, who she knew well. They put a poster in the foyer at the Maple Leaf. Sophie had taken leaflets for her customers to pick up from her counter.

Wednesday evening quickly came around, and the group hoped there would be a good attendance. The band set up, sound checks were made, and the doors in the large concert room opened to the public at 7pm.

Sophie stood by the door in anticipation, ready to hand out raffle tickets in exchange for the entrance money. No one arrived. Seven thirty and only three girls had walked in, but ten minutes later people sauntered in and the room was soon alive. The band, having decided to play reggae, had made the right choice, as dancers were on the dance floor straight away and remained there all night.

When Gina wasn't playing in the band, she was in the middle of the dance floor, dancing flamboyantly to the music, in her tight blue jeans and purple lace-up top, with people clapping her in tune to the music. Sophie thought she was such a showman, but secretly had to admire her.

The band played all night except for two short breaks, when they drew the raffle and ordered their drinks. Alan would be pleased with the money taken over the bar tonight.

One of the raffle prizes, a bottle of whisky, was won by Sheila. She had worked hard at the charity shop for the past five years since it had opened and had helped Tess, picking up and transporting donations from customers' houses, so Tess thought that was fair. Sheila didn't drink, so she swapped it for a giant brown teddy bear that the charity shop had donated and the couple who drew the next ticket were really pleased to have the whisky.

The night was a great success. Tess had placed a collection tin on the table by the door and she noticed people were giving generously. Many of the people who attended lived locally and Tess knew most of them, and at the end of the night she went on stage and thanked the crowd for their generosity. At 11.30pm everyone left. It had been a great success. The group helped Kerry, who was on duty again, clear the tables.

Tess walked over to the table to pick up the collection tin. The tin wasn't there.

Tess asked Kerry if she had seen it.

'It was there a minute ago when I cleaned the table.'

Tess asked around. But Sophie was looking at Gina, who had put her leather jacket over her arm and was leaving. Why wasn't she wearing her jacket as the weather was so cold?

Sophie followed, watching her go to the car park. As Gina was getting into her car she slid her coat off her arm and Sophie saw the collection tin catching the light. Sophie chased after her, wrestling the collection tin from her. Gina snatched it back.

'I was going to take it to the shop tomorrow,' Gina muttered.

'No. You were going to steal it!' Sophie shouted.

'Well, the money is only going to animals anyway,' Gina answered.

'Take it back in,' Sophie demanded. 'Or I will tell the others.'

Feeling really angry and cold, Sophie went back into the club to pick up her bag and coat.

Two minutes later Gina walked in, saying she had found the collection tin on the table in entrance hall.

Everyone rushed up, thanking her. Sophie stood by the door, composing herself.

Kerry looked puzzled. How could she have missed it?

Gina quickly said goodnight and pushed her way past Sophie.

'Don't think you've heard the end of this,' she hissed.

Sophie wondered whether to tell Tess what had happened but thought it would spoil the night for her and that it would also spoil the atmosphere on Thursday nights, so she didn't say anything. Sophie knew that Gina was someone who she would never want to be friends with, but neither would she want her as an enemy, and she began to worry what Gina was capable of.

Eleven

Thursday again. Another late night, after last night's reggae evening.

Sophie settled happily into her usual seat between Tess and Jane. Everyone talked about the night before, saying they had had a great time.

Paul, a stand-in guitarist, was on stage. He had taken Ben's place that evening as Ben was now on holiday for two weeks in Greece. Paul seemed friendly and pleasant, and Sophie liked him straight away. Gina hadn't arrived yet and the band were ready to start. Mark asked Sophie if she would sing more songs with the band. Accepting without thinking, she took a large sip of her house red and followed him on stage, Tess and Jane clapping her. Wearing on-trend black boots, black top and with her new red and white hippy-style skirt floating behind her, Sophie took Gina's place on stage.

The words were on a stand and the band encouraged her throughout the night, and she knew that she had sung reasonably well. The applause confirmed it, and she felt great as she stepped from the stage. She would have been even happier if she hadn't noticed Gina glaring at her. She had arrived late and was taking off her coat in the corner of the room, but Sophie still couldn't stop the glow of excitement. Tess got Mark to announce that they had made £762 from the reggae night. Gina looked across at Sophie and then quickly back at Mark.

At the end of the night, Sophie picked up her bag and was just about to leave when Paul approached her and asked if she would like to sing at a free and easy night on Saturday at a pub the other side of town. The group had no girl singers and he and his sister Jess were going. Sophie, still feeling unusually confident, said she would love to, and they arranged to meet in the Crown car park at 8.30pm.

Sophie took her coat from the peg in the entrance of the club. Her coat, now dry, had been drenched by the heavy rain that she had walked through across the car park. The rain was still beating down, so Sophie hurried to her car, opened the door quickly and drove down the drive. While she sat in her car waiting for the car in front of her to turn into the main road, she suddenly realised what she had let herself in for.

She didn't have Paul's phone number so she couldn't change her mind and would have to go to the Crown pub.

The next morning the rain was still heavily bouncing off the pavements.

Before opening the shop, Sophie walked down the street to post a birthday card to her sister. Pushing her cold hands deep into her pockets, she made her way back to her shop. Pulling out the shop keys from her pockets, a folded piece of paper fell on the ground. Sophie opened the shop, took off her coat and was just about to throw the piece of paper away, together with a receipt and a biscuit wrapping, when she noticed there was something written on it.

KEEP THIS NUMBER. YOU'LL NEED IT.

Sophie reread the number. She didn't recognise it. How did it get there? It was an old coat which she only wore when the weather was really wet. It must be from Paul, Sophie decided.

She sat on the tall chair by the counter and tapped in the number on the shop phone. It rang for a while and Sophie was about to end the call when a man with a low doleful voice answered, 'Smith and Dyer Undertakers.'

Shocked, Sophie quickly put the phone down.
Who had put that note in her pocket?
There was only one person – Gina!

Twelve

Saturday night found Sophie walking into the Crown pub with Paul and Jess. They bought drinks from the bar and sat down and talked for most of the night when they weren't singing. Paul was a plumber at the local firm Westbourne, and Jess was the mother of two small boys. It was unusual for Jess to go out on a Saturday night, but her friend had offered to babysit for her. Her partner, Bob, was on a stag weekend in Ireland, and he had insisted that she should go out and enjoy herself as well.

Jess showed Sophie photos of the boys which she kept on her phone. Sophie thought how nice it would have been if she had managed to go out occasionally when Tom was younger, and wished again that Dave had been more considerate.

She was brought back to reality when the band started playing and she was called up to sing. It was strange singing with a different band, but she got good applause for Adele's "Someone like you" and some of her other favourite songs, and so she was happy and pleased she had been asked to go and hadn't cancelled the evening.

Sophie got on well with Jess. She told Sophie that Paul had talked a lot about her after he had heard her singing at the club and had said that she had a great voice. Sophie learned that Paul and Jess hadn't had many relationships, not having been able to go out often because they looked after their mother part-time before she died, and now they suddenly found themselves free. They sat around talking and listening to the music, enjoying the different atmosphere. Sophie and Jess danced together for a while. At the end of the night, they swapped telephone numbers and said goodbye.

Two nights later Sophie was sitting in the local cinema with Paul. They enjoyed the war film and she felt so relaxed with him. After the film they went for a meal at the Crown pub, where they talked non-stop about music. He told her he was also an artist. Sophie knew a lot of musicians were artistic, so wasn't surprised. He specialised in cars, motorbikes and boats. Sophie told him that she could display some of his canvases in her studio if he was interested. She had never displayed his type of paintings before and was eager to exhibit them.

On Tuesday at lunchtime Sophie and Paul went around the art gallery in Bilberry, which was something that Sophie had promised herself she would do since she had left to start up her shop. After walking around the gallery, they sat in the gallery café, discussing the artwork they had seen. Paul was muscly. His suntan, from the hot summer before, was now fading. He was taller than average, with greying black hair, and kind blue eyes. She enjoyed his company as he was interested in her and was also considerate, which Sophie found refreshing. He was just the opposite of Dave.

After visiting the gallery Paul invited her to his house in the evening to see what paintings she thought she could display. Sophie took two large canvases back with her to put in her studio in the morning; one of a vintage Rolls Royce Phantom car, the other of an old Triumph Bonneville motorbike. They would definitely be something different to hang on her wall. Paul told her he had no idea what they were worth and to get what price she could for them.

Sophie thought that she and Paul seemed so much alike, enjoying talking about the same things.

Perhaps that was the problem.

Thursday night found Paul and Sophie sitting together by

themselves at the club. Tess and Jane sat further along the bench seat. Paul had bought her a drink and had his arm loosely around her, but she felt slightly uncomfortable. Gina walked past, ignoring her as usual, but Sophie had seen her looking over in her direction quite a lot of times during the night. Mark looked on and scowled, seeing Paul sitting so close to her.

This was the last Thursday that Paul would be singing at the club and, despite Paul sitting next to her, Sophie was really looking forward to seeing Ben next week.

That evening Sophie had a decision to make – a safe or an exciting relationship?

She had already made it.

Sophie and Paul parted as friends.

Paul seemed disappointed, but they promised to phone each other should they want to sing together again one night. Sophie told Paul she would contact him when his paintings had been sold and she hoped to see him at the club on the nights when he could go.

Thirteen

Struggling with the mountain of washing as well as pushing the vacuum around at one o'clock in the morning made Sophie decide to advertise for a cleaner. The money she would earn from her Adam James paintings would easily pay for one. She could also offer to pay Dave for helping her keep the shop books up to date, having not been able to afford to pay him before. She knew he wouldn't agree, but it would make her feel more independent, and of course she could send Tom some more money too.

Feeling happy with this decision she put the vacuum away underneath the stairs.

She would advertise tomorrow.

Tuesday, two days later. Sophie waited expectantly at home to interview the cleaners.

Knock on the house door.

'Hello, I'm Kathy, answering your advert for a cleaner.'

Sophie showed her round the house after explaining she wanted help with ironing, washing, cleaning, and cooking. Kathy said she only did housework.

Knock on the house door.

'Hello, I'm Jane. I can only work two hours a week.'

Knock on the house door.

'Hi, I'm Joan. Can't do any heavy work – bad back.'

No knock on the door.

Jake never turned up.

Sophie got out the vacuum from underneath the stairs again and, disappointed, did it herself.

Saturday morning Sophie had to go to the local post office which was now situated in the small convenience store on the high street. She wanted to send a canvas to a customer in Devon. He had bought it while visiting his cousin and was travelling back by train and didn't want to damage the painting on the journey. Sophie decided she would look on the notice board while she was there, as she might find an advert for a cleaner wanting work.

She handed over her canvas and paid for the postage, put the receipt in her pocket, and checked the notice board.

There was just one advert. She took out her phone and put in the number of Janet Frazier.

Walking around the small aisles to buy some bread, she noticed Mark enter the shop, with a blonde woman. He walked ahead, while the woman carried a parcel in one hand and pushed twin boys, aged about two, in a stroller with the other hand. A little girl about three was holding on to the woman's coat. Sophie tried to hide behind the large upright freezer, pretending to look at the vegetables. She watched the woman drop the large parcel on the counter, buy groceries and some sweets for the children and then struggle to open the door and leave, while Mark was already outside, waiting impatiently for her. Sophie didn't think Mark had seen her. Three children? Was that his partner? He didn't seem to bother about her. She watched as he strode down the street in front of the woman, leaving her to carry the shopping and also to look after the children. *Poor woman*, Sophie thought.

When she went home Sophie eagerly tapped in Janet Frazer's number.

Janet arrived two hours later. Early 60s. She said she had been cleaning for years and produced one reference.

Janet started the next day. She wouldn't usually work on a Sunday, but Sophie wanted to get to know her and give her instructions. Janet seemed enthusiastic and had finished by lunchtime. Sophie gave her the key.

On Monday morning Sophie went to work, happy and excited that her house would be tidy and clean when she got home.

She phoned Paul to tell him that both his paintings had been sold to a motor museum in Chellingsford. The buyer was on holiday in Timberry and liked them straight away. He had asked Sophie to get in touch with him if she had any more to sell in the future, and to send photos of them. Paul said he would be over before lunch, and Sophie asked him to bring another two of his paintings in for her to display.

Sophie had sold paintings online a few years previously, but it was too much of a hassle posting and packing them and waiting for customer comments. She had had a few customers send them back, claiming that they were dented when they received them. Some demanded their money back but wanted to keep the paintings, so she now preferred to deal with her customers personally.

Sophie gave Paul his money and the phone number of the motor museum. He could probably deal with them direct in the future as well as placing some in her shop.

Paul was really pleased, and he took Sophie out for an early lunch at The Tavern. Sophie still liked him and enjoyed his company. He was so laid back and still interested in her, asking what she had been doing since he had last spoken to her. They stayed talking and laughing together longer than they had intended. Paul eventually paid the bill while Sophie went to the cloakroom. Sophie left the bar area and walked through the old-fashioned lounge; she was shocked to see Ben and Gina sitting cosily in the armchairs by the log fire, drinking beers and deep in conversation. Wasn't he too old for her? Sophie felt disappointed.

When they got back to the shop, Paul carefully held the stepladder for her while she reached the hooks at the top of the wall. She was used to going up and down the ladder by herself but didn't refuse Paul's offer of help. Sophie displayed his two new motorbike paintings, while he waited for her to climb down and then he put the ladder away. She had this feeling that she would have always been able to trust him. His sister Jess was just as nice, always asking Paul how she was.

But she told herself she had made her choice. She had chosen excitement. Not a safe relationship.

Paul said goodbye and thanked her, saying he might see her one night at the open mic when he could make it. Sophie thanked him for the meal and hoped that his other paintings would sell quickly, and said she looked forward to seeing him at the club soon. She opened the door for him, he kissed her on the cheek and Sophie watched him walk quickly down the street and disappear, his now-familiar aftershave lingering long after he had left.

The afternoon turned out to be remarkably busy. A group of ramblers, on a coach trip, came in on their way back from walking along the nine-mile walk which circled the town and then trailed along the beach. Sophie spent the time trying to find small cheap paintings from the workshop for them to look through, after serving them hot drinks and cakes. The group went out of the shop, quite happy with their purchases, taking photos on their phones. After they left, she mopped water and sand left on the floor by their walking boots and hung up a forgotten wet umbrella on the stand.

After the busy, tiring and somewhat emotional day, Sophie was happy that at least the house would be cleaned.

Sophie arrived home to find Kenny meowing at his dish, the washing still beside the washing machine, washing up in the sink. Sophie tapped in Janet's number.

'Sorry,' Janet said. 'Bad migraine. I will be in tomorrow.'

Sophie sympathised with her, telling her to come in later the next day.

The next day when Sophie arrived home, after another busy nine hours in her shop, the washing was still next to the washing machine, and Kenny was standing at the back door waiting to go out.

Sophie rang Janet again.

'Sorry,' Janet chirped. 'I have another cleaning job which I had to go to. I hope to be in tomorrow.'

Sophie waited impatiently for her the next morning.

'Sorry, Janet, you're not reliable.' Sophie asked for the key back.

Janet shrugged her shoulders.

'Let's hope you don't regret not employing me,' she snarled and left quickly, but not before sliding the £20 note up her sleeve that Sophie had left for the window cleaner.

Disappointed and tired, Sophie carried on as usual.

Fourteen

Two weeks later Paul phoned to say that the motor museum wanted to buy seven more of his paintings, which he was taking to Chellingsford that weekend, and would Sophie like to go with him to look around?

Sophie immediately said yes, she would love to go. She checked that she didn't have any clients coming in on Saturday and put a notice on her shop door saying that she would be closed for two days.

Paul had booked two nights at a small hotel just outside Chellingsford, Sophie making sure he had booked two rooms before she packed an overnight bag. They thoroughly enjoyed the weekend. They went around the car museum later in the morning. It was only a small building but there were such a lot of interesting things to see. They stopped to look at Paul's canvases, which blended in well with the items the museum was exhibiting.

Afterwards they walked around the old-fashioned shops. The weather was cold but sunny, and they stopped to have lunch at a small Italian restaurant, which they had found by accident when they lost their way walking along the narrow streets.

After their meal Sophie took her card out of her bag and offered to pay, as Paul had paid for the hotel, but Paul insisted on treating her, telling Sophie he would pay with some of the money he had earned from the paintings.

Sunday night found Sophie and Paul at an open mic night held in the Lantern pub, next to the hotel. They just sat and listened, enjoying the atmosphere, talking to the singers, and seeing how the evening was organised, disappointed that they had to leave before it ended as they had an early start the next day and had to go to work.

When they arrived home, Sophie thanked Paul for a lovely weekend and told him that she would phone him later in the week. She really had enjoyed his company.

Fifteen

Another Thursday night arrived, and Sophie, Tess and Jane sat on their usual bench seat. Sophie sang two songs: "Perfect", and "Girls Just Want To Have Fun" on stage, and when she had finished, a group of women asked her to sing an Abba song, after which she sat down and Gina then hogged the limelight. Occasionally Gina would look across at Sophie threateningly.

Tonight, Gina was dressed all in black and her purple-black hair was tied in a ponytail, tucked under a black bowler hat. *She looked quite sinister*, Sophie thought, *almost like an undertaker*. Sophie admitted to herself then that it was Gina who had sent her that note. *She's not playing mind games with me*, Sophie thought, although she did feel a chilly uneasiness.

Sophie had to admit that Gina, although a strange person, had a good voice and moved about the stage with ultra-confidence, never wearing the same clothes each week. Sophie thought that perhaps she needed an even better image too. When she went to the charity shop on Sunday she would see if there were any unusual clothes that she could buy.

At the end of the night Sophie was fed up with being stared at by Mark. Knowing that he could have a partner and three children, she certainly wasn't the least bit tempted. Why did he follow her every move?

Ben came over and joined Sophie, Tess and Jane. It was good to see him again, and Sophie told them about the great weekend she had spent with Paul and they were all interested in the open mic night they attended.

Ten minutes later Ben managed to spill a whole glass of beer down her new white top while trying to explain to them how to play the new harmonica that he had recently bought. He offered her a handkerchief and they both stared in embarrassment. Sophie felt the brown beer trickle down her skin. 'I will have to go home,' she said, getting up and placing her scarf artistically round the offending stains. Ben walked her to the door and into the car park. Mark watched.

'Let me make it up to you. Let me take you for a meal,' Ben pleaded, his dark brown eyes worried. Then, suddenly remembering that she might be with Paul, added, 'If Paul doesn't mind.'

'Paul? Oh no,' Sophie said, feeling only slightly guilty. 'We're really just good friends, that's all.'

Sophie, feeling sorry for Ben, and finding him more than good-looking, couldn't refuse his offer to go out for a meal with him.

Although Paul had been the first date she had been on since before she married Dave, she hadn't felt at all nervous. Going with Ben for a meal was totally different. To say she was stressed was putting it mildly.

Ben picked her up from the shop on Friday after work and they went for a Chinese meal in Bilberry. The restaurant was crowded but they managed to find a table for two in the centre of the room, between two pillars. She found him easier to talk to than she had expected, and the food was quickly served by a talkative waiter who seemed to know Ben. Sophie didn't remember the last time she had been to a Chinese restaurant.

She thought of all the things she had missed being married to Dave. Ben interrupted her thoughts, asking her if she wanted a coffee. The waiter brought over two small cups and they sat talking for a long time. Other customers came in, dined and left, without Sophie noticing.

Ben told Sophie his parents died when he was young, and that he was brought up in a caravan by his aunt.

Three years ago, he was living with Grace, his girlfriend. Grace had moved from Wales to Timberry to become an infant teacher at the local school. She wanted to introduce music and singing in her after-school lessons, and after Ben had been recommended to her by one of his pupils, Grace contacted him and he gave her guitar and harmonica lessons at her flat. He taught her twice a week and they became good friends. After a while Grace left her rented flat and moved in with him.

One morning Grace stayed at home, as she had a bad cold, felt dizzy and didn't feel well enough to go into school. Ben left her in bed in the morning and phoned her later, and she told him she felt a lot better, had walked to the nearby shops and was doing some schoolwork. In the afternoon she wasn't answering her mobile, so he went home early, and found her lying in the hall. She had tripped on a pile of books that she had left on the stairs. Ben often wondered if Grace had tried to call him, but she had left her phone on the kitchen table, and it was switched off, something he thought was unusual as she always kept her phone on and nearly always had it with her.

It had been a traumatic time for him dealing with the inquest, informing her family, and helping to arrange her funeral, and Ben didn't have a family to help him.

Afterwards he moved back to the local caravan park as he couldn't face living in the house again. He was brought up living on a gypsy site in Drayston, so he was quite used to the limited space and he was out most of the day and a lot of evenings.

He told Sophie that he still taught the guitar to pupils at their homes and he helped local builders out with any jobs they wanted doing. That type of life suited him.

They sat quietly for a moment, Ben deep in thought, and Sophie not knowing what to say.

Eventually Ben stopped slowly stirring his coffee, which was now cold, and said he couldn't face having another relationship. Sophie tried hard to convince herself she didn't want a relationship with him, either. For her, it wouldn't feel right, after only recently divorcing Dave. They ordered another coffee, drank quickly and left.

Ben dropped her back at the shop, where she turned off the lights, locked the office and closed the shop door. She found him still standing outside in the cold night breeze.

'Car has a flat tyre.'

'Leave it behind the shop in the car park and I will drive you home,' Sophie offered.

They both got into her car and he stretched his long legs in front of him.

Five minutes later she drove through Timberry caravan park, down the narrow tracks surrounded by lawns. Fairy lights twinkled around the small, sculptured trees, and there were pots of winter flowers placed by the caravan doors. Sophie stopped the car at the side of Ben's large cream caravan. Ben leant over her and gave her a friendly kiss. Sophie was disappointed, as she had hoped he would invite her into his caravan so she could see inside.

'I will pick up the car tomorrow.'

'Thanks for the meal, I really enjoyed it,' Sophie replied.

He told her the shortcut way out of the park.

As she reversed between the caravans, Sophie saw the curtains move in the caravans nearby, while a tabby cat strolled in front of her, making its way to the fields opposite. She turned up the heater. Sophie suddenly felt a cold icy chill creep through her body and turned up her collar. The weather was getting colder now. She must think about putting the Christmas decorations up soon.

Thursday nights were good. Ben and Sophie sat by each other when they could and they had quite a few nights out, enjoying each other's company. Ben took her to more clubs and pubs in the area, where she had never been. Sophie again explained to Ben that she didn't want anything serious and again he agreed, much to her disappointment.

She hadn't heard from Paul for a while as he was working in

Scotland on a large contract with his firm. He had phoned her a few times, but he didn't know when he would be back. Sophie couldn't help wondering what he was doing in the evenings.

Sixteen

During the first week in December, Timberry held its Christmas Market over the weekend, where farmers sold their fresh produce, and stalls displayed unusual things suitable for Christmas presents. There were toy and cake stalls, and people came from nearby villages. The town was free of traffic for the weekend, so people could walk safely around the town. Tess had made toys for animals on her stall and was selling them together with healthy pet snacks to make money for her charity.

Sophie had promised to help Tess on the stall and asked Paul if he could look after the shop while she helped on Saturday afternoon. He was happy to do so, arriving wearing a Christmas hat and carrying a box of chocolates for Sophie. She opened the box, and they ate a couple with their hot coffee, sitting in the shop window. Sophie thought how cosy it felt looking through the window, watching the Christmas festivities outside.

Sophie walked slowly between the stalls. Father Christmas was giving out toys from a large sack, and mulled wine was being handed out by his elves to the adults. Children were having rides on his sleigh which was lit up with lights, and children were being pulled along by more elves. She loved Christmas, she thought it came at the right time of year to brighten up the winter. She looked at the large Christmas tree, paid for by the shopkeepers, which was decorated and now glowing in the dusk.

After an afternoon in the cold, Sophie returned to the shop to find Paul, wearing his coat and scarf, waiting to take her to The Tavern for a fish and chip meal.

She was never surprised by his thoughtfulness.

Seventeen

Two weeks before Christmas, Ben invited Sophie to a Christmas dinner and rock 'n' roll night at a large hotel in Brighton. The hotel appeared to be very old; white pebbledash with lattice bay windows and lanterns by the door. Christmas lights were hung around the fir tree at the side of the building, which completed the Christmas scene. This was something different. Sophie felt as though she was in another world as she walked into reception with Ben after the long taxi ride.

The food was delicious, four courses with lots of wine. Eventually, when the meal was finished, the tables were cleared, except for the small flickering candles which were now burning low, and the Christmas snowflake decorations scattered on the tablecloths. The band started playing, and Sophie asked a couple sitting by them if they would take a photo of Ben and her together. It was a beautiful photo of Sophie and Ben dancing. Sophie offered to take one of the couple but they quickly declined.

She hadn't danced on a large dance floor for years, not even with Paul. She had danced at the club, but it was nothing like this and after feeling initially awkward and embarrassed, she was really enjoying herself. Sophie hadn't realised that Ben was such a fantastic dancer and they danced nearly all night, stopping occasionally to walk outside where the air was frosty and refreshing.

The evening went by too quickly. The band said goodnight, the main lights were turned on and after a while turned off, and they were the only ones left on the dimly lit dance floor. The man and woman who had taken their photo had had far too much to drink and were now slumped in their chairs on the opposite side of the dance floor. They were guided slowly to their room by the barman.

Ben and Sophie slowly finished their drinks. Sophie picked up her high heels, which she had abandoned under the table earlier in the evening, and barefooted she followed Ben up the wide staircase which, on the third floor, turned into a narrow attic landing. They disappeared into separate bedrooms next to each other. Sophie watched Ben go in and close his door. He didn't look back at her. She then closed hers. Was she expecting too much?

The next morning Ben was already in the restaurant drinking coffee, talking on the phone, not looking too pleased. He quickly ended the conversation. How did he manage to look so alert and bright, when she felt really rough, and her legs and arms ached?

'Everything okay?' Sophie asked, pouring herself a coffee, and refilling Ben's cup.

'It was Mark, asking if I could give him a hand with a complicated burglar alarm system and some electrics he is fitting today. I told him I was with you and I would get there as soon as I could. He didn't sound too pleased.'

Sophie knew why he didn't sound too pleased.

'I didn't know he fitted burglar alarms,' Sophie said, surprised.

The very mention of Mark's name made her uneasy.

'Yes, that's how he met Julie, fitting alarms in her dad's plastic moulding factory. Her dad's worth millions.'

'Oh!'

Breakfast finished, bill paid, Sophie carried her overnight bag to the waiting taxi. Ben, already waiting for her, was on his phone again. He cut the call when he saw her.

As soon as Sophie arrived home, she downloaded the photo of Ben and herself and put it on her kitchen shelf. She loved it. They looked so good together. She was thinking about framing the photo or even painting it on canvas. Sophie was tempted to send a copy of the photo over to Ben's phone, but decided not to, as it would send the wrong message.

Last night had been a really special night. One she would remember for a long time.

Eighteen

Wednesday was half-day closing. Sophie didn't do any housework, but although it was very cold outside, she tidied her garden, glad of the fresh air. Kenny looked on from the warmth of the kitchen. She booked an online shop for early Thursday evening, and was also able to catch up with her phone calls to her mother, and sister Megan. Since they moved to Cornwall after her father died, she rarely saw them, as they were always busy with their own lives, but they did phone each other occasionally, if they had any important family news.

Megan and her mother both loved Dave and had taken his side in all the arguments that Sophie and he used to have. Sophie never talked to her family about the disagreements, but Dave phoned them to keep them informed on what was going on. They never understood why she wanted to divorce him, and it caused quite an upsetting time for Sophie. Dave sometimes called in to see them when he had a job in the area and always took her mother a bunch of flowers. Something Sophie was never given by him.

Nineteen

Walking past the bar on Thursday night, Mark stood in front of Sophie, put his hand on her shoulder and warned her not to be surprised if she found that Ben wasn't all that he seemed to be, and that she could always go out with him for a meal when he would explain. Sophie pushed away his arm.

'Don't keep asking, as the answer will always be the same.'

Mark huffed and took his beer to his table.

Later in the evening, after washing her hands, Sophie caught her antique ring on the cloakroom tap and the ring snapped and fell to the floor. Upset, she went back to her seat and examined it, showing it to Tess and Jane. Ben looked carefully and suggested he take it to a friend in the jewellery trade, to see if it could be repaired. Sophie hesitated, as it was her great-grandmother's engagement ring. Could she trust him not to lose it? She eventually agreed, saying she would like it back, repaired or not, by the following week.

The week passed slowly, even though she was busy with her artwork and, as Christmas was just a few days away, she still had lots of seasonal things to prepare. Sophie was still convinced she wouldn't see her ring again – not that Ben would steal it, but it could easily get lost, and it was very fragile.

Sophie needn't have worried. The following Thursday night Ben took a small blue box from his pocket which he gave to Sophie. She opened it, and her ring sat shining in the satin interior. She took it out and hugged him.

Ben said he was glad to hand it over to her, as it had been on his bedroom table for the last few days.

'Thank you,' Sophie said, relieved. 'How much do I owe you?'

'Nothing, as Andy, the jeweller, has owed me a big favour for ages. I recommended him to a friend of mine who wanted an expensive necklace and matching earrings for his girlfriend, and she was over the moon with what he bought her. You can take me out after Christmas,' Ben suggested.

Noticing Mark scowling at the next table, Sophie put the ring on, in his view, almost wishing she could put it on her left hand. What was she thinking? They had also attracted some interest from people sitting nearby, who were looking over at them. During the night they sang together, and they even danced on the small dance floor at the back of the room. Sophie felt very happy. Gina watched, but her face, contorted with extreme jealousy, was lost in the darkness.

Twenty

Paul phoned Sophie on Christmas Eve, wanting to know if he could see her. Sophie lied, saying she had a cousin staying and that she would see him next week. Disappointed, he told her to have a good holiday.

On Christmas morning there was a present and a card waiting for her in the porch. Ben had bought her something after all. Why hadn't he knocked at the door?

Sophie sat in her lounge and opened the present, carefully undoing the ribbon wrapped around the expensive wrapping paper. Wrapped in tissue was the gold miniature Indian painting she had admired when she had been in Bilberry art gallery with Paul. Sophie didn't have to read the small card to know who had left the gift for her.

Christmas came and went quickly, Sophie spending it by herself, opening her presents and watching the usual Christmas programmes. There was a three-minute phone call to her mother and Megan, before their neighbours called in to watch the Queen's speech and have Christmas drinks.

Sophie was disappointed that she didn't hear from Ben over the three days and that he hadn't thought to buy her a gift. She had bought him some of his favourite aftershave, but she told herself that they weren't in a proper relationship and he would have a surprise planned for her later.

Twenty-One

The New Year started hectically, after a relaxing Christmas. Adam James phoned, wanting to collect the last batch of artwork at dinner time.

A box of canvases was left on the doorstep and a large pile of faux leather was still on the floor. Sophie was just about to drag the leather through to her workshop when the door clanged, and the phone rang at the same time.

Sophie picked up the phone and pointed to the elderly lady who had just entered to take a seat. After five minutes of conversation about hessian backing, she replaced the phone, only to pick it up again to explain to the next caller the opening times of the shop.

Sophie apologised for the delay.

'Don't apologise. I have been on my feet since five o'clock. I am glad of the sit down.' The elderly lady placed her trolley beside her.

'What are you interested in?' Sophie asked.

'My daughter is getting married, and I would like to buy them a picture. They have been really good to me. It would have to be a small painting as I don't have much money, being a cleaner, and I am about to lose my job next week because the lady I clean for is moving away, so I have to be careful.'

Sophie said she had more paintings in the back which she hadn't had time to display.

'Would you like a drink while you wait?'

'I'll make it myself if you like, you look as if you could do with one as well.'

When Sophie eventually returned from the workroom with the paintings, the cups of coffee were on a tray with some chocolate biscuits which the elderly lady had found and was already eating.

Sophie showed the woman five of the cheapest paintings, in different designs, and asked the colour scheme of the room.

'Cream.'

'Then I think this one would go well.' Sophie pointed to the green and cream abstract design.

'How much is that?' taking out her purse.

Sophie could see that at the most she had £30.

'These paintings are due to go in the sale next week at £10,' she lied.

'Then I'll take it. Can you wrap it in nice paper for me?'

Sophie wrapped it carefully in tissue and placed it in a red gift bag with a tag. She could afford to be generous.

The woman headed to the door, opening it very slowly, dragging her trolley.

'Wait. Do you live locally?' Sophie shouted, and then hesitated. 'I may have need for a cleaner.'

The old lady smiled and turned around.

'Where do you live? As I don't have a car and I'd have to use the bus.'

'Here in Timberry. On the seafront.'

'How much would you pay me?'

'That depends on what you want to do. I would appreciate cleaning, washing and some cooking if possible – anything you see that needs doing.'

'I can't do much heavy shopping.'

'Won't be necessary. I shop online.'

'How many are in the house?'

'Only me. Oh, and Kenny my cat.'

Twenty-Two

Iris started at the end of January, a few weeks after their meeting in the shop.

Sophie thought Iris was wonderful. She let herself in and out and never got in the way. The only rule that Sophie insisted on was not to go in or clean her bedroom. Sophie left messages about things she would like Iris to do.

What would Dave say about her having a cleaner as well?

Sophie learned that Iris lived by herself in Bilberry and had been married for fifty-one years before her husband Tony had died last year. She had one daughter who had recently moved to Forfar in Scotland, because her Scottish partner had recently started a new job there.

Iris wasn't very tall. She had short, straight, dyed black hair, with a fringe, which framed a plump sallow face and alert small button-brown eyes. She wore bright red lipstick, applied quite heavily. She was lonely and hard-up, so Sophie was kind to her, and Iris soon settled into a regular routine, which suited both her and Sophie.

January went by quickly. Sophie and Ben became closer.

In early February, Ben offered to tidy up her garden, but he could only make Sunday mornings. Sophie was pleased as, although she loved working in the charity shop, she looked forward to helping Ben in the garden. Sophie phoned Tess the day before and Tess told her that there would be three people helping in the shop so she would be okay.

Ben cut down branches, which were left hanging down due to the heavy snow and winds that had caused damage during the last two months, and he put new fences up, making her garden safer. He replaced the old rope washing line which had rotted, cleared the gutters, and raked the decaying leaves, which were brown and embedded in the grass. Sophie followed him, sweeping leaves and twigs into green plastic bags. She then mowed the lawn, while Kenny lay under the fir trees, watching.

Sophie offered to make Ben lunch, but he refused, saying he was running late and had to get back to the caravan before one o'clock. Sophie wondered why, but didn't ask.

Twenty-Three

Mid-February brought the sun and more cold winds, and Sophie was looking forward to a meal with Ben for her forty-sixth birthday on the 18th. But Ben had other ideas and suggested that she have a party, inviting just the group. Sophie hesitated, saying she would have to think about it. Ben insisted that it would be great for the band to get together socially when not playing at the Maple Leaf. So, of course, Sophie gave in, but on the condition that he organised it and asked everyone, as she didn't want to. She wasn't looking forward to it, but at least she didn't have to worry about the catering. She would invite Tess and Jane, as she knew they would enjoy the night and it would be good to have them there to talk to.

Thursday, February 18th arrived, and Sophie went to work, leaving instructions for Iris regarding food and drink for the party. The online delivery service would deliver at lunchtime and Iris said she would deal with it.

Sophie wouldn't be back before the party, as she was working late on a particularly difficult extra-large canvas she was painting, so she picked up her clothes for the evening. She would be able to change at the shop.

Sophie cuddled Kenny and poured some biscuits into his bowl. She rushed out and closed the front door, before realising that she had picked up her spare car fob which didn't have her house key on. She had a key hidden in the hanging basket at the front of the house, so she decided she could use that when she returned home. Her shop keys were on a separate keyring in her bag. Sophie got into her car and made her way to work. She wasn't really looking forward to the evening and she could already feel herself getting nervous.

Iris arrived at the house ten minutes after Sophie had left. She let herself in, made a quick cup of tea in the microwave as she was going to be busy today, and started work.

Cleaning, washing, cooking.

At 11.30pm after the open mic night, and leaving their equipment and cars at the club, the group travelled in three taxis and arrived at Sophie's house together. Sophie walked up the drive and, in the dark, searched through the pansies in the hanging basket for the small plastic box which contained the house key, while everyone waited. Entering the house, balloons and the smell of curry greeted them. The table was laid, and the two large pots of curry were simmering on the cooker. On the table were dishes, naan breads and everything to accompany the curry. In the centre of the table was a chocolate drizzle birthday cake covered with chocolates. That was a lovely surprise from Iris. Sophie put the rice on to cook. Iris must have just left.

But an even bigger surprise was waiting for Sophie.

The doorbell rang.

Dave stood on the doorstep, with a woman leaning lovingly on his arm.

Sophie was shocked.

He had never mentioned that he was seeing anyone. He introduced the woman, smiling proudly.

'Emma...'

Ummm.

Tall. Blonde. Slim. Super-confident. Young. Mid-thirties.

'Happy Birthday, Sophie.' Emma radiated a smile of white teeth and red lipstick, and dramatically held out a bottle of white wine. White!

Sophie never drank white. Dave should have known that.

Sophie forced a welcoming smile, accepted the wine graciously and told them to go in.

Sophie disappeared into the kitchen to calm herself.

Mark reluctantly picked up his partner, Julie, from home in a taxi after Ben said she should go. Sophie liked Julie straight away – quiet, friendly and she felt as though she knew her already even after a few conversations.

Deano came by himself.

Pete came with his partner, Joe.

Tess and Jane arrived a little later. Sophie was pleased to see them.

Gina slipped in without saying anything, Sophie noticing that she walked straight up to Ben and they stood talking quietly by the patio doors, while he handed her a beer. Then they walked through the door out onto the patio.

The night started straight away, singing, drinking, and talking. Sophie's eyes were transfixed by Dave and Emma, sitting so close on the floor, as if they had melted into each other. Was she wearing an engagement ring? Sophie tried to look but couldn't quite see, as Emma had put her hand in her jumpsuit pocket. Things quietened down and everyone started to eat.

'Aren't you eating?' Sophie asked Gina, who was now standing by the door.

'There is nothing vegetarian,' she replied in a loud cutting voice.

'There's vegetable curry in the other pot,' replied Sophie. 'They are marked.'

'Thank you, Iris,' Sophie said under her breath.

Gina coloured slightly, walked over to the table and then sat down by herself, with a large plateful of food.

Attention was drawn to Kenny, who was now meowing, staring at the party through the patio window, his fur being ruffled by the cold evening breeze.

'Anyone mind if I let Kenny in?' Sophie asked.

Everyone said no, let him in.

Everyone except Gina, who said she didn't like cats – they were evil.

'Overruled,' said Ben, opening the patio doors, and Kenny sauntered in, shaking himself. He looked up at the table, walked across the room and happily settled by Gina, shaking himself again. Gina moved to the edge of the chaise longue, holding her plate higher.

Sophie walked into the kitchen to make coffee, as the bottles of wine were disappearing fast. She took a bottle of milk from the fridge, filled and switched on the kettle. Iris had left a note that the coffee maker had inconveniently broken that morning, so she had bought a jar of expensive coffee instead. Sophie thankfully took the coffee from the cupboard.

A cloud of expensive perfume made Sophie turn around. Emma towered over her.

'Can I help?' Emma smouldered.

'Thank you,' Sophie replied, smiling. 'That would be great.'

Thinking quickly of all the questions...

'It's lovely to meet you. Dave has talked about you so much,' she lied.

'Yes, he is such a lovely man. He has been so kind to me over the past three years since you have been separated.'

Three years! It was then that Sophie noticed that the ring Emma was wearing was an engagement ring. A huge diamond. Sophie realised she was staring and looked away quickly, but Emma had noticed.

'It's beautiful, isn't it? I am so excited about getting married. I have always wanted to, but never got around to it.'

Sophie realised then that Dave must have been seeing Emma while still married to her. She managed to compose herself by breathing deeply.

'It's beautiful,' said Sophie. 'It's so unusual. Where did you buy it?'

'Oh, we went to Rome for the week three years ago, just after we met, and he proposed then.'

Sophie realised that all this must have been going on without her knowing. That must have been the week he said he was working at the chain of hotels in Wales. Sophie had asked if she could go with him for a holiday, but he had said it would be unsociable hours. She now felt so stupid.

Sophie thought about her ring that Dave had given her – a tiny faux diamond set in even smaller stones, which they had bought from a second-hand antique shop. It was old and cheap, but she had thought the world of it. In fact, she was still wearing it on her other hand. She slid the engagement ring from her finger and dropped it quietly in the bin, watching it fall, blending in with the discarded curry and rice. It meant nothing to her at that moment.

Emma was still looking at her ring, while she poured Dave's coffee, Sophie noticing that he must prefer it black now. She wondered how many other things had changed.

She soon found out.

'And little George loves his daddy so much.'

Sophie listened in a thick fog.

Little George? Sophie tried to focus and look delighted.

'Have you any orange juice?' Emma asked. 'As I am not drinking tonight. I expect Dave has told you that I am pregnant again,' Emma enthused. 'It will be good for George to have a sister.' She patted her invisible bump with her hand, Sophie noticing her perfect long pink nails.

'Oh yes, he did tell me. Lovely news,' Sophie lied again, and now feeling shattered.

'Where will you live?' asked Sophie, trying to sound interested and not shocked or jealous, which she was now beginning to feel.

'Oh, didn't Dave tell you? We are moving to Cornwall. We are selling the flat. I never liked it anyway, although I have only lived there for a few months, but it has nowhere for George to play, and I have always wanted to live in Cornwall. Dave said I could choose the house. I used to live in Newcastle and have never owned a house with a garden. Dave can work from home until he gets an office and, of course, he has your family nearby, who he is very fond of. I expect they will love to see the children.'

Cornwall... my family... of course, Emma must have

been the woman Sophie had seen on Dave's balcony. Their conversation was cut short when Gina walked in, swaying, demanding another tin of beer. *Well-timed*, thought Sophie.

Thrusting a pack of beer towards Gina, Sophie excused herself and went to her downstairs bathroom, forgetting to close the door. She held on to the sink to steady herself. And tears of real hate and jealousy flowed. She was so upset. Dave had lied to her all this time and little George? A baby sister? Dave had never wanted another child, and Cornwall, close to her parents! Sophie tried to breathe.

She felt a warm arm round her shoulders. Ben had come looking for her, to see if he could help in the kitchen. Ben hugged her. Tearfully she explained to him what had just happened.

'Come on. Let's go back into the lounge. It's your party. Show them you don't care – let's dance.'

Sophie blew her nose on the tissue that Ben gave her and wiped her eyes with the hand towel that she was now tightly crumpling in hate.

Ben turned the lights down low, turned up the music and he and Sophie danced together, Sophie thankful that her red eyes couldn't be seen. Others joined the dancing. Pete tried to dance with Gina, but she was holding a can and dancing in a world of her own, so he danced with Joe. Mark was looking through his phone for music. Paul must have arrived with his sister Jess, without Sophie seeing them. Jess was dancing with Deano. Paul was helping himself to the leftover curry and talking to Tess. Jane and Julie were eating birthday cake and looking at Julie's phone.

Dave and Emma slow-danced. How Sophie wished she hadn't suggested inviting him. She was beginning to hate him more every minute. She had never hated anyone like this before. He hadn't even wished her a happy birthday, not even a card. He had certainly moved on with his life, even before their divorce. Three years before.

Sophie went upstairs to find Kenny, who had disappeared after Gina had pushed him off the chair, thinking no one had seen her. He was curled under the spare bed, fed up with all the excitement. She stroked him and left him there, re-did her eye make-up and sprayed her perfume.

Wrong move. Mark was lurking by her bedroom door. He pushed her against the wall and kissed her. Sophie made contact, with her knee.

'Don't ever try that again or I will tell Julie and I'm not joking.'

Mark fell to the floor.

While Mark was making a full recovery, Julie was in the kitchen looking around, and she asked Sophie where she had had her new kitchen units made, as she was thinking of replacing her old ones. She had let her house deteriorate over the last couple of years and Mark hadn't been interested in discussing it.

Julie explained that her dad was seriously ill with a heart condition and was not expected to live, so it had been a struggle for her to help keep the house in order, the factory going and look after their children at the same time. She owed it to her father to look after it and it was so stressful. Her mother had died eight years ago and not having any brothers or sisters she was responsible for a lot of things now.

Julie said she had been worried about coming to the party and was really surprised when Mark had said she could go. She hadn't had much of a social life since marrying Mark. He didn't help her in the house or garden as he didn't know anything other than music and fitting security alarms. He didn't take her out often, as she had to look after the children, and he often worked nights. Sophie explained that she was new to the social scene too, as she was just divorced. How she wished she could have told her all about Dave and Emma; Sophie was sure she would have understood.

'I will give you my number,' Julie said. 'Phone me, and perhaps we can meet for lunch sometime, if you don't mind me bringing the children. Perhaps we both could do with some girl time.' They swapped telephone numbers.

'Of course. That would be great. I would love to see the

children. Let me know when you are free, and I'll try to fit in,' Sophie promised.

Sophie did like Julie, there was no snobbery about her. Mark came downstairs.

'I've got your number. I will ring you tomorrow, Julie,' Sophie said, hoping Mark would hear, but he had already opened the door and was on the drive getting into a taxi. Julie kissed Sophie goodbye and left.

Next to go were Deano and Gina, Gina clinging on to Deano with one arm and holding a beer can in the other, now unable to walk properly and moaning that the horrid evil cat had scratched her.

Paul and Jess left next.

'Thank you for inviting us, we have had a lovely time.'

'How's Bob?' Sophie asked.

'He is at home with a heavy cold, that's why my friend Tina is babysitting the boys at her house.'

'It's lovely to see you again and thank you again for the wine.'

Paul kissed her, saying he would be in touch soon, and gave her a bunch of flowers that he had kept in her porch.

Pete and Joe left, trailing the balloons behind them as they walked down the road to the waiting taxi, shouting that they had had a great night.

Tess and Jane kissed Sophie and thanked her for inviting them and disappeared up the road.

Dave and Emma, the last to go, stood by the door.

'Lovely to meet you, Emma,' lied Sophie.

'I hope we will meet again before the wedding,' Emma enthused again.

'Of course, we must,' Sophie enthused back, 'that would be lovely,' surprised at how she was successfully disguising her total dislike for them both.

Dave didn't bother to look at Sophie as he put his jacket over Emma's shoulders. Emma flicked her blonde hair over the collar. It was the jacket Sophie had lovingly bought him two Christmases ago, having taken ages to choose it.

She had never ever felt this kind of hatred before.

Ben closed the door. Sophie and Ben went upstairs. If Dave had moved on, she was certainly going to.

When Sophie woke up Ben had gone to work, and of course she hadn't bothered to set the alarm. Sophie jumped out of bed and showered. The bedroom was a mess and Ben had dropped towels, a comb, and his watch on the bedroom floor. He must have left in a hurry. Sophie picked up his watch which, although it looked expensive, he had probably bought at trade price from his jeweller friend. The back of the watch was engraved "Love G". So someone else had bought it for him. She would give it back to Ben when she saw him next. Sophie wondered who "G" was but knew she wouldn't dare ask. She put the watch on the bedside table, together with the money he had dropped.

Downstairs Sophie tried to clear up last night's mess. It would have been too much for Iris and it wasn't fair. When she was satisfied that it was reasonably tidy, she went to work, still recalling last night.

Should she question Dave about Emma next time she saw him? She could even phone him. Sophie decided to act as though she didn't care. But she did care. She cared a hell of a lot.

Iris arrived shortly after Sophie had left. She finished tidying the lounge and kitchen. Had a coffee, helped herself to some of the leftover birthday cake and the one chocolate that lay hidden under the plate. She smiled at the thank you note Sophie had left her.

Iris had a dental appointment in two hours, so she quickly cleaned downstairs. Upstairs she cleaned the bathroom, threw bath towels in the washing machine and mopped the tiled floor. Sophie had forgotten to close her bedroom door, and there was a cold wind coming through the window that Sophie had left open. Although Iris knew she shouldn't, she wandered in, closed the window and opened the curtains. She slowly looked around, shook her head at the state of the room, took the coffee cups from the bedside table and went downstairs to put them into the dishwasher. She fed Kenny, put on her coat and warm scarf, pulled her trolley outside, closed the front door and stepped into the cold February sun.

Sophie arrived late at the club the following Thursday as all day she had been working on another set of Adam James's canvases. She had started at 6.30am and she was so tired. She would check them in the morning and tell him to collect them in a week's time. That would mean her studio and workroom would be empty, ready for more designs. Perhaps she could give herself a day off. She could ring Julie.

Kerry the barmaid handed her a glass of her usual house red without having to ask what she wanted, and Sophie looked around the room for a seat. It was crowded tonight. She looked round for Ben, as she hadn't seen or heard from him since the night of her party. She saw him sitting by Gina. They sat close to each other in deep conversation, Ben's arm loosely around her. A surge of jealousy overwhelmed Sophie. Of course. "G" was the initial for Gina. That's why Gina was threatening her. She found a seat where she couldn't see them. Mark watched with interest.

It wasn't a very good evening, as she couldn't seem to sing in tune and when Ben managed to disentangle himself from Gina, Sophie didn't have much to say except to give him his watch.

Later, when Ben saw Sophie to her car, she knew she shouldn't, but she just couldn't help it.

'Who was "G"?'

Ben hesitated for a while and told her that the watch was his father's and when he died his sister Gemma had had her initials put on it and had given it to Ben as a family memento before she left for Australia.

'I thought Gina had given it to you,' Sophie said, feeling really stupid. 'And seeing you with her tonight convinced me it must have been her.' She could hear herself sounding even more desperate now. Ben shrugged.

'Gina, God no. She is very young, and has been in young offenders for violence, drug taking and burglary. I was trying to tell her that she is young and has everything to look forward to, now that she is clean and running her Zumba class.'

Sophie didn't know Gina had been in young offenders.

'When did she go there?' Sophie asked Ben.

'Not too sure,' Ben replied, quickly dismissing the subject. 'I think she has been in twice.'

Sophie shuddered.

Sophie apologised, remembering he had told her he had a sister in Australia.

She drove home feeling tired and foolish, and worried that she was becoming a little too fond of Ben. Perhaps she should cool it for a while.

Twenty-Four

On Friday, Sophie phoned Julie for a catch-up. She felt the need to talk to someone and they agreed to meet for a coffee at 11am, later in the morning.

Sitting by herself in the Coffee Cup Café down on the beach, Sophie gazed across the rough sea and swirling sand. She loved sitting in this café as it was open all year and she enjoyed watching the sea alter throughout the seasons. After a while, Julie came rushing down the promenade, pushing the stroller, holding her daughter's hand. The little girl stopping to shake the sand from her tangled blonde hair and stamped her feet.

Julie and Sophie talked for a while, and then ordered coffee and toast and fruit juice for the children. Sophie ordered a pack of sandwiches to take with her for later in the day.

They carried on talking, while the children, Alice, William, and James, crayoned in their books. Sophie looked out of the café window again, watching the seagulls swoop into the rough sea, white against dark turquoise. Julie buttered Alice's toast.

Julie told Sophie that Mark had persuaded her to marry him when they realised she was pregnant with Alice. They married within two months and had a small wedding, which was what Julie had wanted. Mark was good with Alice to start with, when he was at home, but was never interested in Julie or helped with the house or garden.

Julie told Sophie that they weren't emotionally close. Julie blamed herself for being too busy with her family and her dad's business.

Six months before, when Julie learned her father was seriously ill, she had asked Steve Morris if he would take over the running of the factory. Steve had been there for thirty-two years and had had years of experience. He was also respected by most of the workers, and Julie's father had told her that she could depend on him for advice. Steve agreed he would, as long as Mark didn't interfere with how it was run. Steve had been a great help to Julie. But he detested Mark. He never said why. Sophie thought perhaps he knew what Mark was like.

Julie said that Mark never offered to take her to the open mic night with him and she asked Sophie what the club was like on Thursdays. Thinking quickly, Sophie lied, saying that it was good for people who were performing, but it could be boring for others just sitting there. Julie seemed quite happy with her answer. Sophie thought that Mark wouldn't be very pleased if Julie went with him on his nights out.

Sophie tried to tell her that life was busy for everyone and that soon Julie might have more time, especially when the children were at school full-time. They were only at the crèche in the afternoons, as that was more convenient for Julie and she did like having them at home. Julie told Sophie that she worked at home in the evenings sometimes when the children were in bed, and that worked quite well.

The waitress brought over Sophie's sandwiches and Sophie paid the bill. They arranged to meet again soon at the café, when Julie said she would pay.

'Will you tell Mark we have had coffee together?' Sophie asked.

'No, he won't be interested anyway. He never wants to know what I do. He only ever asks about my father.'

I wonder why thought Sophie.

Sophie stood talking to Julie outside the café for a while, in the wind that was now getting stronger, and then they made their way in different directions. She watched Julie walk back along the promenade and across the sand dunes. Sophie sat on a seat, watching the seagulls again for a while; the cold February wind blowing roughly around her. She wondered if she was being a good friend not telling Julie what Mark was really like. Sophie certainly would have wanted to know about Dave. Perhaps she could tell her when the time was right.

Twenty-Five

The open mic group met early the next Thursday evening at The Tavern to discuss the outdoor music festival they were thinking of holding in midsummer. Paul had spoken to Ben about it at Sophie's party, saying that his uncle owned Seagrove Farm, and also the field which went down to the sand dunes which stretched along the edge of the beach.

He had asked his uncle if they could hold the festival there and he had agreed providing the field was cleared of rubbish during the next day. They would have to erect and take down the temporary fencing which would then divide the field and the sand dunes. There were to be no fireworks. His uncle was already insured as he had let the field out occasionally for pig roast parties, morris dancing and the occasional receptions for weddings which were sometimes held on the beach.

There was now electricity and lighting in the large new barn that had been built, where the band could play, and the grass would be cut for the event by one of the farm workers. Paul's uncle would provide tables and chairs.

In exchange, the group offered to help with a twenty-fifth wedding anniversary party for three hundred guests that Paul's uncle was organising which was being held next year and they told him the band would play free of charge at night if they were wanted.

Midsummer, 21st June, fell on a Saturday which would be ideal, as more people would be able to go. There would be music, dancing, walks along the seafront. Food table. Catering. Marquee. Where would they get the food from? Beer. Drinks. These were the ideas being put forward. Everyone was enthusiastic. Although it was a few months away things had to be organised. They would all meet the day after the festival and clear the field.

They could advertise online, but the group decided that they would prefer to limit the event to local people and have fewer people there. How much entrance fee should the festivalgoers be asked to pay? Would someone stand by the entrance collecting money and where should the profit they make go to? Perhaps some to the local charities. What time should it start? Questions and ideas were thrown around and discussed.

The meeting ended and everyone agreed to think about anything else they should do, as this was the first time that they had attempted something like this.

Two hours later they were back at the club, having had a pub meal after the meeting.

Twenty-Six

In the first week of March, Sophie arranged to see Julie again at the Coffee Cup Café in the afternoon. This time Julie was alone, as her neighbour had offered to look after the children. Julie was wearing a long grey coat and black boots. Her blonde hair was freshly washed and shiny, but although Julie was smiling, she seemed preoccupied. They talked for a long time about Julie's children and her father. He was now not expected to live for more than a month and Julie had resigned herself to the fact that he wouldn't be with her for much longer.

Sophie didn't know whether it would be the right time to mention the festival, but Julie would know about it when the posters went up.

'Do you think you will feel like going to the festival in June?' Sophie asked.

'I asked Mark about it when I heard him talking on the phone to Ben, but he said I wouldn't know anyone, and he would be too busy to talk to me.'

'Well why don't you come, and bring the children. You can help us with the catering. I am sure there will be someone there who would love to look after them.'

'I don't know whether Mark would be happy with that,' Julie sighed.

'He can't stop you going out, especially when he's...' Sophie stopped, biting her tongue.

'I know what you were going to say. I know he is seeing other women, although I really don't want to think about it, and I know he can't wait for my father to die so he can have his money and run the factory, and I also know that he will probably leave me. He has said so, more or less, and...' Julie took a breath.

'I am so sorry,' Sophie apologised. 'I didn't mean to...'

'That's okay. Tell me the truth, has he ever asked you?'

'No, he hasn't,' lied Sophie, interrupting quickly. 'But I do feel that I should have told you, as we were friends, but I didn't want to upset you. I promise I would have done when the time was right.'

Julie wasn't listening.

'It makes me so unhappy to think a large amount of my father's money will go to Mark, when he doesn't care for any of us and never will. He is not even really a father now to his own children,' Julie said, taking off her sunglasses, pushing back her hair and rubbing her forehead. 'The house is mine, as my father gave it to me when my mum died, and when Dad made the decision to move to a smaller house by the factory.'

'Then get your father to change his will if you are serious,' Sophie said. 'It will be too late for Mark to do anything when he finds out. You don't have any other relatives to interfere, and your father could put a suitable clause in saying his will cannot be contested.'

Julie's eyes reflected her thoughts.

'I think I will talk to Dad tomorrow. It's too late now for him to worry about whether I am happily married,' she said. 'He did ask me when I saw him last whether everything was okay.'

'I think he may suspect more than you know,' Sophie said gently.

'Thank you, Sophie. You are a good friend.'

'I would like to think so. If there is anything you want, just let me know.'

They left the café and Julie paid the bill and promised to keep in touch.

Three days later Julie phoned to say that the will had been rewritten by a top solicitor who her father had known for years. Julie had been left the factory, along with her father's house and money. Steve, at the factory, had been left shares, and some of her father's money was being left to her children. She wouldn't have to worry about inheritance tax as her father had left sufficient cash to cover it.

When Julie confided in her father, he was sad, but more than pleased to rewrite his will. He said he had always had reservations about Mark but had given him the benefit of the doubt. Mark had visited him the day before, asking how he was, but didn't stay longer than five minutes. Julie's father seemed pleased that she had now accepted what Mark was like and told her to move on and enjoy life. She held his hand, kissed him and left, tears blurring her eyes.

Mark had no idea about the alteration of the will and Julie was worried and nervous about what his reaction would be when he found out.

Three days later, after a long visit from Julie and the children, her father died.

After the initial shock, Julie was kept busy, organising the funeral and looking through mountains of paperwork, as well as coping with her own feelings.

Sophie offered to have the children, but Julie had arranged for them to go full-time in the local crèche, where they were already attending in the afternoons. Steve was looking after the factory. Julie said she would be grateful if Sophie could help with her father's personal paperwork.

Sophie closed the shop for the rest of the week and helped Julie sort through her father's household bills and insurances, taking her to the undertakers and helping Julie decide what to do with her father's house. Julie thought she might ask Steve if he wanted to rent it cheaply, as he lived in a flat, ten miles away. He might want to be nearer the factory now.

When Mark found out the following day that he had been left nothing by her father he was furious. He insisted on seeing the will, and when he saw when it was dated, Mark accused her of telling her father to rewrite it when he had been too ill to understand what he was doing. Mark said he would challenge it, but Julie told Mark that her dad had said he would need a lot of cash to contest the will through the courts, with very little chance of winning. That's why her father had used top lawyers.

Julie asked him why he should be included when he was hardly ever at home and she told him she knew that he had other women throughout the few years of their marriage.

'I suppose that Sophie woman told you,' Mark shouted. 'I know you're friends. I've seen you together in the high street.'

He stormed into the hall, picked up his "always ready" overnight sports bag and grabbed his car keys.

'Don't bother coming back!' Julie shouted. 'By the way, your car belongs to me; it was bought by my father, but you can keep it – you may need to sleep in it, if none of your girlfriends will let you stay with them.'

Mark picked up the art deco ornament that had been on the hall table for years and threw it at the wall. It shattered into orange confetti.

He hadn't been in touch with her since.

The following Monday, Sophie called in to her shop to collect the mail and check everything was okay, forgetting to lock the door. A customer walked in, wanting matching canvases for his large office boardroom. She didn't like to say she was closed, so she let him look around. After liking most of her paintings, he bought four, all with an abstract orange and brown leaf design. Sophie was pleased with the sale, but her thoughts then quickly turned to Julie. She was worried about her and whether she should have interfered between her and Mark.

Deciding to keep the shop open, after the last customer had left before lunch, Sophie phoned Julie to tell her she had been delayed and would be with her soon. She was just about to head back to Julie, when Mark stormed through the door, red-faced, eyes screwed-up, and angry. He slammed the door, slid the door catch closed and banged his fist on the counter, which sent Sophie's shop cards and leaflets scattering to the floor. Sophie, although shocked, thought how desperate he looked.

'You made her change the will, didn't you?' Mark shouted, now inches away from her face. 'What's it got to do with you?'

'No, I didn't,' Sophie replied, surprised by her confident calm reply. 'Julie at last realised what you were like. I only confirmed it.'

'You'll really regret that you interfered. You really will. You'll see. You really will,' Marked raged, flapping his arms in the air. 'You've no idea what I'm capable of. You'll see.'

He pushed past her, unlocked the door and headed across the road to his car, just as a traffic warden placed a ticket on his windscreen. Sophie saw his arms fly up in the air again. He got into his car and roared away, oblivious to the cars sounding their horns around him.

Sophie decided not to tell Julie about Mark's rant. It would only worry her. She might tell her later, as Julie had too much to think about at the moment.

You don't scare me, thought Sophie, as she closed the shop and headed over to Julie's house.

Twenty-Seven

Friday, March 25th was the day of Julie's father's funeral. The day was unusually warm and sunny, and the funeral passed off quietly. Julie was surprised by the number of people who attended the crematorium. Many of the factory workers were there, as Julie had closed the factory for the day as a mark of respect. She had also arranged security cover at the factory for the day, as well as for the night shift.

Julie had asked Sophie if she would look after her children in the morning until after the service, and Sophie agreed willingly. She decided to take them down to the beach. They collected shells and stones as a surprise to give to Julie. Alice paddled in the sea and then they had an ice cream at the café. Julie didn't want them to go to the funeral as they were too young and wouldn't understand what was going on. She would explain to them when the time came.

At 2pm, after a lovely morning on the beach and after a quick wash and change, Sophie took them to the wake at the Maple Leaf and Julie was so pleased to see them. She was also relieved to see Sophie, the only person who really understood how she was feeling.

Sophie walked over and talked to Steve, from the factory, as he was standing by himself eating a sandwich from the buffet table. Sophie didn't realise just how hungry she was and put four sandwiches on her plate, together with some chocolate cake.

Steve suggested they sit down, and he pulled out two chairs from under a table away from the rest of the group; their conversation soon turned to Mark. Sophie, not wanting to comment, just listened and nodded her head. Steve didn't like Mark at all and totally understood why he wasn't there.

He told Sophie that Mark had been calling into the factory, walking around as though he already owned it, and telling everyone that soon he would be in charge. Mark had also told Steve off for being late one morning, when Steve was caught in heavy traffic, due to the road being flooded. Steve had already phoned Julie to apologise, and she told him not to worry and to get there when he could. Steve added that he hadn't said anything to Julie about the incident, as it would cause even more trouble between her and Mark.

Sophie, still listening, also learned that last year one of the women in the factory had an affair with Mark. Steve had pleasure in sacking her after she almost hit another woman with a chair, when she thought the woman was spreading rumours about Mark and her. Steve had seen the incident and told the woman to leave. Sophie should have been shocked, but it was sad that nothing seemed to shock her anymore.

Julie, after going around talking to everyone, eventually joined them, sitting down for a while. Sophie gave her some food and a coffee. Julie was reassured when Steve told her that she had done the right thing in changing the will, and if there was anything she wanted, to let him know. He also added that her father had asked him to make sure she was all right when her father wouldn't be there to advise her. Julie took a deep breath; her dad had thought of her right up until he died.

There was no sign of Mark at the funeral. Julie made the excuse, when asked, that he had been called out early that morning by an emergency job and hoped he would be there later, although one of the men at the wake told Sophie that when he had called in at The Tavern pub for a quick pint before the funeral, he thought he had seen Mark with a girl with black and purple hair.

Julie asked Sophie not to mention Mark or the will to anyone at the open mic club and Sophie promised not to say anything, as it would cause a lot of stress for Julie, and it would make life very unpleasant for everyone.

The funeral was over, and everyone left, except Julie, Sophie and Steve, who helped to clear the tables. They didn't have to, but they felt the need to tidy up and to keep talking. Afterwards, Steve asked Julie if she wanted a lift home and they left, leaving Sophie thinking how good they would be for each other. Was this going to turn out eventually the way that Julie's father would have wished for her? Sophie hoped so.

Sophie went to Julie's house the next day. Julie seemed more relaxed and asked Sophie how she and Ben were. Sophie explained that she thought she was relying a little too much on him lately so she might stop seeing him for a while, although she was very fascinated and attracted by him.

Sophie told her all about Dave and Emma. She hadn't meant to, but she just couldn't stop. About him getting married, moving and that he must have been having an affair for a long time while they were married. Julie listened and shook her head in disbelief.

'Sorry, Sophie, I thought I had problems. Why didn't you tell me? I know we have only known each other for a short time but I thought we were good friends now.'

'I have only really just come to terms with it,' Sophie said. 'They've even invited me to the wedding.'

'You should still have told me,' Julie said again. 'Will you go?'

'No. I just don't care about him anymore.'

After talking for two hours, Sophie left, because she had to reopen the shop after it had been closed for a week. Julie walked part of the way with her, gave Sophie a hug and then she and the children walked back home. They promised to ring each other regularly.

Sophie thought it was good to have a close friend again.

Twenty-Eight

Sophie didn't open the shop on the last day in March, as she spent most of the day painting a portrait on canvas, of Pam and Adrian, a couple who wanted it for their silver wedding anniversary in a month's time. They had phoned to make an appointment the week before. It was ages since she had painted portraits, but Sophie really enjoyed talking to the couple and getting to know them. They were both tall and slim and were good subjects to paint.

They had decided to wear blue and silver as a colour scheme, Adrian in a light blue suit, white shirt with silver tie, and Pam in a silver-grey off-the-shoulder dress and light blue bolero. Sophie decided to paint the background light grey, mixed with light blue swirls. The blend of colours worked well. She didn't show the couple the painting as she wanted it to be a surprise. She took photos of them so that she could finish the canvas after they had left the shop. At the end of the day Sophie was really pleased with the result.

It was late at night when she signed the canvas, put the hanging cord on the back and washed her brushes. She placed the portrait on the wall to dry. Their daughter would come to collect and pay for the painting, as her anniversary present to them, in two weeks' time.

Sophie left the shop tired but pleased with the day's work and pleased she hadn't lost her touch.

Twenty-Nine

At the beginning of April, on a lovely sunny day, Sophie started to think more about the festival and found herself climbing up the loft ladder. She opened the door, stepped in and switched on the light. She hadn't been in the loft for years. She made her way through the black bags and boxes, now covered with years of dust. Sophie looked around.

She recognised her old photo album, which was jutting out of a wooden box. She took it out and wiped it with her hand. She sat on the box and looked through the photos. Sophie had almost forgotten her life as a teenager. A time so uncomplicated and optimistic. She sighed and promised herself she would take it down from the attic and have a better look at the photos soon; perhaps she should put them on her computer. She put it away carefully.

Sophie carried on looking for her guitar. She found it wrapped in two large pillowcases which she had had on her bed before she moved in with Dave. She picked it up, switched off the light, carefully climbed back down the steps carrying her guitar, and closed the loft door.

Sophie cleaned and dusted her guitar, using beeswax that she had in her cupboard, and she tried to play, but it needed new strings and tuning. She knew Ben would enjoy fixing it, so she phoned him, telling Ben she could take it to him. He said he was just on his way out and would see her Thursday night. Sophie, again disappointed she wouldn't see inside his caravan, left her guitar in the hall so that she wouldn't forget it.

The next evening Sophie took Ben her guitar to look at. He said he would bring it to her house when he had fixed it, and that it would be great to hear her play at the festival. Gina, sitting nearby, looked on, saying that it would take Sophie ages to play it again properly.

'Not with lessons from me,' Ben retorted.

'We'll see,' Gina said sarcastically.

In the middle of April, after Sophie had painted the wedding anniversary portrait, Jenny, the florist, arrived at the studio, carrying a bouquet of flowers from Pam and Adrian with a thank-you note, saying how pleased they were with the painting, which was now hanging in their lounge.

Sophie was happy that the painting was a success. Perhaps she should put a notice in the shop advertising portraits, but decided that, for the moment, she didn't want any more work.

Thirty

The next evening when Sophie arrived home from work there was a note from Iris saying that Kenny wasn't in the house. Had Sophie let him outside before she went to work? He hadn't had his food as his bowl was still full. Sophie was sure he had been in the house before she left. At nine o'clock that night, in the dark, she strolled down her garden, which was now quiet, calling him and picking up pieces of paper that had blown into the garden. Kenny quite often refused to go inside if he was hunting, so Sophie wasn't too worried.

As she walked behind the small green garden shed Sophie's legs buckled. Kenny was hanging on the washing line, wet, ginger and limp, tail dangling, lifeless. Sophie stood still, unable to move. After a while she dared herself to walk up to him and take him down from the line. When she was closer, Sophie realised that it wasn't Kenny but a large ginger toy cat, similar to those sold in charity shops. She found herself crying with relief. Sophie tried to pull it from the line, but it was tied securely with a guitar string. She managed to undo it with trembling hands, dropping it on the ground. Sophie left it there, unable to pick it up to put it in the bin. Quickly turning to hurry back into the house, she heard a familiar sound. Kenny was locked in the shed. Sophie opened the door, and he flew down the garden, into the house and hid behind the sofa.

Reluctantly, Sophie called Ben, and he came over to her house straight away. By now the sky was dark and a cold damp breeze was blowing round the garden. Sophie was shivering when Ben walked in.

'Who could hate me enough to do this?' Sophie said, trying to control her voice.

'It must be someone whom you have upset recently,' Ben replied, belatedly realising that he could have put that better. He handed Sophie a large brandy and made himself a coffee.

'Do you want me to stay here tonight?' Ben asked.

'Can you get rid of that fake cat straight away?'

Ben disappeared into the garden and Sophie heard the sound of the bin being opened and closed. She was scared now as someone must know where she kept the spare key. They must have entered her house and taken Kenny.

Ben came in, worried.

'Someone has taken the spare key.'

No one knew where she kept it, only she and Ben.

'Oh no,' Sophie thought out loud. 'The group saw where I had hidden it when they came to the party.'

At 1.40am her mobile rang. Worried, Sophie stretched over the bed to answer it. All she could hear was the purring of a cat. Ben took the phone and said, 'Hello?' The phone went dead.

While cuddling Kenny the next morning, she told Iris what had happened. Iris was upset, as she had grown to love Kenny, and said that she would stay until one o'clock but after that she had to meet a friend for lunch; she couldn't put it off as it was her friend's birthday.

Sophie thanked her, and as she was leaving Iris said, 'You'd better get the locks changed.'

'Yes, I will. Ben wanted to change them today, but tomorrow is the earliest his friend can do it. Ben's staying the night, so I'll be quite safe. Kenny's shut in the spare bedroom with his tray and food. Don't let him out. I'll walk round the garden with him when I get home.'

Iris told her not to worry and waved her off, tea towel in hand.

After what seemed a long day Sophie came back earlier than usual and went upstairs to find the spare bedroom door open and Kenny missing. Her heart sank. A note was on the kitchen counter from Iris saying that she had changed his tray and shut the door again and she had left a chicken casserole in the oven.

Again, she rang Ben. She hated being so reliant on him, but she couldn't cope. She stood by the window, waiting for him. The April evening seemed to be getting dark quickly. Dark clouds seemed to have gathered and she certainly wasn't going down the garden by herself.

When Ben arrived, they searched around the house, Sophie wondering what they might find. Iris had left at one o'clock and Sophie had come home at 5pm. So someone must have watched the house, and come in during that time.

Ben went out into the garden and told Sophie to stay in the house. After a while he came back looking pale and upset. He had found Kenny dead on the lawn. Sophie collapsed in a chair.

'Are you sure it's Kenny? What happened to him?' Sophie asked, when she had eventually taken in what Ben had told her.

'He must have been poisoned. I'll bury him,' Ben mumbled, and he turned around and went back out into the garden.

'Somewhere by the apple tree,' Sophie managed to say.

Sophie phoned Iris, who was inconsolable. 'I know I shut the door, I even locked it. I'll be round early tomorrow, when Ben's gone.'

'Shall I phone the police?' Ben eventually asked Sophie, but she said no, as she couldn't face it at that moment. She washed Kenny's bowl and put it in the cupboard under the sink. She had a shower and went straight to bed.

Who could have done it? Mark? He certainly had a large grudge against her. Or was it Gina? Gina certainly hated cats and didn't like her. Janet, the cleaner she sacked? She said she would regret sacking her. Perhaps she had taken a copy of the key. But Sophie went to bed convinced it was Gina.

Sophie intended to take the next day off. She had phoned Paul to see if he was free to open the shop and just be there in case customers came in. He happily agreed and he called in to collect the key. She didn't tell him why.

As Iris was fussing her so much, Sophie decided to go to work in the afternoon even if she closed the shop after Paul left. She could think there and be by herself.

When she arrived at her studio Paul was having a coffee at a table in the window with Jenny from the flower shop. They were deep in conversation and laughing. Why did Sophie feel slightly annoyed about that; probably because she was so stressed. Jenny hurriedly finished her coffee and left.

If Paul could see she was upset, he didn't ask any questions. He was pleased he had sold a painting and had replaced it with another one. He told her that he had left the money by the till, as he didn't know how to work it and had written a receipt out and had made a note of who had bought it.

Sophie thanked Paul and told him he had been a great help. He was always so helpful. She desperately wanted to tell him about Kenny but knew she would break down.

Should she go to the club again? Could she face it? Sophie decided she should go as she might see if there was any indication of who had poisoned Kenny. Sophie phoned Tess to make sure she was going as she would then have someone to sit and talk to. She decided not to tell anyone about it and would try to act normally if she could.

On Thursday night Sophie arrived at the club trying to look upbeat. Kerry handed Sophie her usual red and asked her how her week had gone. Sophie told her she'd had a busy week and she decided Kerry was not a suspect and asked her how she was.

'Tired,' said Kerry, yawning. 'The club has had a lot of late-night events, so it's been well after midnight when I have got home. Then up at 7am to catch the train for my day job. I never seem to have any time for myself. I would love a holiday – somewhere warm where I could lounge by a pool.'

Sophie said that sounded wonderful. She could do with a holiday herself, after all that had happened.

In fact, why shouldn't she go away for a few days?

Sophie sat down in her seat, where she had sat since joining the club. She thought of where she could go. She took out her phone to look for holidays, but Tess walked in, so she put it back in her bag.

Only Tess came tonight, as Jane was getting ready to go to a hen party at the weekend, and they talked about their week, Sophie saying that she had had a good week as she didn't want anyone overhearing about Kenny. Sophie added she might go on holiday in the next few days. Tess said Brighton would be a good idea, but Sophie thought it would be too busy.

Sophie managed to sing as normal, which surprised her, and she looked around for any sign of people looking at her differently. Gina was wearing a new orange tiger-striped top and jeans. She looked away when Sophie was watching her, and Mark was following Sophie's every move, so everything was normal. Was someone playing the same game as her?

On Friday, Sophie looked for hotels on her laptop – just out of interest – where could she go early in May? She wouldn't want to go too far. Somewhere quiet. Somewhere she could be alone.

Having not been on holiday for years, and never by herself, she decided somewhere in the Cotswolds, where she could walk and take picnics. She realised that sounded a quiet holiday but that was what she felt like doing. Get away from everyone and everything and especially Ben as she was relying on him so much. Sophie eventually found a large hotel where she could stay without anyone questioning her. If she stayed in a smaller one, she would have to be sociable.

Sophie took out her phone and found herself tapping in the number of the Chalet Hotel. She booked a week Monday for four nights and asked for a room with a view, balcony, an early check-in, as she didn't know what time she would arrive and didn't want to wait until three in the afternoon to get into her room, and did they do room service? She might even treat herself to room service on the balcony. The hotel had a swimming pool, spa and evening entertainment, where she could watch from her dining table. The basic price of the room had now become more expensive – view, balcony, room ready on arrival. Sophie didn't care. She put her phone back in her bag.

What had she done?

The following Thursday Sophie told everyone she was going away, and she might not be at the club next week. Kerry said she was envious, but she, personally, would have gone to Spain for a fortnight. Everyone was interested and Sophie described the hotel and that she was looking forward to the break. She knew that she had to go now that she had told everyone.

'See you soon,' Gina commented sarcastically as she walked past.

Sophie asked Paul, who was now a regular at the club, if it would be possible for him to look after the shop while she was away. He said he was too busy that week, but he would have loved to have helped her. Sophie thought that it would have taken her too long anyway to explain everything to him.

When she next saw Iris, she told her she would be away the next week so she could have the week off with pay. Sophie asked Iris, when she was in Timberry shopping, if she could pick the post up from the porch. Iris said she would look after everything. At least Sophie didn't have to worry about her house, *or Kenny*, she thought sadly.

Thirty-One

A day later, after placing a "SORRY, CLOSED UNTIL FRIDAY" sign on the shop door, Sophie found herself driving to the Cotswolds. The towns and hedges disappeared, and stone walls took their place. The roads became narrower, with less traffic, and she found herself relaxing. Sophie stopped at a roadside pub for a sandwich. It was strange going into the pub by herself, but it was something she would have to get used to, now. She then continued down the uneven road, which was fast becoming a narrow track – following the satnav instructions. Sophie hoped that it was taking her the right way.

Sophie eventually drove into the hotel's secluded car park, and sat looking at the large cream building. Was she doing the right thing? She turned off her phone, and put it in her glove compartment, not wanting to answer any calls or be tempted to make any. Staying at the hotel would give her time away from Ben, as in the last week she had relied on him too much, and Sophie was shocked at how much she had wanted his help. She had always thought she was an independent person.

She took her warm coat from the boot and threw her travel bag over her shoulder, locked the doors and walked towards the hotel, pulling her suitcase behind her.

She was welcomed by the doorman, who asked her for her room number and took her luggage. A porter labelled her suitcase and bags, and put them on a trolley, and disappeared in the lift together with her suitcase. Sophie checked in at the large reception area and the receptionist gave her the key card, and leaflets, and wished Sophie a pleasant stay. She told Sophie reception was open twenty-four hours, so if she wanted anything, to let them know, and then went back to her computer.

Sophie walked past the lift and climbed the wide plush carpeted staircase. She said hello to a couple who were closing their door, making their way downstairs.

She was pleased at how easily she found her room along the never-ending corridors, and when Sophie opened the door, she was pleasantly surprised. It was much larger than it appeared on the internet.

Sophie looked out of the window. The room was on the second floor, with a view that went on for miles over the countryside. She could see church steeples, and white and yellow stone cottages, set against a deep blue sky.

Sophie sat on the balcony eating biscuits and drank a cup of tea from the welcome tray, and closed her eyes, enjoying the quietness. An hour later she woke up. She must have drifted off to sleep. Sophie stepped back into her room and put on her jacket, as the air was getting colder. She took a book that she had bought from the charity shop out of her suitcase and started reading. A murder mystery. She didn't read many books, as she didn't have time, she had never bothered with e-books, neither did she have a large bookcase; she preferred to surround herself with art.

Sophie found it hard to concentrate at first but after a while she was enjoying being transported into a different world of poisoned wine and love affairs. Two hours went by quickly and she had read over half of her book.

Feeling hungry, Sophie looked at the menu which had been left on the bedside table. She could help herself from the buffet or have table service.

She showered, dressed and made her way down to the restaurant, feeling quite nervous.

The waitress showed her to her small table in the corner, which she liked, as she didn't want to mix with people. The couple she had seen earlier were sitting talking at the next table. They smiled and carried on talking between themselves. Sophie chose chicken and salad from the long buffet counter, followed by licorice and blackcurrant sponge. After her meal she sat for a while, watching the waiting staff quietly glide between the tables, serving meals. She looked at couples having quiet intimate conversations and suddenly wished Ben was with her.

Leaving the restaurant and walking through the bar, Sophie stopped and asked for a bottle of wine. She gave the barman her name and room number and took the bottle and a glass upstairs to her room.

Sophie had enjoyed today and planned in the morning to pick up a packed lunch, that she had ordered earlier from reception, and tour round the villages.

After drinking a glass of wine, she got into bed, and watched the television for a while. She eventually fell asleep looking at the twinkling lights in the windows of the faraway cottages.

The next day Sophie woke up quite late and went downstairs for breakfast in the restaurant, which was almost empty. Everyone must have already been down. She sat for a while reading the free newspaper.

She left the hotel later in the morning, got into her car and spent the day driving and walking around the small villages, stopping for coffee in the quaint old tea shop in Snows Wood. She studied the pictures that were hanging on the café walls, trying to get ideas for her shop. She asked the friendly waitress, who was filling the plates on the counter with fresh cakes, the price of the paintings. They were quite cheap, compared to those in her studio, and were all painted by local artists. There were also children's paintings displayed. Sophie thought that was a nice touch as it encouraged children to paint, and probably brought in more customers. She could try this at her shop.

She had her lunch sitting on a long bench overlooking a stream just outside Snows Wood. The stream ran down the steep hill and trickled noisily past her and disappeared under a low narrow wooden bridge, taking leaves and small sticks with it. Sophie picked up a stick and threw it in the stream and watched it slowly drift away from her. She was really enjoying her break and could feel the stress getting less. She didn't remember when she had been so close to nature, even though she lived by the sea. She should have brought her sketch pad.

Sophie returned to the hotel in the afternoon to read her book out on the balcony again and to pour herself a glass of wine. She wondered if anyone had called her. She hadn't checked her phone since she had arrived at the hotel and Sophie thought how great it was not having to answer it.

The following day, after breakfast Sophie decided to go down to the indoor swimming pool. She hadn't been to a pool for years; in fact, the last time she had been swimming, besides swimming in the sea, was when she and her friend Joanne joined a gym years ago, when they worked together at the art gallery in Shertsbourne.

She walked down the long corridor and then followed the smell of the swimming pool down another corridor and through the double doors. Sophie changed quickly into her online-next-day-delivery swimsuit, remembering just in time to remove the price tag, and, very self-consciously, walked out of the changing room and down the steps into the pool.

The pool was empty, and she splashed about, getting used to the cool water. After a while she was confidently swimming up and down, hardly noticing the other swimmers who had gradually joined her. Feeling really refreshed, she climbed the steps and sat on the side of the pool and shook the water from her hair. A man wearing a tight swimming hat and goggles surfaced from the water beside her and sat next to her. Not interested in starting a conversation or maybe getting involved with him, Sophie excused herself, saying she had to meet someone. Disappointed, he dived back into the pool, sending a shower of water over her. She didn't want another man in her life; this was definitely going to be a man-free holiday.

After changing out of her swimwear, Sophie went for another drive, to an old castle which was advertised in one of the leaflets she had picked up at the hotel. The castle was on a steep, uneven hill. She parked the car, slowly walked up the incline, went through the cold entrance and climbed up the never-ending narrow winding stone steps, which were just wide enough for one person. At the top she looked through the telescope over the miles of countryside. She thought she could see her hotel in the distance, with its distinctive high chimneys. Sophie wished she had her phone with her to take photos, but she certainly wasn't prepared to climb up and down the steps again.

Sophie decided that tomorrow she would buy the large sketchbook that she had seen in the charity shop in the village. There was a pencil in her bag, and she would have an afternoon sketching. She would also buy another mystery book.

While dressing for dinner, Sophie sat on the balcony in the sun, drying her hair and putting on her shoes. A few minutes later, after enjoying the warmth of the sun, someone knocked on her door.

She looked through the spy hole but couldn't see anyone. They must have knocked on the next door. Earlier she had hung the "Do Not Disturb" notice on the door, as she didn't want to be interrupted by cleaners or housekeeping. Sophie walked into the bathroom to finish putting on some mascara. She hadn't worn much make-up over the last few days and even doing that was liberating. Her hair had gone back to its own way, curly and wild; she thought she looked like a different person. She would never let it look like that normally.

Someone tapped quietly on the door again.

Sophie opened it, annoyed at being disturbed.

Paul was standing there.

'What's wrong?' Sophie heard herself say, shocked at seeing him.

'Not me – you. Ben told me about Kenny, and I just had to come and see if you are okay here, all by yourself. I tried to phone, but your phone was switched off and then I was really worried.'

Sophie was close to tears. How thoughtful Paul was. It was a shock to see him, but she was so pleased.

'Are you stopping here?' Sophie asked, hoping he was.

'Yes, but I won't be in your way. Tomorrow I have to go back.'

'Oh.'

Sophie was disappointed.

They arranged to sit with each other at dinner in the evening, the waiter setting an extra place. Paul, hungry, piled his plate high with food from the buffet counter and didn't stop eating until the plate was empty.

He then helped himself to fruit crumble and large scoops of ice cream.

Sophie thought he couldn't have eaten all day. He hadn't thought of himself.

After dinner they watched the show together, an eighties band, and then danced. Sophie was pleased that Paul had travelled the long distance to see her. She hadn't heard from anyone since she had been at the hotel, but then it was her fault for having turned off her phone when she had arrived.

'How did you know my room number?' Sophie suddenly realised that no one knew it and the receptionist certainly wouldn't tell him.

'I saw you on the balcony when I walked around the grounds, so I knew you were on the second floor at the end of the building. I saw the "Do Not Disturb" sign and thought that must be you.'

The evening finished and Sophie and Paul said goodnight. He said he would see her at breakfast before he went home. He kissed her on the cheek and went into his room and she carried on down the long narrow corridor. Her room was hot, so she opened the large balcony window and lay in bed, watching the lights in the distance again, feeling happier than she had in ages.

The next morning, she woke late. She looked at her phone

– it was 9.30. She must have been more tired than she thought. Not being able to resist, she checked her phone, which she had taken from her car after dinner last night. There were five calls and three messages, all from Paul, and two messages from a familiar work number. There was no message from Ben.

Breakfast didn't finish until 11am, so she still had time to shower. Walking out of the bathroom she noticed an envelope pushed under her bedroom door. It couldn't be the bill, as she wasn't leaving until Thursday. Sophie picked it up. The envelope was stamped and addressed to her, but the stamp hadn't been franked, just crossed with a line.

Opening it, a photo fell out. A photo of the ginger cat swinging on her washing line. There was something else in the envelope – ginger fur. Sophie dropped it on the floor. She sat on the bed and tried to phone Paul's number, but her hands were shaking. Her third attempt got through to him.

'Where are you?' Paul asked. 'I'm starving. I am waiting in the restaurant.'

'Can you come to my room?' Sophie tried to speak, hardly able to breathe.

He was there within seconds.

'What's wrong?'

Sophie pointed to the photo and the clump of ginger fur.

'Oh my God,' Paul said, visibly shocked. 'Ben told me it was bad, but I didn't realise it was this bad. It looks so real.'

'The fur is real!' Sophie shuddered.

'I'm going home,' she said, gathering up her clothes in a pile.

'You've got to get dressed first! I'll drive you,' his blue eyes showing deep concern.

Paul put the envelope and contents in his jacket pocket.

Sophie forgot she still had only a towel wrapped around her.

'What about the cars?'

'We will go back in yours. I'll drive. I can easily get someone to pick up mine,' Paul offered.

Sophie dressed quickly.

She was so thankful that Paul had come to the hotel, and

she insisted that he had breakfast. Sophie just sat at the table, sipping coffee and nibbling at her toast.

An hour later, after Paul had paid Sophie's hotel bill, they were driving down the lanes, Sophie taking no notice of the countryside.

Who had sent that photo?

Sophie didn't think she had any enemies, but she thought of Gina again. Gina certainly didn't like cats and she didn't like Sophie either; and she was capable of doing something like that. Sophie didn't say anything.

'You should go to the police,' Paul suggested, driving fast along the straight roads.

'No,' snapped Sophie. 'I just want to forget it.' She sat beside him, staring blankly at the road ahead. Paul shot her a glance and remained silent.

They made it back in two and a half hours, stopping once to have a coffee.

At home Paul took in her luggage and checked around the house and in the garden. Everything seemed normal. He stayed until mid-afternoon and then left to go back to work. Sophie thanked him and told him she was sorry she had upset his day.

'I'm just pleased you are okay. I will ring you later.' He called a taxi and left. Sophie watched as the taxi turned out of her drive. She was so grateful for his help.

Later in the afternoon Sophie tried to get back to normal, but still couldn't think logically about who had sent the envelope. She had told a lot of people she was going to the Chalet Hotel, so it could be anyone.

The next morning Sophie went back to the shop and let herself in. Although she had only been away for a few days there was a lot of post, and messages flashing on her phone.

She consoled herself with the thought that Kenny was dead, and no one could hurt her anymore. She should move on.

Sophie spent the whole morning catching up with phone calls. Dave had left a message for her to ring him back. But she ignored it. She couldn't deal with him at the moment.

Feeling hungry now, after not feeling like any breakfast that morning, Sophie went to the sandwich shop and decided to stay and have soup and pizza. She stayed there longer than usual, talking, then called in quickly to see Jenny at the florist. After a while Jenny asked how Paul was. Sophie answered abruptly that he was okay and then hurried back to the shop.

When Sophie opened the door, she stood in horror. Orange paint was dripping down one of her walls, just missing her paintings. Someone had been in her shop and in her workroom after she had left for lunch. Sophie checked her paintings again; only the corner of one painting was marked, and she could soon remove that.

Sophie looked around in disbelief. *Could Mark have done this?* she wondered, remembering his rant.

'When will this stop?' she muttered, thinking she couldn't cope anymore and slumped down on a chair, staring at the paint.

Sophie closed the shop and washed down the wall and floor, thankful that the paint was still wet. After an hour of hard work, the wall was back to normal again. Who had done it? Someone must have come through the back door so that they wouldn't be seen. She checked. The door was open. The large paint pot was on the ground in the courtyard.

She would go to the police tomorrow, or even better, she would install a security camera. She would ask Ben to fix one when he could.

Thirty-Two

On May 13th the awaited wedding invitation arrived, enclosed in a white envelope embossed with flowers and hearts. Sophie took a deep breath and opened it.

DAVID JOHNSON AND EMMA JONES
invite
SOPHIE TOMKINS AND GUEST
to their wedding...

'Two weeks' time!' Sophie said out loud. She noticed he had used her maiden name.

The wedding was being held at the Castle Mansions, close by. She read further down the invitation. RSVP was dated last month. Why did they send the invitation out so late? Was it so that she wouldn't go, or because someone had backed out?

And guest? She knew Paul would definitely want to go, but that would send the wrong message to him. She didn't want to invite Ben, although she would love to arrive with him, but she didn't want him to think their relationship was that serious.

Sophie phoned Julie.

Julie jumped at the chance of going to a wedding at the Castle. She had walked past it many times, wondering what it was like inside.

Sophie now had to find a dress. Julie said she already had one she had worn for a work's posh do that she had attended last year with her father. Sophie bought an acceptance card and posted it in Dave's postbox outside his flat. She wondered if they really wanted her to go. She was going anyway.

Sophie closed the shop door at lunchtime and spent the hour on her phone. She took a long time searching but eventually found an exclusive dress website with next-day delivery. She chose eleven dresses in different sizes and colours, clicked them into her basket and then paid quickly. What was she doing? Did she really care what she looked like? Yes, she definitely did.

Julie arrived at Sophie's house the next afternoon. They waited for the delivery van, and watched it turn into the drive. The driver didn't have to knock on the door as Sophie was standing outside. She signed for them and he handed her the heavy parcel.

They began opening the packets, taking out the dresses carefully. As soon as Sophie saw the green dress, she knew it was the one she wanted to wear. Jade green, fitted, sleeveless, with a narrow belt and low, round neckline, and knee-length. Sophie held her breath as she tried it on and prayed that it would fit, as she had only ordered the dress in one size. She looked in the long mirror they had brought down from Sophie's bedroom.

'That is absolutely beautiful,' gasped Julie. 'You have got to wear that one.'

'I've got some shoes to match and a clutch bag,' Sophie said, thinking out loud.

Julie was busy looking through the other dresses.

'Can I try this one on?' Julie asked, holding up a deep blue dress. She liked it better than the one she had at home.

'Of course,' Sophie said excitedly. She and Julie were almost the same size.

Julie wiggled into the dress and stood sideways in front of the mirror. She looked lovely. It went well with her blonde hair and pale complexion.

'Have it!' Sophie insisted.

'What about this pink one?' Julie asked, waving a long dress in front of Sophie.

'No. No. Have the blue one.'

They didn't bother about the price. They wanted to treat themselves to something that would make them look and feel good, as they both thought they deserved it.

They parcelled up the other dresses, and carefully hung up the chosen ones safely, upstairs.

Now, they were both looking forward to this wedding.

On Thursday night Sophie told her friends at the club about the invitation to Dave's wedding, showing them pictures of Julie and herself in their dresses. Jane asked if she could do their hair on the day and Sophie told her that they would love her to.

Gina who was sitting at the next table, muttered that she would never get married in a silly meringue dress, and finished drinking her beer before going on stage. The evening passed quickly, with everyone enjoying the usual Thursday night.

Thirty-Three

On Tuesday evening, four days before the wedding, Sophie decided to have an early night. She felt stressed and exhausted from an extra-long day at the shop, trying to finish a commissioned canvas, which she had had to concentrate on more than usual to finish before the weekend.

Sophie showered, put on her dressing gown, got into bed, and switched on the television to watch the James Bond film that was on at nine o'clock. She sipped her glass of red and, totally relaxed, fell asleep before the end of *GoldenEye*.

After three hours of sleep, Sophie woke up with a start. She listened and was sure she could hear someone downstairs. Her heart was thumping heavily and then it began to race faster. Sophie reached for her phone but realised she had left it charging downstairs. She listened again for a while, but everything seemed quiet. Sophie silently got out of bed, still wearing her dressing gown from last night. Without putting the light on she stood on the landing, listening again. She heard a quiet thump and the creak of the lounge door.

Sophie tiptoed quietly downstairs. If Gina was there, she was ready for her. She froze at her own shadowy reflection in the hall mirror, her heart beating twice as fast now. She waited for a moment, looking around for something with which she could defend herself. She quietly picked up her hairspray from the hall table, which she hoped would immobilise the intruder. Sophie squeezed through the half-open lounge door, hoping it wouldn't make a sound. She quickly switched on the light. Nothing. No one was there. But the patio doors were open, and the wind was noisily blowing the curtains against the table. Sophie had been tired last night, but she was sure she had checked the patio doors. It had been a warm evening and she had opened them earlier. She locked the door, checked downstairs and took her phone upstairs.

The security light on the front of the house flicked on and then went off.

The next morning, after a sleepless night, Sophie was still feeling concerned about leaving the patio door open. She went downstairs, took her breakfast into the lounge, opened the curtains and switched on the television. Seeing that she had left her dress for the wedding on the sofa, after trying it on again yesterday, she picked it up. The dress fell from the coat hanger. It was cut to ribbons.

Sophie gasped, and picked up the dress again – how could this have happened?

She heard Iris opening the front door. Iris shouted to her that she had brought back the pie dish that she had borrowed.

'Someone has cut up my dress,' Sophie tried to shout, but her voice turned into a whisper.

'What?' Iris shouted.

'Someone has destroyed my dress.'

'What? Which dress? When?'

'Last night.'

'Who was here?'

'No one.'

Iris walked into the lounge, carrying the pie dish.

'Did someone come in?' Iris said, still shouting.

Sophie said that she must have left the patio door open.

Iris shook her head, seeing that it was the dress Sophie was going to wear for the wedding.

'Why would they come in just to cut up your dress?' Iris asked. 'Did they steal anything?'

'I don't know. I haven't looked.'

Iris walked around, looking.

Sophie was just staring at her dress.

'Everything looks normal to me,' Iris confirmed.

'You must check that you have locked up at night. It's not as safe as it used to be around here. Especially in the summer nights,' Iris lectured. 'There have been some break-ins recently where I live.'

Sophie wasn't listening.

'Don't worry, give it to me and I will take it home to mend.'

'That's impossible. My beautiful dress,' said Sophie, as she sat on the floor and just stared.

Iris put the pie dish down on the chair and picked up the dress; Sophie watched as Iris shook her head again.

After realising that the dress was beyond repair, Iris advised Sophie that if she acted quickly she should be able to get another one just in time for the wedding.

'Someone must have been in my house last night,' Sophie shuddered. 'I've had enough. I'm going to the police today.'

Iris advised her to change her locks again and make certain she closed the doors. She told Sophie that it seemed like an act of revenge, and that the person who did it probably wasn't interested in hurting her, just wanted to frighten her.

Iris made Sophie another cup of tea and more toast and took the dress with her, leaving Sophie to order another one, saying she would be back in the afternoon to make sure she was all right.

'No need,' Sophie snapped. 'I am going to the shop later.'

Iris tutted and left.

Now disheartened, Sophie went online again, and was lucky to find the same dress. There was just one available in the same size. Sophie paid for next day delivery.

Later in the afternoon she returned from work, had the locks changed yet again and felt safer.

When the dress arrived the next day, she tried it on. There was no excitement like the first time, but she was relieved she had managed to replace it. When she phoned Julie to tell her what had happened, Julie offered to keep all her wedding clothes at her house.

Sophie was now very worried – she didn't scare easily. But Iris was probably right. The person who did it wasn't interested in hurting her. But to think that someone had been in her house at night while she was asleep – it must have been Gina. But how could it be her? She didn't have a key. She must have walked round the back of the house and seen the patio door open. Should she confront her on Thursday night before going to the police?

Sophie did confront Gina, and Gina just shrugged and laughed.

'Why would anyone want to waste money on a dress for a wedding anyway? Or celebrate someone spending their whole life with the same man?' She picked up her glass of beer.

'There's only one man I might consider giving up my freedom for.'

Gina walked away, laughing.

Sophie was now convinced that Gina had done it. She didn't know why, but she would find out, and go to the police next week.

Sophie decided that she had solved the mystery and she would try and forget it, if she could, until after the wedding.

Thirty-Four

May 25th. The wedding day had arrived. As promised, Jane styled Sophie's and Julie's hair early in the morning and helped them get ready. Julie promised to take photos of themselves at the wedding to show Jane when they got back. Sophie was relieved that Iris had popped in, saying she would look after the house while they were out.

Sophie drove Julie to the Castle, and they were now starting to feel excited again after her dress ordeal.

Arriving in good time, they drove up the long wide drive, where they were greeted and shown where to park. They walked across to the venue carefully in their higher-than-usual heels.

After visiting the huge, magnificent cloakroom, decorated in black and gold, they were shown to their seats by the usher. The seats had place names in silver and their seats were situated at the back of the room, almost behind a column. Sophie hadn't expected it to be any different. She was glad she was with Julie, as they both understood what the other would be thinking.

Sophie and Julie looked around the room, which was full (probably a hundred guests). All seemed to be aged under fifty, except for an elderly lady who managed to slip in, and sit on the unnamed spare seat behind Sophie, just before the ceremony started.

Soft music played and Dave and Emma entered the room and walked up the aisle slowly together, both dressed in white: Emma in a long fitted satin dress with see-through lace bodice and sleeves, her face half covered by see-through lace falling from her small white fascinator – she looked more pregnant now; Dave in a white suit, pale grey shirt, white tie and white shoes. Little George was a pageboy, and he was also in white. They looked like models in *Vogue*. For a fleeting moment Sophie couldn't help thinking what a great canvas portrait they would make.

Dave and Emma pledged their vows, looking lovingly into each other's eyes, while Emma held George's hand. The sun suddenly shone on them through the long window, adding to the atmosphere. Julie looked at Sophie and squeezed her arm. The elderly lady sitting behind them said something quietly and coughed.

For half an hour poems and music floated around the guests and the room was filled with quiet sophistication.

Then cameras flashed and phones appeared. The ceremony ended.

Music played again and Emma and Dave slowly walked down the aisle, blissfully smiling at everyone, conveniently turning to look at guests on the other side of the room as they walked past Sophie, and then glided out into the corridor. Little George, having forgotten to pick up the dress, skipped behind them. He looked straight at Sophie and smiled. Sophie ignored him. *Horrible brat*, she thought, but then felt guilty – it wasn't his fault.

The guests, talking quietly, slowly followed the bride and groom out of the room, leaving Sophie and Julie the last ones to leave, except for the elderly lady, who was just getting up from her seat.

'It's all wrong,' she muttered, but before Sophie could comment she had disappeared out of the door.

'What was that about?' wondered Julie. 'Who is she?'

'No idea,' replied Sophie.

All the guests made their way outside, where, for a whole hour, cameras flashed, Emma posed, and Dave just stood smiling.

Not wanting to be in the photos, Julie and Sophie walked around the large grounds and sat in the spring sunshine on one of the benches which were scattered on the lawns, partially out of sight of the wedding crowd. They agreed that they had chosen the perfect dresses for the occasion, and they took some photos for Jane to see.

When, eventually, the last of the wedding photos had been taken, they wandered into the dining area, looking for the board with the seating plan.

'We'll be at the back,' Sophie anticipated. 'Out of the way.'

Sophie was right. They had been placed right in the corner at the back by the open patio windows. A table laid for two. They wandered over and sat down, kicking off their shoes, pleased that they were at the back as they could see everything that was going on.

Guests were still walking around, talking and trying to find their places.

As Sophie and Julie sat watching, the waitress suddenly appeared from nowhere and laid another place on their small table. Sophie and Julie looked at each other.

The old lady from the ceremony walked over and sat down, adjusted her yellow hat and took off her yellow chiffon scarf.

'I shouldn't be here,' she said, sitting down. 'I wasn't invited, but I wouldn't miss this for anything.'

Sophie looked at Julie.

'Are you a relative?' Julie asked.

'Yes. I'm Emma's great-aunt Hettie, although I don't like admitting it.'

The waitress interrupted, bringing the bread rolls.

'Why didn't you have an invitation?' Julie questioned.

The waitress interrupted again, placing the bowls of watercress soup in front of them.

'I doubt if anyone in her family has. I haven't seen anyone I know,' Hettie said taking a bread roll from the plate. 'All these people must be new friends and colleagues and are probably David's side of the family.'

Sophie suddenly realised that she didn't know anyone either. How did he know all the guests? He really must have had a secret life.

'How do you know them?' Hettie questioned.

'Work colleagues,' Julie quickly replied.

Hettie carried on, 'Emma was such a lovely girl. She used to stay at my house at weekends and we used to be very close, until she married that Australian bloke, then she changed and became hard.'

'Australian bloke?' Sophie could feel herself getting hyper. 'She was married before?'

'Why did they divorce?' Julie now took over the questioning.

Hettie didn't answer; she was too busy spooning her soup and buttering her bread roll.

'How did you manage to attend the meal then?' Sophie asked, trying to get her attention.

'I went up to David after the ceremony, when Emma was busy talking to someone and showing off her dress. I said that I had come all the way from Newcastle to see the wedding and did they do sandwiches here.'

Sophie thought that was clever.

'He must have taken pity on me and said he might be able to find me a seat. He didn't even ask who I was. Too busy taking photos of the pageboy.'

'My next-door neighbour and his wife gave me a lift from Newcastle, as he is a retired chauffeur and they like getting out and about. We are going to stop at a local bed and breakfast tonight. My treat.'

The waitress interrupted again, serving the chicken main course, and placing the plates on the table.

'Why did they divorce?' Julie tried again.

'Do you want more water?' Another waitress pointed the jug at them.

Hettie was engrossed in eating her meal and helping herself to more potatoes.

They lapsed into silence. Sophie looked around; everyone was busy eating. She glanced at Julie. Julie raised her eyebrows.

There was no main table. Dave, Emma and George were sitting together by themselves. Dave was kissing Emma and pouring her a glass of iced water, while George was playing with the silver horseshoes and bells which were scattered on the table.

The wedding cake was large, white and four-tiered. White chocolate drizzled over the cake with chocolate horseshoes placed around it. A happy wedding couple stood on the top, also dressed in white. The cake had been placed on a round table in the middle of the room. The table was surrounded by presents, wrapped in shiny paper, and gift bags. Little George was now sitting on the floor looking at the labels.

Sophie thought of Dave and her wedding. Twenty people, registry office, a pub meal, and a homemade cake which she had made, and it looked homemade.

The sweet arrived, ice cream and lemon soufflé.

Sophie nodded to Julie to ask more questions.

'Where is her ex-husband now?'

'Oh... Zac?' Hettie replied, now wanting to talk, having quickly finished her sweet, and wiping her chin with her serviette.

'He's gone back to Australia after he and Emma had a furious row. Emma decided to use his money from their bank account to buy a fashion boutique in Newcastle without telling him. He went to visit his relatives in Sydney and when he came back there was hardly any money left.'

'So, when did they get divorced?' Julie tried yet again.

'Well, she never did divorce him. That's what I'm on about.'

Sophie and Julie looked at each other.

'I must go, as I'm being picked up,' Hettie said. 'And I really don't want her to see me.'

Hettie picked up her bag, put a small bell table decoration in her pocket, and left unobserved through the open patio window.

Sophie and Julie watched her go. They each picked up their glass of wine and drank at the same time.

'I don't think Dave knows that she is still married. At my party she said that she had lived with someone but told me she never married.'

'Are you going to tell Dave?' Julie asked.

'No, I'm not,' responded Sophie. 'I will feel guilty not telling him. But he treated me badly so let him get on with it.'

They sat back, drinking more wine than they should have.

The speeches were now taking place. How Emma and Dave had met – love at first sight. What a wonderful couple and family they were. Sophie slid quietly out of the patio window and sat out of sight on the patio chair. Julie followed, carrying their glasses of wine.

'I had to escape,' Sophie explained, 'otherwise I would have stood up and screamed.'

'It's nice out here anyway,' Julie said, breathing in the fresh air. 'What a day and what a revelation.' They each finished their wine at the same time.

After a while they walked back into the function room. They must have been outside for quite a while as the cake table, together with presents, had been moved to the edge of the room and Dave was now on the dance floor, dancing the first dance with Emma.

A slow rumba.

Sophie and Julie overheard the couple on the next table say how wonderful they looked; apparently Dave and Emma had been having lessons for a month at the local dance studio. Dave didn't want them, but Emma had already paid and booked.

Dave and Emma were still dancing in the middle of the large round dance floor, Emma swinging slowly from side to side, Dave slowly turning her under his arm and then Emma walking around him. She had definitely practised her moves and was certainly enjoying the exhibition; Dave was only moving when he had to.

Others joined them on the dance floor, and they then became

invisible in the crowd. Sophie suddenly felt sorry for him. Did he really deserve to start a new life under false pretences?

Sophie and Julie put on their shoes and made their way to the cloakroom. They washed their hands in the expensive soap and combed their hair. Sophie had taken a lot of care trying to look good this morning. She then applied her very red lipstick. Julie sat in the beautiful gold armchair and took off her shoes, slowly rubbing her feet, trying to rub away the red marks that her shoes had made. She redid her makeup in her small mirror and stood up.

Just as Sophie closed her clutch bag, Emma walked in. Sophie froze and a feeling of hatred overwhelmed her. She could hardly look at Emma.

Emma adjusted her dress and reapplied her make-up.

After a long silence, 'It's been a lovely wedding,' Sophie enthused, now trying her best to disguise her feelings.

'And the food was really delicious,' added Julie, who had sat down again and continued to rub her feet.

'And the rumba looked so professional,' lied Sophie, digging her fingernails into the palm of her hand.

'We had a couple of spare seats available, due to a cancellation. We thought it would have been too late for you to accept,' glowed Emma.

'Not at all,' Sophie replied. 'We wouldn't have missed it for the world, although we did have to cancel another dinner date and I'm afraid it was a bit late to buy you a wedding gift.'

'Don't worry. I have everything I need now.'

Opening the door to leave, Sophie replied, 'Enjoy the rest of the night.'

Sophie and Julie left the cloakroom.

'Wait a minute, Julie,' Sophie said, unable to stop herself.

Sophie opened the cloakroom door again. Emma was pinning back a stray strand of blonde hair.

'Oh, sorry, Emma,' Sophie smiled apologetically. 'I forgot to say Great-Aunt Hettie sends her love and she told me to tell you she enjoyed the meal.'

Sophie closed the door. She and Julie walked happily arm in arm down the hall and into the reception room. They ordered another bottle of wine and finished the evening by dancing.

Later in the evening most of the guests left the Castle Mansions in taxis and some disappeared to their rooms.

Julie asked at the reception desk if there were any spare rooms available.

'Only one,' replied the receptionist. 'Someone has just left, not wanting to stay the night.'

'Then we will take it,' Julie said, without consulting Sophie.

'It's £390 a night,' warned the receptionist.

'That's fine. I'll pay for it now.'

'What are you doing?' Sophie whispered, pulling Julie away from the reception desk. 'We can call a taxi.'

'Let's treat ourselves,' Julie slurred. 'Steve's babysitting for the night.'

At the end of the evening Sophie and Julie made their way out of the function room, which meant they had to go past Dave and Emma, who were standing by the door.

'Thanks for a lovely day,' Julie sighed, slightly slurring again, and shook hands, and kissed Dave and Emma.

'Yes, it has been lovely,' Sophie added. 'A bit different from our wedding, Dave.'

Dave didn't reply. He hardly looked at her.

'Was your wedding to Zac as lovely as this, Emma?' Sophie asked. 'I'm pleased your divorce papers came through in time,' and, not waiting for a reply, walked through the doors.

'I wonder what's happening in there now?' Julie said, as they swayed up the stairs.

'I don't know, but at least Dave will now know the truth about her, so it's up to him. I couldn't let him be made a fool of any longer, for Tom's sake.'

She was glad that Tom was in Scotland on a music course and hadn't been able to attend the ceremony. She would leave it to Dave to explain; if he wanted to.

'You're too nice,' Julie said, stumbling up the last stair.

Julie fell asleep straight away, snoring and still dressed in her wedding clothes.

Sophie, realising she'd left her clutch bag downstairs, dragged herself off the bed and staggered downstairs again. The waiting staff were still working and had found her bag under the table and, after a quick security check, handed it to her.

Too tired to climb the stairs again, Sophie pressed the button for the lift.

The lift descended and opened.

Dave was standing there! He was by himself, hair dishevelled, tie undone, cigarette packet in hand.

Each was shocked at seeing the other.

'Did you know before the wedding that Emma wasn't divorced?' Dave demanded, in a low troubled voice.

'How could I have known? I have only met her once. Have you started smoking again?'

Dave put the cigarettes in his pocket.

'I don't care anymore about you, Dave, as you certainly don't for me, but please don't let Tom suffer through your actions.'

Dave leaned against the lift wall.

Sophie pressed the button to take her to the second floor. The floor that Dave had just come from. She couldn't bear to look at his troubled face.

The lift stopped, and Sophie stepped out.

'Goodbye, Dave,' Sophie said quietly.

She then sent the lift down to basement level.

Sophie had first met Dave in a hotel years ago, in the early hours of the morning, and she had probably seen him for the last time in a hotel in the early hours of the morning.

She stood outside the lift, feeling sad.

Sophie woke late the next morning, wondering where she was. Julie was drinking tea and on her phone to Steve, who was looking after the children.

They ordered breakfast on their balcony. The cleaner had already knocked on the door, wanting to clean the room, but Julie had given her a tip asking if she would give them an extra hour.

Sophie and Julie talked about last night and how strange it all was, Sophie telling Julie about meeting Dave in the lift and how she felt sorry for him.

'Did Dave feel sorry for you, when he got engaged while you were still married?' Julie asked.

Sophie shrugged. At least now she could move on, knowing everything. What would have happened if Aunt Hettie hadn't turned up at the wedding? She just hoped she hadn't caused any trouble between Hettie and Emma.

Still feeling slightly drunk after drinking far more than they should have last night, they called a taxi and left Sophie's car in the car park.

Thirty-Five

Two weeks before the festival, the group were busy organising the event. Sophie and Paul had made posters, banners and tickets, working happily together late into the evening in her workshop. Sophie hadn't seen much of Ben, as he was planning the music that was going to be played, together with Pete, Deano, and Gina. Paul's uncle was helping by supplying the tables and chairs, and cutting the grass, and would erect the temporary fence when the time came. The weather forecast predicted a hot day so everyone was happy that there would be no rain. Mark was supposed to be on electrics, but he had disappeared for a few days and no one had heard from him. He wasn't needed yet, so no one was worried. Sophie made a note to phone Julie.

Sophie had arranged for the food to be delivered to the farm the afternoon before; it would be put in the farm's large spare fridge. She asked Iris if she wanted to help, but Iris said it would probably be too much for her and she didn't like crowds, but if she could help at Sophie's house, she would. Sophie, Tess, and Jane offered to prepare all the food for the barbecue the morning of the festival and make the large quantity of curry sauce the night before. Gina said she knew where to get some cheap beer and cider, and she would help Ben set up the stage. Sophie thought some flowers would look good on the stage and she could arrange to get those from Jenny at her shop if she gave her enough warning.

Some of the entrance fee would go towards the expenses. The festival was due to start at midday and finish at midnight, so there would have to be a regular supply of food. They had borrowed two large barbecues; one for meat and one for vegetables. Some festivalgoers would probably bring their own snack. Tess suggested large bins to put the litter and unwanted food in afterwards.

This all had to be arranged in a short time. Sophie was a bit worried about Gina supplying the drink but didn't say anything.

Hopefully, there would be over two hundred people throughout the day. The group planned to play for an hour then invite other entertainers onto the stage.

Paul's uncle would supply the marquee should they want it.

After weeks of intense practice, Ben told Sophie she was more than capable of playing the guitar at the festival. She had been playing every night when she had the time and found it quite easy to remember how to play after such a long time.

Sophie had chosen the songs she wanted to sing, and Ben said he would put her on stage late in the evening, which suited her. By then she would have had a few glasses of wine.

Everyone was looking forward to the evening.

Thirty-Six

A week later Sophie decided to go and see her mother, and sister Megan, in Cornwall.

She chose not to drive, as the six-hour journey there and back would take too long; she was only going for the weekend. She would fly there from her local airport.

Three hours after leaving the house and taking a taxi to the airport Sophie was sitting in her mother's kitchen, drinking coffee.

'How are you, Sophie? How are you coping by yourself? Have you seen Dave lately? Have you met Emma? She is a lovely woman. They are well suited. Are you jealous?'

Sophie smiled. Her mother harshly getting to the point, as usual.

'Yes. I'm great. Yes. I saw Dave not long ago. We are both moving on.'

Sophie didn't tell her that he was married to a bigamist and that she had been to his wedding.

'He sent us a lovely bouquet of flowers, together with ballet tickets for the Palace Theatre,' Megan now joined in.

Sophie so wanted to tell them the truth.

'We told Dave we were so sorry we couldn't attend the wedding, but we did speak to Emma and she sounds so nice. Dave said he would send some cake and wedding photos, but we haven't received them yet. I keep checking the phone and email. I expect they have gone away for a while. They may even pop in to see us. That would be nice, wouldn't it, Megan? What do you think about them getting married? Do you regret getting divorced now? How's Tom coping?'

Sophie listened to her mother endlessly droning on.

'Where's Freddie?'

'He's in the veranda, asleep in his basket.' Megan pointed.

Sophie put her cup down and escaped from the kitchen.

She stroked Freddie's ears. He had become fatter since she had last seen him, *not unusual for springer spaniels when they got older*, she thought.

'I am going to take Freddie for a walk!' Sophie shouted.

'Good luck with that,' Megan said, now standing behind her, passing Sophie the lead.

'Shall I come with you?'

'No. It's fine.'

Freddy reluctantly left his basket, shook himself, and Sophie put him on the lead, wondering why, as he wasn't capable of running off. He stood by the door, refusing to go out. After being tempted with some treats, Freddie slowly walked down the path and along the narrow lane, stopping occasionally. After a while Freddie stopped altogether and lay down. Sophie sat on the grass next to him, stroking his speckled long nose.

She looked around her; the lane was quiet, with just the sound of traffic in the distance. The sun was warm, and she enjoyed the quiet, away from her mother's interrogation.

Sophie wondered why Megan and her mother had quickly taken Dave's side when she had decided to divorce. They never listened to her side of the story. But then, it had taken ages for Sophie to learn that Dave was good at lying.

So Dave couldn't have been in touch with them after the wedding. Sophie wouldn't tell them what she knew. She just didn't care anymore. They would always think he was wonderful whatever he did. But she would love to know if she was only invited to the wedding because her mum and Megan didn't go.

Sophie got up from the straw-like dry grass, brushed the bits from her trousers, and tempted Freddie back home with another treat.

After a weekend made bearable only when Sophie's mother chose to babysit the three children next door in the afternoon and overnight, and Megan decided to stay over at her boyfriend's, which meant Sophie had time to herself, early on Sunday morning she packed her bag and stroked Freddie, *probably for the last time*, she thought sadly. She left her mother and Megan a note.

Why did her mother and Megan choose to go off and leave her by herself when she had put herself out to go and see them – and why didn't they take an interest in her life?

Sophie made her way to the airport, pleased that she didn't have a long drive back after a wasted weekend.

Thirty-Seven

June 21st, festival day, arrived and was already being warmed up by the midsummer sun. The forecast was good for the next few days.

The night before, Sophie, Tess, Jess and Julie had worked hard, preparing all the food for the following day. Mountains of onions peeled and placed in large pans of water. Burgers and sausages placed in the fridges. A small amount of salad was prepared. This morning, Julie and Jess were preparing vegetables for the curry. Bread rolls had already been delivered.

Gina arrived, driving a large black van containing vast amounts of beer, wine and soft drinks. She drove fast into the farmyard, just missing stray chickens which had wandered into the yard.

She jumped down and started to take out the crates and tins of drinks, carrying some of the crates down the field to the marquee. Tony, one of the farmers, got into his 4x4 and took the rest down for her, driving over the newly mown field. After they had finished unloading, Gina sat talking to him while drinking from one of the tins.

The boundary fence was already in place, leaving a narrow gap for people to walk through.

The marquee had been erected; this would shelter festivalgoers from the hot sun while they sat at the tables inside.

The barbecues had been cleaned and were now ready. Paul's uncle had provided portable toilets which were put at the end of the field amongst the trees.

Ben had arrived with Mark, after picking up Sophie's guitar and amplifier from her house, and they put up the lights around the stage and checked the electrics again. The stage lit up. They then did a second sound check with Ben walking further down the field.

Jenny drove up in her van with Paul and they placed the fresh flowers around the stage. Everything was going to plan. Paul's uncle and cousins said they would take it in turns be on the gate to collect the money. They dragged a wooden bench down the hill to sit on as they knew they would be there quite a long time. Paul's cousins expected to know most of the people who would pass through the gates, as Timberry on Sea was only a small town.

At twelve o'clock midday the festival began. People carrying rolled-up mats and picnic bags queued and then made their way through the gate and drifted in. Others carried guitars and an assortment of instruments – saxophones, accordions, and flutes. Ben was going around to everyone with a clipboard, booking them an appearance time. He then placed a large board by the stage so that anyone else could add their name and a suitable time.

Ben had also phoned entertainers who he thought would want to play, and he had had a good response. He knew he could rely on them to turn up and he hoped that there might be enough people to fill in the twelve hours.

The barbecue, which had been fired up earlier, was now producing appetising smells of sausages, burgers and onions. The curry they were leaving until later in the evening.

Ben and the group had played for an hour and the second group were on stage. The sounds of loud live music now filled the field and surrounding area. Ben looked at the playlist board and was satisfied that there would definitely be enough people to entertain all day.

Sophie, Jane, Julie and Jess sat on the grass bank, which they covered with an old blanket. They weren't needed at the moment as all the food and cooking for the afternoon had been prepared.

Sophie noticed how well Tess and Paul were getting on, laughing as they walked around the field together pulling a rickety trolley, selling sun hats, sun cream and water that they had bought cheaply on the internet. They must have been making a profit, as people were thankful for them now that the sun was strong and it was still only early afternoon.

Afterwards, Tess and Paul sat on the grass near the stage, eating burgers and drinking coffee from the urn in the marquee. They then disappeared into the farmhouse. Ben appeared from nowhere and sat down by Sophie. He was really pleased everything was going well.

They all sat waiting for Gina's first session. Sophie tried to speak to Ben, but he was transfixed, watching the way Gina was playing the guitar. She played to the crowd and they all loved her as she took control of the stage. Gina sang for half an hour, dressed in black leggings and boots, denim waistcoat, white T-shirt and a straw hat. The audience were taking photos or videoing her.

After great applause Gina left the stage, drank another can of beer and sat with Mark, who had just walked down the field. Sophie looked across at Julie and Julie just shrugged, not in the least worried. The group knew they were no longer together, but didn't ask any questions. Sophie was pleased she had invited her to the festival and that she was enjoying herself.

Julie had left her children with Paul's aunt in the farmhouse, and she said she would bring them over to Julie when they were bored. Later in the afternoon, Alice came running down the field, tripped over an uneven mound of grass and fell flying onto the ground. Julie lifted her up and Sophie went over with her first aid box. Soon, after having a plaster on her knee and drinking a cup of orange, Alice was dancing to the music; she didn't go over to see Mark. He had noticed her fall but was still too busy drinking with Gina. Julie and Sophie looked at each other and knew then that Julie had made the right decision.

Jenny came over and said goodbye, as she had to close her shop and make another delivery by five o'clock. She hoped she might drop by later in the evening. Ben thanked her for supplying the flowers free of charge and said that if she wanted anything doing in the shop to let him know.

At six o'clock some parents with young families went home, children reluctantly, dragging their feet and squealing, and the field was worryingly quiet except for the bands playing. At eight o'clock a new crowd of festivalgoers arrived and headed for the beer tent.

Sophie and her friends made their way to the farmhouse to prepare the curry, naan breads and rolls and more burgers, sausages and onions. Sophie hadn't had much to eat, as she had lost her appetite preparing all the food, so Paul made them burger buns which they ate while waiting for the onions to cook. Then he went back to the barn.

More people had arrived and added their names to the playlist and the festival was proving highly successful. Some people were sitting on the sand dunes looking out to sea, listening to the different types of music being played, from jazz to folk.

As there were a lot of customers queuing at the barbecue, Tess and Paul quickly cooked the sausages and burgers in the farmhouse and took them down to the barbecue, where Deano, wearing a woolly hat and an apron with a large rock 'n' roll motif on the front, finished grilling them and dished them out with the onions to the large crowd that was waiting to be served. People queued, wanting a selfie with him, and he was more than happy to oblige. Vegetarian food was being cooked and served by Jess with the help of Julie. They left Sophie in the kitchen, tidying up and preparing the next batch of food.

Cooked food finished being served at 10pm, which allowed everyone helping to enjoy the evening. The beer tent was now extremely popular, but no one dared asked Gina where she had got her supplies from.

Sophie was sitting in front of the stage watching a reggae band. She looked across the field at Tess and Paul and was convinced that there was a friendship starting. Sophie knew that she could have easily had a close relationship with him if she had wanted to and wondered now why she was feeling slightly envious. Tess would be very lucky to have a man like Paul in her life.

Sophie, still sitting by herself, was thankful that everything was going smoothly. The midsummer sun was fading behind the trees and the air was becoming cooler. Festivalgoers were waving their phone lights to the music and there was a good atmosphere. Sophie pulled her wide scarf around her shoulders.

Paul strode over to tell her that his uncle was pleased with the way that the festival was going, and Sophie stood up, facing him. She looked up at his concerned face and sad blue eyes.

'Sophie...' He was about to say something but stopped. Then he added, 'Thank you for helping out today.'

They both looked at each other for a while, somehow understanding.

He strode away toward Tess.

Sophie felt part of her heart break. But she knew she had made her choice.

The evening now was getting noisy and almost everyone was dancing to the variety of music being played by enthusiastic artists.

Sophie sang on stage for half an hour. She was pleased she had chosen to wear the sleeveless, pale yellow jumpsuit and gold roman sandals, and she suddenly realised that she was moving about the stage naturally.

She hadn't seen much of Ben, but she knew he was busy. The success of the evening depended on him. Deano would be taking over from him soon, after he had finished with the barbecue, so she and Ben would be able to be together for the rest of the evening.

After singing, Sophie walked into the marquee, collecting used paper cups and clearing rubbish from the tables. It was then that she saw Gina talking to Ben, sitting close together in the marquee. They were in deep conversation with their backs to Sophie. Gina looked around but Ben didn't see her. Sophie doubted if he had even heard her sing.

Sophie walked out and went around the field, annoyed that he had found time to talk to Gina and not her. She slowly picked up rubbish that had escaped from the bins. Why would Ben want to spend time with Gina? She replaced the black bag and dragged the full bag towards the farmhouse. Sophie placed it with the mountain of others, against the wall. She turned the corner of the building. Gina was now standing in front of her, another can in her hand.

'Not playing guitar tonight?'

'I'm going on at about eleven o'clock,' Sophie replied, trying to sound friendly, although feeling slightly threatened.

'I'll definitely be watching,' Gina slurred.

Sophie shuddered; a cold breeze seemed to touch her. She went into the outside cloakroom to freshen up.

The group were on stage next. Ben picked up his guitar and the band started playing again and Sophie sat on the grass to watch with her friends. The group, who for tonight were calling themselves The Timberries, were now playing their eighties music set, and they looked and sounded great. While playing the third song Ben's amp started to break up and, after trying to fix it, he shouted at Sophie, asking if he could use hers.

Ben unplugged his guitar lead from his own amp and moved over to her side of the stage and plugged his guitar into Sophie's amp. The lights flickered and a large flash from Sophie's amp sent Ben flying across the stage.

People screamed and while the group stood looking on in horror, Sophie ran to switch off the electricity, and then went over to Ben. A doctor in the audience called an ambulance and attended to him. He was taken to hospital within twenty minutes. Gina just sat in a huddle on the grass, shaking and traumatised. Julie sat with her.

The festival was over, festivalgoers left, and the field was in darkness.

After being thoroughly checked out at the hospital, Ben came home early on Sunday morning.

Later on Sunday they all met up at the farm and, as promised, cleared the field. They were all in a sombre mood, trying to figure out what had happened. Taking a break, they drank coffee and sat on the grass outside, Ben saying that he had done a safety check the night before the festival and again yesterday, together with Gina and Mark.

Sophie told Ben to take it easy, so he helped in the kitchen, tidying up. Sophie was shaken because, if Ben hadn't wanted her amp, it was she who would have been electrocuted.

'It was supposed to have been me that was electrocuted!'

She kept repeating the words out loud. She immediately thought of Gina, but didn't say anything. Gina hadn't turned up today to help, but neither had Mark.

Thirty-Eight

Arriving at her shop on Monday morning, before pulling up the blinds and opening the door, Sophie sat for a while, thinking about the weekend.

She made her usual coffee, still thinking about the festival. Could Gina have been responsible for what happened, and if so, why? She knew Gina was jealous of her being so close to Ben and that she had been to prison for violence. But would she go that far?

Gina had been very upset when Ben had been electrocuted, so perhaps there was something going on between them. Sophie had seen them quite a few times recently, talking secretly together. Or could it have been Mark? He didn't turn up the next day either and he had threatened her.

Sophie took Tom a mug of tea and biscuits. He had arrived much earlier, to help her with the accounts and he probably hadn't had time for breakfast. She put the tray on the desk. He thanked her and she closed the office door and went through the post, throwing most of it in the bin.

After making some phone calls, and deciding what canvases she should display that week, Sophie stood on the stepladder and carefully placed her new designs on the wall. She went into her workshop and picked up the remaining canvases. She pulled the stepladder to the opposite wall and climbed up, carefully holding the paintings under her arm.

The door clanged.

'I'll be with you in a minute,' Sophie said, unable to look around as she stretched up to place the last painting on the top hook above the others.

No one answered.

'Wait just a minute.'

Still no answer.

Just as she was positioning the canvas, Sophie felt a rough hand grip her ankle. The stepladder rocked violently, and she fell onto the hard floor, hitting her head on the wall.

Sophie tried to stand, but she was pushed back onto the floor again. She felt sharp pains in her hand and shoulder. Blood trickled down her arm. She was being stabbed.

Dazed, Sophie looked up. Iris was standing over her, a blood-stained knife gripped in her hand.

'Now, perhaps, you will leave my Ben and his money alone,' Iris shouted hysterically, her small brown eyes filled with hate, her red lips in a tight line.

Iris was now kneeling on the floor, leaning over, stabbing Sophie's hand and arm violently again. Sophie screamed and then fainted.

The office door flew open, and Tom ran out. He dragged Iris away and lifted his mother from the floor, took off his T-shirt and wrapped it around her arm. Shaking, he then phoned the paramedics and the police.

'Now keep away from Ben. I'm warning you for the last time.'

Iris dropped the knife on the floor, wiped her hands on the inside of her coat and walked slowly out of the shop, pushing her trolley. Tom, looking after his mother, watched but was unable to stop her.

Sophie found herself in hospital, her hand and arm heavily bandaged. She had been traumatised. She was very shocked that Iris would hurt her. And the look of hate in Iris's face when she was stabbing her – Sophie closed her eyes. It was all too much for her to take in.

Sophie's hand and arm were so severely damaged that the doctors warned her that she might never be able to paint again. Sophie looked at the bandages. She could never imagine a world without art. She drifted off to sleep in the depths of depression.

Later that day in hospital, Sophie was questioned by DI Jones, whom she had known for a long time. Tom was thankfully by her side.

Sophie explained to DI Jones that she had asked Tom to go to the shop early as he was going to do her accounts – something he did now, when he was home from university, as Dave no longer helped her – and later that day, Tom had to go back to university as he had an important lecture to attend.

Tom had been working in the office, listening to music on his phone. Sophie would be forever grateful to him. He was just taking a break and drinking his tea when he heard her scream and ran into the shop; but by the time Tom had taken care of Sophie, Iris had managed to escape.

The police looked at the film on the shop camera, which Ben had insisted that Sophie have installed two days after the paint incident. At the time, she thought that she would never ever have need of it. The police had recognised Iris straight away. She had been interviewed when Ben's girlfriend, Grace, had fallen down the stairs when Iris was cleaning for them. Iris would now probably be interviewed again for Grace's death, as there were unsolved suspicious circumstances.

Sophie asked if they had talked to Iris.

'Her name isn't Iris, it's Gemma. Gemma Slater. She is Ben's older sister,' Tom explained.

'Sister?'

'Yes. Ben's older sister,' Tom repeated, putting his hand on Sophie's other arm.

Shocked, Sophie couldn't say anything. She just stared blankly.

DI Jones tried to explain to Sophie that Gemma lived on the caravan site. Apparently, according to neighbours who had lived on the park for years, Ben and Gemma had been there for a long time. A few years ago, Ben had left to live in a house in town but had returned after a short while and had moved back into his caravan next door to Gemma. Gemma had always been very protective and possessive towards Ben, as she was a lot older than him. Neighbours also said it was strange that friends or girlfriends were never seen visiting or staying at his caravan.

'That's why he never invited me there,' Sophie thought aloud.

'We also found out,' DI Jones continued, 'that Ben had a daughter when he was in his twenties, when he was living at the caravan site in Drayston. His daughter's mother was a young gypsy girl, no older than seventeen. Ben didn't know about his daughter until last September. She's called Gina.'

'Gina,' Sophie gasped.

DI Jones continued, 'Gina had tracked Ben down through the old community that is still there. Her grandmother looked after her, after Gina's mother died. Now they have both died Gina is on her own, with no family. She has become remarkably close to Ben, as you can understand. We know she has been in trouble for half her life, but since last year she seems to have been okay.'

After trying to process the information, Sophie asked, 'What does Iris... sorry, Gemma, think about her?'

'She loves her, we are told. Well, she's her only niece, isn't she, part of Ben. At the moment Gina lives with Gemma in her caravan. Although I probably shouldn't say this, but as Ben is very wealthy, he will probably buy her a house when she can prove she's changed.'

'Wealthy?' Sophie was shocked again.

'Yes, he is. His uncle left him a large amount of land, which Ben sold not long after he had inherited it.'

'How do you know all this?'

'As you know, Sophie, this is a small town, and we have contacts who have been keeping an eye on the family for a long time.'

'So that's the reason Gemma hated me.' Sophie was now beginning to understand.

'I couldn't say for sure,' DI Jones interrupted, 'but presumably Gemma didn't want anyone else having his money, and also Ben was their rock. Someone who was always there for them.'

'Gina must have thought the same thing,' Sophie said, wondering if they had both wanted to kill her, but she still didn't think Gina would have gone that far.

But surely Ben could have broken away from the hold that his sister had on him if he had wanted to? Sophie was upset that he hadn't told her about Gina; he had had the opportunity. Ben should have broken free and lived his own life. He was a grown man.

'What about Iris's daughter? I'm sorry, but to me she will always be Iris,' Sophie commented, suddenly remembering she had a daughter.

'She never married. We don't think she had any children,' DI Jones replied.

'She lied again,' thought Sophie out loud. 'Ben lied as well. They both lied and lied.'

She leaned against the pillow, her head thumping.

Sophie knew that Ben had a sister. But Ben had said she lived in Australia.

'Why would he have lied about her?' Sophie said, not meaning to say it out loud.

'Well, he wouldn't want you to know what she was like. As I said, Gemma was under suspicion when Ben's fiancée died but we couldn't prove anything, and she used to clean for them occasionally; probably, they really appreciated her being around.'

Sophie knew that feeling.

'We are now also looking into the electrical incident at the festival, although it hasn't been reported officially. We think Gemma was responsible for that.'

'How could she be? She wasn't there,' said Sophie, now exhausted.

DI Jones told Sophie that Ben and Mark had been to the

police station last night to confirm that they had both checked the equipment together with Gina and they were all cleared of any responsibility.

After Ben had left the station, Mark had told DI Jones that Gemma and Ben used to play in a group years ago, and that Gemma would have known all about electrics as she used to help Ben set up on stage. She even played the guitar for a while until she decided the nights were too late for her. She often used to drive them to gigs.

Sophie realised that Gemma could have fixed the amp any time while cleaning her house. But Sophie had played the guitar the night before, so Gemma must have disconnected the earth wire before Ben connected it up on Saturday.

'We have no problem with Ben, he is a good bloke,' DI Jones added, as he left her ward to speak to the nurse. Sophie watched him disappear.

'You may not have a problem with him, but I certainly do,' Sophie said out loud. She felt heartbroken, realising that her relationship with Ben would never have gone anywhere.

So, Mark had known about Iris. He and Ben had been friends since teenagers, but did he know about Gina? Ben may have told him when she turned up out of the blue. Gina never did tell anyone who she was, but then she never talked much to anyone anyway.

And Kenny, poor Kenny. Sophie couldn't bear to think of him. Iris must have killed him while she was at work. How could she have done that so cold-heartedly? She shuddered to think that Iris could have done anything to her at any time.

Her heart crashed.

Tom said goodbye, saying he would go and sort the shop out for her, as it was a mess. He then had to go back to university. She kissed him and then she was left very much alone.

Sophie thought of the many times Iris had been in her house. She must have planned it the very first time she came into the shop. She shivered. It was all thought out. Sophie had told Ben she was thinking of having a cleaner and he must have mentioned it to Iris. He must have talked to Iris a lot about her and made her jealous. Ben had no idea she was cleaning for Sophie. They never met at her house. Of course, Iris always disappeared if she knew Ben was going to be there. Sophie thought, *how could I have been so stupid, to be taken in like that?*

Iris knew about the key in the hanging basket; Sophie had told her that if ever she got locked out, she could use that one. Iris must have taken it herself so that she wouldn't be suspected. So it wasn't any of the group, as she had thought, who had taken it.

Sophie thought about all the kindness that she had shown Iris. She probably had snooped around and looked into every drawer in her house. She would have certainly seen the photo of Ben with her, taken at the Christmas dance. Iris must have been jealous, seeing that. She must have gone into Sophie's bedroom and had probably seen things that Ben had left there occasionally. Sophie was sure Iris had seen the ring as well, on Ben's bedside table in his caravan. She must have been filled with hate – just waiting for the time to end Sophie's relationship with Ben, not caring how she did it.

Sophie's mind was now very tired, but she couldn't stop thinking.

Could Iris have put the small broken crystals of glass in her bath last month? It hadn't been the wind through the open window that had blown the candle holder off the windowsill, after all. What if she hadn't seen them before she stepped in?

Iris must have been the person who threw paint up her wall in her art shop. It wasn't Mark.

She seemed such a lovely kind person; how could she have done it?

Sophie was shocked by Ben as well. He should have told her about Iris. No wonder he didn't want a serious relationship.

All those lovely nights she and Ben had had together. He never told her that he was wealthy, but then she wasn't bothered about that. He could have told her Gina was his daughter. She would have understood the situation more and got to know her better.

Her thoughts went back to Iris; she could have been killed by her. Sophie shuddered. She tried to sleep, but all she could see were Iris's small brown eyes staring at her.

Ben certainly wasn't the man she thought he was.

That was what upset her most. He wasn't strong minded, independent or sexy now.

'Oh God, Mark was right,' Sophie whispered – Ben wasn't the man she thought he was. Why hadn't she questioned Mark more? He had tried to warn her in his strange way.

Her heart crashed again.

Ben hadn't phoned when she was in hospital and Sophie didn't feel like phoning him.

Thirty-Nine

The next day Sophie was home. Although it was mid-June the house felt cold, quiet and somehow lonely. She had the feeling that she would hear the door open, and Iris would walk in, offering to make a cup of tea.

Who could she call to get the locks changed? Ben hadn't been in touch and wasn't there to recommend someone. She found the number of a local locksmith on the internet and he was there within hours, as she had requested emergency callout. He changed the locks on all the doors and Sophie felt a lot happier, even though it had been expensive.

She phoned Julie.

Julie was still very shocked about what had happened and couldn't believe that Iris was such a horrible person, but she was having lunch with Steve so couldn't talk at that moment. She was very supportive and told Sophie they would come and see her, on Wednesday evening when they had finished work at the factory. The children would be in the crèche full-time from next month, which would allow her more free time. They must meet up regularly again soon and keep in touch.

DI Jones called in two days later, saying that Gemma would be charged for the murder of Helen, attempted murder of Ben, and also for attacking Sophie. Did she want her charged for her cat, the paint, and the dress incident?

'Of course, my lovely dress.' Sophie thought back to when Iris had been so concerned about it. It was Iris who had been in the lounge that night.

Sophie shuddered and prayed she wouldn't see Iris ever again.

Sophie said, 'No, it's over now. At least I know who did it.'

She wanted to talk to Dave, but she knew he had moved to a small flat in Cornwall after learning the truth about Emma, and after having a very upsetting time telling everyone. Her sister and mother hadn't been in touch with Sophie to tell her he was living nearby, but Sophie wasn't surprised.

Emma had moved to France, taking George, the unborn baby and a lot of Dave's money with her. Tom told Sophie that Emma had admitted to Dave that the children weren't his. She had been seeing a much younger man throughout their relationship, while taking money from Dave's bank account, and they were now all living together in nice accommodation in Paris.

Dave hadn't been in touch with Sophie since their meeting in the lift. Sophie was sad but life had changed such a lot since their divorce.

Tom also had some surprising news of his own. He and Zoe were going to America to study music for a year in September, and they were looking forward to going.

Sophie said she was very pleased for them, trying not to let him see how totally devastated she was.

At least, Sophie had Tom for another three months and he would visit her whenever he had time off from university and wasn't seeing Zoe. She was so thankful for that.

Forty

Sophie thought about Paul, and the good times they had had, and how worried he had been when she was in the hotel by herself. She thought how well they had got on together. No one else had bothered about her. How could she have turned him down when he had been so loving and caring towards her? Tess was so lucky. She couldn't phone him now that he was in a relationship with Tess.

But Sophie couldn't help herself – she phoned Paul's number.

'Hello, Sophie. How are you?' Tess answered. 'We were just talking about you. We were going to call in today, to tell you our good news.'

Sophie caught her breath. She knew what Tess was going to say.

'What news?' Sophie tried to sound excited.

'Paul and I are engaged.'

'That's wonderful. I am so happy for you both. Can you call in next week, though, as I am still on painkillers and not really with it yet?' Sophie said quickly, not feeling able at that moment to talk to Tess. She had to have time to process the idea of them being engaged.

'Of course, it will be great to see you. Pleased you are getting better.'

Sophie could hear Paul's voice in the background.

Her heart sank.

'Oh, by the way Paul sends his love.'

Sophie ended the call.

'Where's Ben?' Sophie said out loud. 'I must see him.' She tapped in his number. He didn't answer. She tried again. No answer.

A message came up on her phone from DI Jones.

'We have obtained a warrant for the arrest of Gemma Slater later today. She won't have gone far.'

Forty-One

Ben's phone rang again. It was Sophie. He deleted her number and blocked her calls.

An announcement echoed through the airport.

'This is the last call for passengers going to Thailand. Please go to gate number ten.'

Ben, Gina, and Gemma picked up their hand luggage and walked quickly to the waiting plane.

OR DID SOPHIE GO THROUGH THE DOOR
ON THE RIGHT?

Forty-Two

'Let me help!'

Sophie had caught her large clutch bag on the door handle, scattering the entire contents on the floor, and was now on her hands and knees rapidly trying to retrieve the items from under the chairs and radiator. She came face to face with a man who was smiling cheekily, also on his hands and knees. He stood up and handed Sophie her shoes and phone.

'My name's Ben,' Sophie heard him say. She was now standing up, struggling to quickly take off her jacket.

'Sophie,' she managed to mumble, embarrassed, as she was convinced the whole room was now watching her. She noticed her tights were laddered.

'Let us get started.'

The teacher introduced herself.

'My name is Gina.' She flicked her black and purple hair from her face. 'It's lovely to see you here tonight and it's great that you are all interested in learning Latin dance. Latin dancing is very expressive and a lot of fun and I'm sure you'll all enjoy it. I'll be partnering Mark for this session. Please find a partner and we will go slowly through the rumba steps.'

Ben, who had decided to sit by Sophie, offered to partner her and, as she was still in a daze, she agreed.

He waited patiently for Sophie to struggle into her dancing

shoes. Admittedly she had bought them from the charity shop, but they had fitted her perfectly yesterday when she had tried them on. She managed to buckle the left shoe and was now trying to squeeze her right foot in, while Ben watched her. Sophie stood up, trying to wiggle her toes into a comfortable position, and looked around for the first time.

There were about ten couples, from all different age groups, in the room. The women were dressed in suitable clothes, the men more casually.

Then she saw him.

Dave! Standing in the middle of the dance floor.

What's he doing here? Sophie couldn't believe it. He was partnering a woman who was wearing a short flared red dress and very high heels. *How will she dance in those?* Sophie thought, embarrassed by her own ancient Cuban heels. She couldn't even hide them.

Dave didn't like dancing. He had certainly never danced with her, and he hadn't watched it on the television the few times when he was at home.

He shrugged and smiled at Sophie across the dance floor. She somehow shrugged and smiled back. Could she just leave now before the lesson started? She started to walk back to her chair, but Ben swung her round and she found herself following him as he danced his way to join the others.

'Oh God, an extrovert,' Sophie said under her breath. Enthralled, they watched Gina perform the rumba moves beautifully while she professionally guided Mark at the same time. Even Sophie could see he wasn't a natural dancer, but he didn't care, he was enjoying himself.

'Now that *Strictly* is on the television again, try to watch it and you will get some idea of the moves, but don't expect to be as good as the professional dancers,' Gina was saying, twirling around in her black rumba skirt and red top, admiring herself in the long mirrors. 'Remember, dancing is for fun.'

Sophie was yet to be convinced.

She wasn't really listening. Sophie was looking at Dave

again, dressed in black trousers, black shirt, and black and white dancing shoes. His shoes must have been new. She had never seen him dressed like this. Usually, he wore ripped jeans, T-shirts, and trainers.

After a long hour of dancing and total concentration everyone thankfully went to the bar. The group were friendly and Sophie realised that Gina wasn't as formidable as she first appeared. She told them that she had been dancing for twenty years and had just finished teaching on cruise ships. Although she had enjoyed her time cruising, she wanted a change, so she had started up her own dance club. She advised the group where to get dance shoes from if they decide to stay with the club and if they needed them. Sophie hoped Gina hadn't seen the ones she was wearing and was referring to her.

'For the second half,' Gina now reverting to her teaching mode, 'we will now change partners for fun. Pete, you partner Julie, Jess, you can partner Paul. Ben with Jane. Sophie, you can partner Dave...'

After wondering how Gina remembered everyone's names, she suddenly realised that she was partnered with Dave. Could things get any worse?

They shuffled awkwardly towards each other and stood together.

'What are you doing here?' Sophie hissed.

'I have more time now, and Tom said I should get out more.'

'But you don't like dancing.'

'I may do! Why are you here? I didn't know you liked dancing.'

'You never asked me!' Sophie retaliated.

Gina switched on the music and Sophie found herself stumbling around Dave, being flung out to his side, and her arm being twisted into unnatural moves. She pulled her arm away and rubbed it, telling him to be less aggressive.

'The Hockey Stick is a difficult move, but the man should lead his partner gently and not throw her around,' Gina added, looking around the room.

'Exactly,' agreed Sophie.

Gina, noticing their argument, as she was dancing next to them, said quietly, 'If you hadn't arrived separately, I would have said you were a couple.'

Sophie and Dave just looked at each other.

Dave raised his eyebrows.

'That's our secret,' Dave suggested.

Sophie, who had now almost forgiven him, and surprised by Gina's comments, agreed.

'Who's your partner?'

'Oh, Emma, I met her when I walked in,' replied Dave. 'But she's been having lessons for years and hasn't got much patience.'

'Mine's Ben.'

'I know, I saw you come in.'

'Oh,' replied Sophie, embarrassed.

'Dancing is fun,' Gina told the group again and smiled at Sophie and Dave as she walked past to change the music.

Dance lesson finished, Sophie levered off her dance shoes with great difficulty and slipped her hot painful feet into her cold comfortable flats.

Dave returned to his chair.

Ben, having attached himself to Sophie at the beginning of the evening, came back rubbing his calves and shoulders.

'I have really enjoyed tonight.'

Sophie nodded, but still had to be convinced.

The group talked for a while and then said goodnight and looked forward to seeing each other the next week.

Sophie walked through the car park and sank into the car seat.

'What am I doing?' she sighed aloud.

Did Tom know that Dave was intending to go tonight? If he had known, he should have warned her. Sophie was slightly annoyed.

As Sophie drove home in the dark, she couldn't decide whether or not she had enjoyed herself.

Sophie let Kenny out into the garden and made herself a cup

of tea. She would have preferred a couple of large glasses of red wine after her dancing ordeal, but she could no longer afford any. She was pleased Dave had offered to buy her a glass tonight.

Sophie looked at her shoes; compared to the other women's, they really did look old and worn. But she might not go dancing for long and a new pair would be a waste of money. She would try and polish them again tomorrow.

Her green top looked okay. Although it was also from the charity shop, it was brand-new and fitted her well. Her black skirt was passable. She just wished she had some spare money that she could spend.

Sophie opened the kitchen door to let Kenny back in.

An hour later she went upstairs and had a shower, the warm water splashing soothingly on her feet, and she then climbed into bed. Why had Gina partnered her with Dave?

The following week was less stressful.

During the evening Gina told them that there was a possibility the Maple Leaf might be closing down, due to lack of attendance, generally, in the club.

'I have given it some thought and have been in touch with other dance studios in the area to see if they are interested in having dance competitions here, starting in a few months' time, and then perhaps every month. They won't be serious competitions. They will be friendly, but it will give us something to aim for, as well as bringing in more people and money for the club. Alan, the owner, likes the idea. Anyway, it's just a thought; let's see how it goes. Remember, it won't be competition dancing, it will be fun. Something to bring people to the club.'

There was a hum of excited conversation.

'We'll have to practise,' Dave interrupted Gina.

Trust him, thought Sophie, *never danced in his life, and now he's an expert.*

'Alan has offered us the small room upstairs. It has a dance floor, but it will be cold as the heating won't be on. It should be available Monday to Friday if anyone wants to use it. But remember to bring warm clothes and perhaps hot drinks.

'If you want to put your names down for the competitions, I have a book here, then I can see how many are interested. Anyone who doesn't want to enter can help in other ways, should they prefer.'

Dave made his way to sign the book first, encouraging Emma, who wasn't too sure. They wrote their names, together with telephone numbers.

Pete and Joe.

Mark and Julie.

Paul and Jess.

Deano and Jane.

Sophie and Ben.

Sophie was hesitant, knowing that she wouldn't be able to afford to carry on.

Carole signed in by herself. She didn't as yet have a partner.

Anthony, who had arrived alone that night, also signed in without a partner.

Everyone in the dancing group added each other's telephone numbers to their phones, all except Anthony, who said that he had left his phone at home and would do it next time.

'I think we may attempt the cha cha next week,' Gina added. 'I have written down some of the steps as they won't be in the same order as shown on YouTube.'

She handed out sheets of paper.

'I hope you will use the room upstairs and I look forward to seeing you up there when I can make it.'

Gina closed her large book, took off her black Latin shoes, put on her biker jacket and boots, flicked her hair, checked herself in the mirror, said goodbye and left.

Everyone agreed they would practise when they could find time after work, promising that they would phone each other and probably arrange to go for a meal first at The Tavern.

Sophie was the last to leave, as she was looking at photos and pictures of dancers in gold frames on the walls, admiring the women's dresses and shoes, a world away from what she was wearing. She was really worried that she wouldn't be able to afford the clothes which she needed to wear for the competitions.

Sophie found herself taking a deep breath just as Anthony walked past her.

'Goodnight, Sophie.'

'Goodnight.'

How had he remembered her name? She remembered his, as Gina had asked him to sign his name in the book.

Did she catch him looking at the shoes which she was holding? She pushed them into her bag.

When she eventually made her way to her car, she saw Anthony on his phone as he walked to his taxi.

Strange, she thought. *He did have his phone! He hadn't left it at home.* Sophie wondered why he had said he had, and why he was using a taxi.

While at work in her art shop Sophie practised the rumba steps every day, when she didn't have any customers, and even her abstract artwork suddenly included flashes of dancers in red and black. She just wished she was selling as many paintings as she used to. She was now beginning to worry more about her money situation. Perhaps she could run an art class at night. But that meant she would have to buy more equipment. She quickly gave up on the idea. Perhaps she could get a bar job.

Sophie had agreed to meet Ben on Monday for a meal at The Tavern and then they were going to the Maple Leaf to practise, but later in the day he messaged her, apologising. He had to work in Southampton for a few days so he wouldn't see her either at The Tavern or on Thursday night. Sophie wondered if she should go alone to the dance lesson. She spent the rest of the day persuading herself that it was a good excuse not to go to the dance club as she wouldn't have a partner.

But Sophie decided to go. She arrived at the Maple Leaf much too early for her lesson, as she had driven there straight from the shop. She was still worried about who she would be partnered with, or if she would even have a partner, but she thought she would give it one more chance. She sat in the bar, trying to memorise her dance steps, which Gina had written on the piece of paper and had given her the week before.

A man and woman in their mid-fifties walked in. The woman, slim, with blonde hair and wearing a short brown jacket, sat down at a table close by while the man, who was thickset, wearing glasses, dressed in blue shirt and black trousers, ordered two beers, and then sat next to her. Sophie could tell from their faces that they weren't very happy, and they started to argue quietly while leaning over the table. Sophie found her mind wandering over to them. She tried to listen, but they kept their voices low and then left without finishing their drinks. Sophie watched them leave, the woman walking quickly ahead of the man, who was still trying to reason with her.

Sophie gazed through the window and she saw them walk even more quickly across the car park and get into separate cars, the man slamming his door. Realising that the woman had left her mauve scarf hanging over the chair, Sophie quickly picked it up, followed them, knocked on the woman's car window and handed it to her. The woman thanked her and drove away; the man drove fast in the opposite direction, scattering gravel behind him.

Sophie sat down again. She hadn't noticed Anthony sitting opposite, watching her. He was the oldest of the group, well-groomed, and quite good-looking. Tall, slim, well-toned, black-grey hair. Sophie thought he was about sixty-five. They acknowledged each other, he came over, sat by her, and introduced himself.

'Anthony.'

'Sophie.'

'Are you a people-watcher like me?' Anthony asked, placing his glass of brandy on the table.

Sophie noticed his expensive dance shoes as she put her bag on the floor. They looked hand-made.

'I suppose I am. I have always found people fascinating.'

Anthony nodded, deep in thought.

After talking for half an hour, they agreed to dance together that evening as Ben was away.

She learned that he was Anthony Oliver, a semi-retired property developer, who had recently moved from London when his wife died. He was now living in the vast new exclusive complex on the edge of Timberry. His company had developed the site. He had sold his house and was waiting to see if everything went well with the development, and then he was off to the South of France, as he didn't have any children or anyone to keep him in England.

His wife had been a very keen golfer, spending her time on the golf course most of the day, while Anthony loved vintage cars and dancing. His former dance partner of many years, Bernice, had also retired from the company, at the same time as him, and had recently moved from London down to Devon to be with her daughter.

Anthony asked Sophie about herself. She shrugged, saying his life was far more interesting than hers, and cleverly changed the subject, asking him how many vintage cars he had and where he kept them.

She thoroughly enjoyed dancing all evening with Anthony, as it was a totally different experience from dancing with Dave or Ben. Gina complimented them, saying they were totally in step to the music.

After dancing, and before leaving the club, Anthony asked Sophie, as she had shown interest in the complex, if she would like to look around the following Tuesday night. If she agreed, they could also practise the new dance steps for the competition in their new village hall.

Sophie thought that the complex might want new paintings, so she accepted his invitation, hoping she would make a sale.

Feeling inquisitive, after Sophie arrived home from dancing, and after putting Kenny outside, she searched Anthony's name on her phone. There were lots of Anthony Olivers, but there was nothing that matched. Disappointed, she put down her phone, picking it up again to search the complex where he lived.

Nothing really interesting – basically a complex for people who have money. No description, just a phone number.

Forty-Three

Tuesday night arrived. Instead of looking around the complex, Anthony took Sophie straight up to his luxurious penthouse suite. Stepping out of his lift, Sophie had never dreamed she would find herself in a place like this.

Anthony admitted that he had purposely not told her he owned the penthouse, and apologised, saying he wanted people to like him for himself and not for his money.

So Sophie found herself sitting looking out at the twinkling lights across the town, drinking coffee and talking to a virtual stranger, but somehow she was enjoying it and didn't feel at all threatened. She tried to look around without making it too obvious – extensive lounge, large wide windows, expensive furniture, fully stocked bar, typically a man's residence.

Anthony asked Sophie about her life.

She told him she was recently divorced – she didn't go into all the details – and that she had an art shop which was not going very well. She had a son at university, which was proving very expensive, and she helped out in a charity shop. And now that she was dancing, she didn't know whether she could afford to carry on with the lessons, as she realised it was going to be expensive buying new clothes.

Anthony was so easy to talk to unless it was the brandy, that she was now drinking from the large brandy glass, that was making her think aloud.

'Sorry,' Sophie apologised, realising she must now be boring him with her worries.

Anthony asked if her ex-husband contributed. She told him he did, towards Tom. He had given her the house but that was all. She hadn't wanted anything from him, but she still had the mortgage. She didn't want Dave's help.

Why am I telling him all this? Sophie thought.

Anthony sipped his brandy, now staring out of the window.

'You are a natural dancer,' Anthony breathed deeply, his eyes still fixed on the view. 'Try not to give that up.'

It was so relaxing, sitting in the plush armchair sipping her brandy. She'd never drunk brandy before – well, she couldn't afford it.

'Have you thought of selling the shop?' Anthony added after a while, not looking at her, his gaze still fixed out of the window, his legs stretched out in front of him, exposing his bright orange and white socks under his jeans.

'I couldn't. My father left the money for me to buy it when he died,' Sophie answered, more sharply than intended.

Anthony now looked at her, with his dancing grey eyes.

'If you want my advice, you should sell it before you start losing too much money. I think your father would think that would be the best thing to do. You could use the money to help with other payments.'

Sophie told him that this had crossed her mind, but it would be too emotionally difficult for her.

'You can always buy another shop when you have fewer commitments, should the cash become available one day.'

Sophie knew he was right and they both sat in silence.

Anthony suddenly stood up, walked over to the window and turned to face her.

'The complex is opening up an art activities workshop soon, when the room in the village hall is finished. Would you be interested in running it?'

Surprised, Sophie just looked at Anthony.

'I would love to, if you think I could do it.' Then she

added, 'But I don't think I would be able to afford to run it properly.'

Anthony laughed.

'You will be paid, of course. I will have to check whether they have advertised yet. As I have said, it will be in the village hall. The hall is almost finished now. The room is just being decorated.'

Sophie sat in silence again. It would be a big step to take and a big commitment.

By the time she had drunk the second generous glass of brandy, which Anthony had automatically poured, she had said she would love to run the activity club. How could she refuse him?

Anthony stood up, walked across the room to his private lift and took her down to the main entrance. They walked along the long corridor where he let her through the large glass doors with his key card. Anthony said he would be in touch by the end of the week.

It was good that she had walked to the complex as, after her brandy binge and the strange events of the evening going round in her mind, she wouldn't have been able to drive back. Sophie made her way home and was now trying hard to understand what she was letting herself in for and why she had let him influence her.

On Friday, as promised, Anthony phoned and Sophie confirmed she wanted the job at the complex, and after thinking about what Anthony had advised, she got in touch with Jordans, the local estate office, who by Tuesday had taken videos and photos and had placed her art shop on the market.

Sophie felt sad, but Anthony was right; she could always buy another shop later, and she did feel that a weight had been lifted.

Forty-Four

Ben was back at the dance club on Thursday and danced with Sophie, while Gina danced with Anthony. Sophie thought they looked so professional. Anthony acknowledged her, but nothing more. She thought he almost ignored her.

The evening went well, Gina explaining that she was still trying to organise local dance competitions.

In the second half Gina told them to swap partners again.

'Sophie, I would like to partner you with Dave for the competition – you seem to gel well together. If you're not happy with that arrangement, let me know.'

'Oh no,' Sophie sighed.

Dave swaggered over.

'We can win this.'

Sophie shook her head. Where had this dancing confidence come from?

Gina went around the room, re-partnering people who weren't a couple.

'Unfortunately, Anthony won't be coming again, as he has other commitments,' Gina explained. She thanked him for being such a good partner and told him he would always be welcome.

Sophie looked at him. But Gina had taken his hand and she was beginning the cha cha.

The evening ended, Sophie thankfully took off her shoes,

rubbed her feet and slid them into her boots. She looked around for Anthony, but he had already left.

Dave interrupted her thoughts, suggesting they should get together for practising; Sophie reluctantly agreed, but secretly thought they would never get on together without arguing. It was going to be a very exhausting and irritating time. Not what she had anticipated at all.

The following week the estate agent phoned to inform Sophie she had received a good offer for her shop with all the contents, and that it would be kept as an art shop. She asked who the buyer was. The estate agent told her it was Dawn Tomlinson, who was new to the area, and she had liked it straight away. He had shown her around the shop just after Sophie had left for home. Sophie said she didn't want to deal with the buyer, and accepted the offer, resigned to the fact that she would miss it terribly. But she would be pleased to have the money in her bank.

Forty-Five

To Sophie's surprise, Anthony phoned her two weeks later, saying that the village hall was almost complete, and asking if she would like to see it. She met Anthony the evening after the phone call, in a dark quiet part of the garden next to the car park. He took her first around the outside of the complex. It was very impressive. She hadn't taken much notice of the building the last time she was there. Sophie could tell from the cars parked in the covered car park that only people who had money were living there, as the cars were worth a fortune, and as she walked around the gated complex it certainly had the feeling of grandeur.

They walked across the vast gardens and went through the back doors of the village hall. The entrance hall opened onto a large dance floor, with a glitter ball on the ceiling and large comfortable armchairs with a long pub bar. The smell of fresh paint lingered. Sophie just stood looking in amazement.

'Your workshop will be in here.'

Anthony opened another door to the side of the ballroom and Sophie walked into a huge empty room with large windows. Cupboards, chairs, and tables were stacked in the corner. 'You will be able to order what you will need to set it up.' When Sophie had taken everything in, she thanked him, saying she hoped she could make it work.

'I know you will,' Anthony replied, closing the large doors after her.

He opened another set of doors which led back into the grand corridor of the complex.

'Come up to my suite. I have something else to discuss with you.'

Sophie hesitated slightly, but Anthony was now walking quickly. How could she refuse him? So she followed, trying to keep up. She followed him along the never-ending corridors, passing a large lounge, where people were drinking in the bar, and a door marked cinema on the right. They carried on along another corridor, and Sophie could see a swimming pool with a glass roof where swimmers could swim under the stars. They eventually turned into a quiet hallway and after Anthony had keyed in six numbers, they went up in the plush large lift marked "Private". The doors opened directly into his suite. She would never remember her way around.

He poured a coffee, handed it to Sophie and told her to take a seat. She sank into the deep black leather chair and waited for him to speak. He sat in the chair opposite and it was quite a while before he spoke. Sophie thought he looked embarrassed as he flicked imaginary fluff from his trousers.

'I have a proposition to put to you,' Anthony said, his eyes quickly leaving her and looking out of the window.

Sophie held her breath, without realising it.

'Since moving from London, it has been difficult for me to make genuine friends. Something that I really miss. Most of the people living in this complex are married, and others have busy lives, or they don't share my interests.'

Sophie put down her cup on the side table, making sure her slightly shaking hand placed it exactly on the square bamboo mat.

'I was wondering if you would like to dance with me in my ballroom. Perhaps practising would help you with the competitions you are entering. I miss dancing so much and we could both benefit from it. But there is one condition. I would like you to be discreet and not tell anyone. It's important that I keep up an appearance living here. People see me as the rich man who has everything.'

Sophie thought it would be a change from dancing with Dave, and the idea of dancing around a large ballroom with an experienced dancer, well, she didn't even have to think about it. She said she would love to.

But then Anthony looked at her and said, 'Of course, I will pay you for the time you spend with me.'

Shocked, Sophie got up quickly, picking up her bag and sending the carefully placed cup flying onto the polished floorboards.

'I don't need paying,' she gasped and headed blindly for the lift.

Moving even more quickly, Anthony blocked her way.

'I'm sorry if I have offended you.'

'I'm not interested in your money,' Sophie half-lied, feeling slightly insulted, although admitting to herself that a little more money for doing something that she loved would really help her financial situation.

Somehow, Sophie found herself sitting back down in the chair. Anthony started talking again.

'Please don't be offended. I am paying you for your time. Okay, you will have money from the shop sale but that won't last forever.'

He offered her a brandy, carefully stepping over the upturned cup still on the floor.

She drank it quickly, not realising that she had almost finished it by the time he had poured his.

'Will there be anyone else dancing in the ballroom?' Sophie asked, shocked by her interest.

'No. Just you and me.'

'Follow me,' Anthony ordered, and walked towards one of the walls of his large lounge. Sophie stood up and obeyed. He punched three numbers into the small bronze keyboard beside the light switch. The panelled wall slid open, exposing a large room which lit up immediately on entering. The room was designed for dancing; wooden floor, glitter ball, lights, seats, windows, again looking out over the lights of the town. Sophie's jaw dropped.

'It's a shame, it's never been danced in since I moved here. I had it specially designed,' Anthony's sad voice trailed into the distance.

The phone in his lounge rang, interrupting. Anthony walked out of his ballroom and answered it. He excused himself, saying he had to go to reception, and disappeared in his lift.

Sophie walked around. She noticed that there was a small stage in the corner of the vast room and that the coloured ceiling lights changed to different shades. How could she not dance in here? She spun around on the floor two or three times and then stared out of the window again.

The phone rang again; she automatically walked towards it. After only a few rings it went to answerphone.

'Gerald, this is Anthony. Sorry to ring on this phone, but I must speak to you. I am on a different number now.' Anthony quickly said the number and ended the message.

Why was Anthony called Gerald? Sophie didn't understand.

That wasn't Anthony's voice. Had Anthony been lying to her? Was his name really Gerald and not Anthony?

Confused and very curious, Sophie mentally made a note of the number and then put it into her mobile, hoping she had remembered and tapped it in correctly, in the hurry.

She heard the lift stopping. Sophie walked quickly to the bathroom, locking the door.

She heard Anthony calling her.

Sophie made her way to the lounge, trying to make out she wouldn't have heard the phone's low purring ring.

'Sorry, I should have told you where you could freshen up.'

Anthony keyed in the numbers and the ballroom door closed automatically. He asked again if he could pay her. Sophie, now intrigued by him, and needing the money, quickly forgot her pride and agreed. Well, it was his idea to pay her.

She picked up the cup from the floor and offered to clean the coffee stain from the floorboards, but Anthony said his housekeeper would do it in the morning.

Before she stepped into the private lift Anthony gave Sophie a box. She looked at him, surprised, and started to take the lid off, but Anthony told her to open it when she got home. As she left his suite, he watched her on his camera. Sophie made sure the corridor was clear and walked through the long hallways, hoping not to meet anyone. Anthony had instructed her to tell any residents who questioned her that she was his PA as well as part-time art teacher. Should that have sent warning bells?

Anthony was certain he had chosen the right person for his future plans.

Sophie eventually made her way out of the complex, not feeling guilty about taking money from him. She put the lift code number which Anthony had written on a piece of paper and the two key cards in her pocket; one for the complex and the other to his suite.

Back home, Sophie took out her computer. She would use the computer in case she mislaid her phone. She typed in Gerald Oliver's name. She found three in the London area. An MP, an ex-criminal and a schoolteacher. She closed the computer. She could always phone the number that she had tried to remember. But what phone could she use? Sophie pulled out her old pay as you go phone from her wardrobe and charged it. She would wait a couple of weeks before phoning, to let some time pass after being in Anthony's suite.

Sophie, suddenly remembering the box, opened the lid, thinking it contained something for her art class. Inside was a beautiful pair of black Latin dance shoes. She tried them on quickly and they fitted perfectly. How did he know her size? He had noticed her old worn-out ones.

She felt embarrassed and then pleased. Anthony must have wanted to spend money on her. She phoned to thank him.

Two weeks later Sophie tapped in the number and waited.

After what seemed like two minutes a man replied, 'Hello, Oliver's Antiques.'

Sophie knew she had dialled the right number. Even after practising what she was going to say her mind went completely blank.

'Hello, Oliver's Antiques?'

Trying to disguise her voice, Sophie asked to speak to Gerald.

'Who is this?'

Panicking, Sophie ended the call quickly. She looked up Oliver's Antiques on her computer. She didn't use her phone as she was still worried that she might leave it at Anthony's. Again, there was nothing. She closed the computer.

Sophie started her job at the complex and she settled in straight away. She found it easy showing her classes how to experiment with ideas using arts and crafts; it was fun, with no pressure. She never spoke to Anthony if they saw each other accidently. It was important to him that he made sure that no one knew about their arrangement. He was talked about occasionally by people in her workshop, when they saw him drive into the car park or walk to or from his car, but she just listened, not saying anything. They all seemed to be distant from each other. Not too friendly. Sophie didn't notice him walk past occasionally, glancing through the open door.

After two months Sophie's finances improved enough for her to go shopping for a new dress and pay off some of her small debts. She even gave Kenny some special expensive food, which he ate appreciatively. She always looked forward to seeing him sitting on the windowsill, patiently waiting for her, when she turned into the drive.

Forty-Six

At her Thursday night dance lesson Sophie wore her new shoes; they were so comfortable and fitted her perfectly. She wondered again how Anthony had known her size.

Later in the evening, just as she was going to bed, Anthony phoned, saying he had a business meeting at a hotel in London, and offered to take her there for the weekend if Sophie wanted to go. She accepted immediately, as she hadn't been to London for years, and she knew she would be paid for it. She enjoyed being paid by Anthony now; there was something secretive about it and of course, she still needed the money.

He instructed Sophie to wait at a bus stop five miles along the deserted coast road, as he didn't want to be recognised with her. This area was one of her favourite places as it was so quiet. The local bus only ran twice a day, but she was happy to take a taxi and go along with his plan. She wondered which of his cars he would use.

Fifteen minutes after getting out of a taxi with her new small on-trend suitcase, she was sitting in the bus shelter, which was almost hidden by overgrown bushes. Sophie was enjoying the quiet, looking over the beach and the lapping waves, until the sound of Anthony's car could be heard. The Aston Martin screeched to a halt.

Sophie got in and they sped along the coast. After a

couple of hours they arrived at the Dormston Hotel, which was extensive and set in perfectly manicured gardens. She was surprised that Anthony was known personally by the staff and that he was treated like royalty. His car was parked for him and they were shown to his suite, which contained three bedrooms.

Sophie suddenly realised that she hadn't given any thought to where she would be sleeping. She just assumed she would have her own separate room.

Anthony told her to order what she wanted and to choose any room she liked, and he went downstairs to meet a colleague in the lounge, leaving her by herself.

After looking around the large high-ceilinged suite Sophie chose her bedroom. They were all different, but she liked this one as it had a roll bath in the bay of the window. She put her overnight bag on the massive bed.

Sophie then became curious about who Anthony was meeting. She picked up the spare door card and took out one of her earrings. She could always tell him that she had lost it and was looking for her earring, should he see her. She then left the suite and made her way carefully down the staircase.

Sophie walked into the empty lounge, which was beautifully decorated, with large armchairs and a wide fireplace. Although it was a warm November day there was a log fire burning.

Anthony was sitting with his back to her, talking to a woman with black hair who was wearing a short fur jacket, white top, and black trousers. They were deep in conversation. Anthony was drinking his usual brandy and the woman was drinking white wine. They were sitting quite close together – *too near*, Sophie thought, *to be colleagues*. Anthony didn't get close to anyone. He got up and went to the bar.

Sophie, suddenly feeling nervous, turned and left the lounge quickly.

'Can I help you?' the receptionist asked, making Sophie jump as she walked past the reception desk.

Sophie felt herself freeze.

'I have lost my earring,' Sophie replied, stroking the one in her ear. 'I may have lost it down here.'

'I will tell everyone to look out for it.'

'Thank you, that would be great.'

Sophie quickly made her way to the lift, opened the suite door, walked through to her bedroom, and collapsed on the bed. Why had she gone downstairs?

Two hours later Anthony returned.

'Did you find your earring?'

Sophie couldn't look at him. How did he know?

'No. I could have lost it when I put my scarf on in the car park. They weren't expensive. Don't worry about it.'

Sophie replaced them with another pair she had brought with her, carefully putting the missing earing in her coat pocket.

After a weekend of shopping, offers to buy her dresses, another pair of earrings which she had tried to refuse, fantastic expensive meals and dancing on Saturday night to the hotel's resident band, it was time to leave the hotel. Sophie had had a fantastic time. The Aston Martin had been valeted and was waiting for them outside the main door. When Anthony was talking to the doorman, Sophie carefully placed the "lost" earring on the floor of the car. They then made their way back to Timberry, Sophie oblivious to the envious looks of the drivers they were overtaking.

Anthony dropped her close to her house around midnight. He shocked Sophie by leaning over and kissing her on the cheek. He said goodnight and thanked her for her company. Anthony placed the expected envelope in her hand. Sophie thanked him, saying she had had a wonderful time. She walked the rest of the way, carrying her shopping bags and overnight case. Anthony watched with interest, until she disappeared out of view.

Sophie was now perfectly happy that he was paying her for their secret rendezvous. Why not? But who was the woman he had met at the hotel? She didn't look like a colleague. Would a colleague leave bright red lipstick on his cheek? Why did Anthony seem pleased enough to kiss Sophie when they parted, leaving his expensive aftershave lingering on her coat? That was so out of character.

An hour later Anthony phoned her, pleased, saying he had found her lost earring. She faked her happiness and thanked him, apologising for being so careless. She breathed a big sigh of relief.

Anthony smiled, raised his eyebrows, and closed his phone.

Sophie's dance lessons were going well, better than she had anticipated, and Dave, she had to admit, was a fast learner and they were managing not to argue too much. In fact, dancing with him was proving to be quite enjoyable. Perhaps Gina had seen the potential they both had. The group had become close friends, meeting two or three times a week and going through the dance routine. Not having the shop to worry about, Sophie found she had more time in the evenings. Sophie could now afford to buy wine when they went out.

Gina had managed to arrange a rumba and cha cha newcomers' competition between four interested dance schools in two weeks' time.

Dave and Sophie practised hard together, Dave asking Sophie where she got her dresses and shoes from. Sophie told him they were cheap off the internet. Should she tell him about Anthony? She was sure Dave wouldn't say anything, and she did want his opinion.

The competition afternoon was to be held at the Maple Leaf. Posters were displayed locally. The judges were going to be four people picked from the audience and the dancers would be judged on entertainment value and not technique.

Forty-Seven

Sophie enjoyed her evenings dancing in Anthony's luxurious ballroom. He was such a fantastic partner; he was also teaching her other dances and, of course, she was being paid regularly.

Afterwards, when they sat and drank brandy, he had started asking all about her friends, which she found strange, and he mentioned her ex-husband. Did she still see him? She lied, saying they didn't get on and she rarely saw him. Anthony raised his eyebrows and drank from his large brandy glass as if in deep thought. He turned quickly towards her.

'Sophie. I'm sorry, I have a confession to make; I have been testing you. I knew that you hadn't lost your earring when we went to London, as I saw them catch the light when we were in the hotel suite and I am aware that you followed me down to the lounge. I also understand that you made a phone call to Oliver's Antiques. The way you remembered the telephone number was very impressive. That was my brother, Gerald. We wanted to see if you were inquisitive enough to try and find out who I really was.'

Sophie went hot and cold and tried to stand up to go, but she couldn't move.

'But then, I have been lying too.' Anthony put down his empty glass. 'Yes, I am a semi-retired property developer, but I also run Oliver's Private Detective Agency. Oliver's Antiques is a codeword we use sometimes.

'The moment I saw you watching the couple in the Maple Leaf, when we first met, I knew I wanted you to work for me.

'I apologise for secretly testing you, but I really think that you would make a good private detective. Working, we like to call it, in our domestic side of the business. You wouldn't need any formal qualifications, just patience, an ability to observe people and judge situations as they arise.'

Sophie was now totally confused.

'I'm so sorry,' Sophie said. 'I was intrigued.'

'That's what I mean. It would come naturally to you to investigate people. Would you be interested in a trial case? I would only give you cases where you wouldn't need formal training.'

Sophie, totally surprised and very shocked at being found out, told him she would have to think about it.

'I'll give you a week.'

Anthony got up from his chair.

'Give my regards to Dave – your dancing secret is, of course, safe with me.'

'How did...?' Sophie answered.

Anthony raised his eyebrows.

'Of course.' Sophie understood.

Forty-Eight

The first dance competition was the following Saturday afternoon.

On Thursday at the dance club, Gina told the group there would be general dancing after the competition, for the audience as well. She went through all the rumba and cha cha moves, making sure that everyone had the right clothes and shoes.

Sophie thought that she certainly wouldn't have had any suitable dance clothes or shoes if it wasn't for the money Anthony gave her, or, as she preferred to think of it, paid her for working for him. She listened to Gina again.

'I know you will make our visiting competitors feel welcome. The trophies for the winners will be awarded after the general dancing.'

The next evening, Dave and Sophie practised until 10pm and they were pleased with their progress. They had only two arguments; one when Dave almost tripped Sophie up doing the Turkish Towel in the cha cha, and the other when Dave pulled her arm in the rumba's sliding doors. They agreed if anything went wrong, they would try not to draw attention to it and just smile.

*

Saturday afternoon arrived. Sophie drove Dave to the Maple Leaf. The women disappeared into the cloakrooms to finish getting ready. The men stood around talking.

Alan, the manager, and Gina had arranged for a local band to play, which gave a better atmosphere in the large room.

Most of the visiting dancers were friendly, except for a couple from Texbury who didn't appear nervous, saying that they had been dancing for years and had entered a lot of competitions and loved dancing in front of audiences. Stuart, their dance teacher, came over to them and wished them well and Sophie heard him whisper, 'No contest.' He then sat down.

At 2pm the audience arrived, shuffling their way into the best seats, while talking excitedly.

The band had set up and were now playing.

Four people, two men and two women from the audience, who were not from the towns involved in the competitions, were chosen as judges. They took their seats at the side of the stage, where papers, pens and glasses of water were arranged on the long table.

Sophie looked around and saw Anthony sitting at the back, talking to a woman with black hair. It was the woman she had seen him talking to at the hotel. The woman was wearing the same fur coat again. Who was she?

A few minutes later Sophie was on the dance floor. The dancers were given numbers, which the men wore on their backs. Dave and Sophie were number eight. There were ten couples. They would be divided into two sets, one for the rumba and one for the cha cha.

The band started playing the cha cha, and Dave squeezed Sophie's hand hard. She flinched, just remembering in time that she had to smile through everything.

Dave began dancing on the wrong foot, but Sophie managed to compensate for it, and she thought they were dancing well, and in time to the music. She couldn't see the other dancers, as they were just a blur of colours and black. The audience watched quietly until one of the dancers performed a move that was outstanding or unusual. Then they clapped and whistled.

Dave, now feeling overconfident, let go of Sophie's hand too soon, just as she was turning, which sent her spinning round by herself. Luckily, he had done that before in practice and so she wasn't too surprised. As she spun around, she then spun round again in the opposite direction, ending in front of Dave; something that Anthony had suggested that she could do. Dave adapted to the move. The audience, seeing this, clapped, thinking it was part of the dance. After five minutes, the cha cha dancing finished, and the first competitors left the floor for a while, relieved that the dance for them was over. It was now time for the next set of dancers to take the floor.

Sophie quickly looked at Anthony; he was still deep in conversation with the unknown woman. She was slightly disappointed that he hadn't acknowledged her.

The rumba dance went well. Sophie thought that she and Dave did have a natural feel for it. There was only one mistake; when she did the Hockey Stick her foot almost caught Dave's, but it wasn't noticeable.

The whole competition didn't last very long, and Sophie was pleased to sit down and watch the audience dance around the floor.

Anthony danced with the dark-haired woman, who had now taken off her coat, exposing a beautiful red fitted dress. Sophie watched, mesmerised by their dancing. Did she look that good when she was dancing with Anthony? She knew she didn't. Why did she feel slightly jealous? Even Dave noticed them.

After a while Sophie danced with Dave and the rest of the audience and competitors, Dave, of course, adding some unconventional steps. The couple from Texbury flew around the dance floor, bending, stretching, spinning, weaving. They looked professional, but so serious, and didn't appear to be enjoying themselves.

The afternoon went by quickly and the time came for the prizes. The band stopped and played a drum roll. The dancers stood in nervous anticipation, forgetting that it was just for fun.

The three judges passed their papers to the nominated judge.

He stood up, coughed, straightened his tie, and told everyone what a fun afternoon it had been.

'Second prize for rumba goes to number six, John and Sarah from Texbury. Congratulations to you both. A splendid effort. We can all see that you have tried really hard.'

They walked onto the dance floor and took their small medal, without thanking the judge, and not looking at all happy.

'First prize goes to couple number eight, Dave and Sophie from Timberry.'

Sophie stood there, not hearing, as she was watching Anthony and his mystery woman, and Dave had to escort her to the front of the stage.

'Well done! We all enjoyed your dance. You both have a natural dance rhythm. We were all spellbound.'

The local Timberry audience clapped and whistled, together with the rest of the audience.

Dave thanked them, accepting the trophy, saying how much he had enjoyed it. Sophie just smiled blankly, still trying to believe it.

She and Dave had won a prize!

Dave went to the bar and returned with a beer and a glass of red wine.

'And for the cha cha,' the judge continued. Sophie had now zoned out.

She watched as the two other dance couples from different dance clubs were presented with their trophies.

The head judge thanked the Maple Leaf for giving him the opportunity to judge such a wonderful event. He was in Timberry for the weekend, working, and he hoped future competitions would be just as successful.

Everyone started to leave. Sophie looked around for Anthony, but he had disappeared. Dave was at her side, saying what a great afternoon it had been. Their friends congratulated them. Gina hugged them, saying she always knew they had something special. Dave looked at Sophie and she just shook her head. She told Dave he could keep the trophy as he deserved it. She honestly thought he did.

Anthony phoned her later in the evening, saying that he and his sister had enjoyed the dancing. He thought that Dave and Sophie's rumba was danced really well. He congratulated her on her spinning move in the cha cha, and asked if, when she had time, she would see him some time, other than on their dancing night.

She arranged to go on Sunday night.

So, the mystery woman was his sister, Marion! Sophie didn't know why but she felt relieved and pleased.

Forty-Nine

On Sunday, Sophie walked in the heavy rain to Anthony's complex, not wanting to park her car next to all the expensive ones. Even the visitors' car park was full of high-priced cars. There was a separate car park for staff, but she wasn't exactly staff.

She let herself into the building and went straight to the large cloakroom which was situated in the hall. Sophie made herself look a bit more presentable by combing her wet hair and reapplying her makeup, leaving her wet coat hanging there until she left.

She walked along the maze of corridors and keyed in the number Anthony had given her. The lift door opened and closed and took her smoothly and quietly up to his suite.

Anthony was waiting for her. She realised that Anthony had a hidden screen which activated when someone keyed his number into the lift.

He welcomed her. He was looking through a pile of papers, which he was putting away in folders, and asked if she had given any thought to his offer to take her on as a private detective. She was honest and told him that she had been thinking more of her dancing in the past week.

'Of course. But is it something you would consider?' Anthony pushed her.

'It does appeal,' Sophie replied, now having at least five minutes to think about it.

'It's just that I have an interesting local case for you,' Anthony tempted her. 'You realise that you wouldn't be able to discuss any cases with anyone else. Would that be a problem?'

'Not at all,' Sophie lied slightly.

'I can arrange for you to fit the job in with your art projects here, of course.'

'What is the case?' Sophie asked, now tempted.

Fifty

'A local man believes his wife may be having an affair. I know it's nothing unusual, but if he is willing to pay us for information, we will be happy to take it on. I would like a woman to investigate this, and as my sister has now given up working with me, I am sure you'll find this an interesting and easy first case.'

'What will I need to do?'

'That's up to you; I can't advise you how it will play out.'

They talked all evening, Anthony going through how to approach cases and deal with clients, but he was totally confident that Sophie would be more than capable of carrying out the investigations without many problems.

Anthony checked through the file and gave Sophie copies of the details.

'These are the details that Mr. Conway has given us.'

Sophie read through them.

Woman's name: Angela Conway. Married 35 years.

Age: 54.

Job: Part-time hairdresser and receptionist at Wavers hairdressers in Packton, a small village about a ten-minute drive into the country.

Hobbies: Slimmers' club and a book club.

Sophie thought that Angela didn't sound like a woman who

would have an affair. But she knew she had a lot to learn in this job.

Description given: Blonde, 5 ft 2 inches.

Husband: Peter Conway.

Age: Also 54.

Owner and managing director of the Conway Engineering Company on the small industrial estate, hidden away up a long drive behind trees just outside Timberry. He has worked there since he left school at sixteen, and later took over from his father.

Sophie put her copy of the information into the folder that Anthony had given her.

'Do I get in touch with Peter?'

'Yes, he has given his number, but only phone him in office hours on his mobile and never at home. He will be expecting someone to phone in the next few days.'

Sophie found his number in the folder and made a note of when to phone him.

'You'll see all the information in this envelope. Our telephone number is in there. But there is another private number which our clients can use if they are concerned about anyone knowing that they are using our firm. If they do use the second number, then as you know, we will answer it as Oliver's Antiques.'

Sophie finished her coffee, which was now nearly cold, and picked up her scarf, handbag, and folder, telling Anthony she would keep in touch.

'Good luck. I know you'll enjoy investigating this case.'

Sophie did feel quite excited.

She had now joined Oliver's Detective Agency.

Sophie, or Jackie Hunter, the name she had decided to call herself, made an appointment at Wavers, asking especially for Angela.

On Tuesday, at 10.15am, sitting in the chair, looking at herself in the mirror, she saw Angela walk towards her. She was just as Sophie had imagined her to be. Angela introduced herself. She ran her fingers through Sophie's hair, asking what she would like done.

'Just a shampoo and trim today, as I need a boost. I have had a bad weekend, arguing with my husband about where to go on holiday. He insists on staying at home and spending the money doing all the house improvements instead,' Sophie lied, enjoying using her imagination but suddenly realising she wasn't wearing a wedding ring. She would have to get one from the market.

'I know what you mean,' Angela smiled, leading Sophie to the wash basins. 'My husband won't spend any money on anything, including me. I even have to ask him for money for books I want to buy. He doesn't even pay me when I work in the office at the factory. Working here doesn't pay very much – just enough to run my car. Peter always finds money for his golf though. I enjoy working here so I'm happy to get away from the house.'

Wow, thought Sophie. *I won't have too much trouble finding out about Angela's life.* Sophie wondered how many times she had talked about her husband to other clients.

'What car do you drive?' Sophie asked, changing the subject.

'A yellow Fiat 500. I have had it for years.'

Sophie, finding it difficult to talk, let Angela shampoo her hair, while she thought of the next questions.

'I haven't been on holiday for ages,' Sophie lied, now sitting back in the chair, looking at Angela in the mirror, trying to engage her in more conversation. 'Hopefully, I will be able to persuade him to go somewhere really cheap.'

'Don't hold your breath,' Angela said sadly. 'Men can be quite selfish.'

'I know,' Sophie lied again, quite enjoying herself.

Sophie, now wishing to change the subject, asked Angela what hours she worked.

'Just mornings.'

Sophie couldn't help noticing the bracelet that was now dangling from Angela's wrist; it must have been under her sleeve. She had seen one like it in London when Anthony was trying to persuade her to buy some earrings. It must have cost a lot of money. Should she say anything? She decided she had enough information for the moment.

Sophie thanked Angela, saying she would make another appointment soon.

Sitting in her car she wrote down the information that she had gathered.

Didn't seem like a woman who would have an affair.

Very talkative, but underneath very inoffensive. Lives quite a boring life.

Negative opinion of men.

No money.

Expensive bracelet.

As Sophie was writing she suddenly remembered the bracelet. It was in the London shop, featured as 2020's latest design.

Worked for husband, not paid.

She looked at Angela's address.

The Briars, Bracken Lane, Packton.

Sophie drove slowly up Bracken Lane. It was winding, narrow, and getting even narrower. She hoped another car wouldn't be coming the other way, as there was no way she could avoid it. The Briars was the only house in the lane. An old barn, caravan and a tractor were in the fields close by.

Sophie slowed down her car and stopped outside the metal gates of The Briars, realising that she would not be able to park in the lane without being seen, so she would have to park somewhere before turning into it.

The Briars was an impressive large, converted barn building, painted white with floor to ceiling patio windows. Sophie couldn't imagine Angela living there unhappily, but it was a massive house for two people. The front gardens were immaculate with lawns, apple trees and a large pond. She took a photo and a video to add to her collection.

She drove slowly back down the lane and onto the quiet road leading back along the coast. Should she have checked if there was a CCTV camera covering the gate? She hoped there wasn't.

At home, Sophie poured herself a coffee and looked through her information. There wasn't much but it was a start. She knew that Angela didn't work in the afternoons so she would wait for her at lunchtime and see where she went.

Sophie, worried that Angela would see her when she was following her, decided to buy herself two hair pieces, one black and one blonde. She looked on the internet, found the ones she liked and ordered them for the next day. She also ordered three different bobble hats and called in at the local cheap chemist to buy an assortment of glasses that she could wear. They had to be low prescription so she could see through them. Sophie had an assortment of coats and scarves which she might need. She then walked through the market stall and bought a cheap wedding ring. She had given her wedding ring back to Dave.

Two days later, instead of parking at the end of the lane as intended, Sophie parked close to Wavers. Their small car park was at the rear of the shop and Sophie would be able to see when Angela left at twelve o'clock. She had already checked that Angela drove a yellow Fiat as she had driven past The Briars at seven o'clock the night before to take a second look.

On Monday at 12.14pm, in disguise, Sophie waited for Angela to finish work and followed her car, disappointed that she went straight home.

On Tuesday, she waited again. At 12.34pm the yellow car appeared, coming out of the car park, and headed towards Timberry. Sophie followed, two cars behind, disguised, wearing long black hair and a bobble hat. If needed, she would put on the glasses later.

Angela drove into The Tavern pub car park.

'Oh no,' Sophie muttered. She went to The Tavern pub regularly and hoped she wouldn't see anyone she knew there.

She checked herself in the mirror. Black hair, eyebrows darker. Bobble hat and scarf, complete with glasses. She walked into the pub, ordered a sandwich and orange juice, and sat in the corner at the darker part of the room with her back to Angela. Luckily, the pub was quite busy, so Sophie didn't feel too conspicuous.

Eventually a man in a dark suit walked in and sat by Angela.

'Yes!' thought Sophie, aloud. But there was no kiss or hugging. The man picked up and drank the beer that she had already bought for him. Sophie's sandwiches arrived at the same time as Angela's ploughman's lunch. Sophie ate as she slowly turned herself towards them. Angela gave the man some papers and he handed her a long envelope. Sophie quickly took out her phone, half wrapping it in her scarf, and took a video of the pair of them. No one was watching as they were too busy talking and eating.

She placed the phone back in her bag and waited. The man quickly finished his lunch and left the pub, leaving Angela looking around. Sophie bent her head, pretending to read the menu, her new black hair falling over her face. When she looked up Angela had gone. Sophie waited a while and then headed for the door, just as Mark and Julie from the dance club walked in. Sophie quickly bowed her head, forgetting that she was still wearing her glasses, which fell off her nose and on to the concrete floor. Mark stooped down and picked them up and gave them to her. Sophie snatched them quickly from him, muttered a thanks and headed to her car.

'How rude,' she heard Julie comment.

Had her disguise really fooled them?

Back at home Sophie looked at her video taken in The Tavern. Who was the man and what were the papers that Angela had given him?

Sophie decided to find information on the factory that Angela's husband owned.

She looked up engineering companies in the area. She found Conway Engineering straight away. A picture of Peter Conway appeared several times. Sophie thought he looked quite pleasant. He didn't have a Facebook page, but what she read was quite okay. Family man, married, hobbies golf and fishing.

The page suddenly disappeared, and Sophie found herself looking at another engineering company on the same Timberry industrial site. She was about to delete the page, when she was surprised to see the face of the mystery man who had met Angela in the pub.

John Fisher, owner and MD of Fisher Engineering. She read further but nothing too interesting. What was Angela doing with John Fisher? She printed the relevant pages and double checked it was him. Should she now get in touch with Peter Conway? But what could she tell him?

Sophie sat down and went through all the information she had. She could ring Anthony for his help. But she wanted to prove that she could do this herself.

John Fisher and Angela were definitely not having an affair, so Peter had got that wrong.

Why did John Fisher give her an envelope after she had given him papers?

She had to get closer to them in the pub next time. Did they meet every week?

Sophie headed back to the pub, this time without her disguise. She asked the waitress, who she hadn't seen before, if her friends had been in, the ones that sat at that table, pointing. The waitress said they had.

'When will they next be in?' Sophie asked casually.

'They have been having lunch here every week for months.'

'Oh great,' Sophie said. 'I'll come in next week and surprise them.'

She had a week to plan her next move.

Sophie was pleased that dancing took her mind off her detective work. She was getting on with Dave much better than she had for ages. And she saw Anthony regularly for his dancing session. Sophie was still enjoying the evenings with him. Anthony was now combining them with some tuition. He didn't ask about her progress with the job, he just casually enquired if everything going okay. She might consult him later should she want advice.

The next day she phoned Peter Conway, saying she was willing to take on his case. She wouldn't tell him yet what she already knew. He asked if she would mind meeting him at the Forest Hotel, ten miles away, so that he wouldn't see anyone he knew.

The following evening, Sophie booked herself into the hotel for the night. She would then have time to write down and take in all the information that Peter had given her. It would also be a treat to have a night away; the agency would pay for it. Was she becoming money-grabbing?

Later at the hotel, after showering and practising what she was going to say, Sophie met Peter in the lounge, and he suggested they have a meal. Sophie was grateful and, although she was nervous, looked forward to choosing something special from the menu, as she had only had a cheese sandwich before she left home. She hoped the restaurant wouldn't be noisy as she wanted to hear everything he said.

Sophie needn't have worried. Ten minutes later they were sitting in a deserted bar, eating vegetable lasagne and bread rolls, Peter choosing a cheap white wine without asking her what she would like. They made small talk regarding food and restaurants, Sophie surprised that he ever went in one. He droned on and on about how he had become a successful businessman. He never asked her anything about herself. Sophie made a mental note never to go on a date with him.

Sophie offered to share the bill with him. Peter didn't protest. Sophie made another mental note. Tight with money.

Sitting in the chairs in the lounge, Peter explained, 'I have got in touch with you as I think my wife Angela is having an affair. She used to be at home most afternoons, but now when I phone the house she's never there and doesn't answer her mobile either. I have asked her where she goes, but she says I am being controlling. When I go out at night, I know she goes out as well, as I have checked her car mileage. She says she belongs to a book club and a slimmers' club. I also go out a lot, playing golf most weekends, together with meetings during the week and sometimes in the evenings. I really do not know what she gets up to when I'm not at home and I always like to keep a check on what she does. She works at the factory when I need her, and she has a little job at the hairdresser's which pays for her car bills.'

Sophie listened.

'Do you have any evidence of an affair?'

'No. To be honest, I am shocked that anyone would want to have an affair with her but why else would she go out?'

Sophie had to stop herself from expressing an opinion.

'I'm afraid I shall have to ask you some personal questions,' Sophie said in an official voice.

'Fire away.'

'Do you and your wife have a happy marriage?'

Sophie didn't make notes as she didn't think it looked professional. She knew she wouldn't find it difficult to remember what he had said.

'Of course. I have provided her with a lovely house. I have worked hard and if she asks for money, I usually transfer or give her a small amount of cash. She didn't want children, but I told her we should have two, as one day they could take over running the business. She looked after them well, until they left home. I was always too busy to be able to give them much attention.'

'Of course.' Sophie faked sympathy, realising how draconian and controlling he was.

'Has she had an affair before?' Sophie asked.

'Good God, no. As I have said, I am surprised that any man would find her attractive now.'

Sophie still tried not to show how shocked she was by his comments. She wished that she could lie and tell him that Angela had been having an affair for years.

'Have you ever had an affair, Peter?'

Peter paled and was visibly shocked by her question.

'Of course not!'

Sophie wasn't too sure, but this wasn't about him.

'What does Angela do when she comes to the factory?'

'She potters in the office; she is not very qualified for anything else.'

Sophie was now not liking Peter at all and she confirmed to herself that Angela was telling the truth.

She closed the meeting, saying that she had all the information needed and she would be in touch with him.

He shook her hand, thanked her, and then made his way to the entrance and disappeared into the car park, leaving Sophie to pay the drinks bill the next morning.

Sophie thought her hair needed attention again and made another appointment with Angela, saying that she was going out on a rare night out.

Angela asked her how her week had gone. Sophie lied, making her life seem very dull. She asked Angela if she had been to the factory and Angela told her that she had, early on Tuesday morning for an hour before Wavers opened. She had just popped in for a while before Peter arrived at work as he wanted her to clean his office; his usual cleaner was away for a few days.

'They are quite flexible here, so as long as I tell them what I am doing I can work to suit myself,' Angela added. Sophie noted that was the same day she had seen her in the pub with John Fisher.

'I am going out for lunch tomorrow,' Sophie lied. 'Do you know of any pubs that do great meals in the area?'

'No,' Angela replied, not looking at Sophie. 'I hardly go out during the day.'

'It's a bit of a treat. A friend is paying,' added Sophie.

'I would love some of those friends. "Friends that pay",' Angela said, drying Sophie's hair slightly roughly.

'My husband wouldn't treat me,' lied Sophie, glancing at the fake wedding ring. 'But he would treat his girlfriend.' Lying again.

'Same here.' Angela surprised Sophie. 'Peter has had a girlfriend for the last five years and he thinks I don't know. He thinks I am stupid, but he'll soon find out that I'm not. I wouldn't say anything as he would make life even more difficult for me.'

'Who is she?'

'I don't know, but she works at the factory as he stays late sometimes. I sat in the car park one night when he was supposed to be working, but he left by himself. Then he wanted to know where I had been when I returned home later than him.'

'Would you like to know?'

'Of course. I have tried to find out, but he thinks he is being clever. But as I have said, he will soon find out that I am cleverer than he is.'

Sophie thanked Angela and paid her. Angela told her to have a good time.

Sophie sat in the car, confused. She must write all this down.

Peter's having an affair with someone at factory.

Peter thinks Angela is having an affair.

Angela has a meal with MD of another engineering company. Giving him papers in exchange for an envelope.

Angela is going to get her own back on Peter?

Tuesday lunchtime arrived again, and Sophie found herself at The Tavern, sitting at the table next to where she hoped Angela and John Fisher would sit. Heavily disguised and now feeling quite warm, she sat waiting for them. She bought a newspaper that she could read, but decided she would look too conspicuous, so she settled for holiday brochures from the travel agency which she had passed earlier in the morning. She ordered her sandwiches but before she could open the brochures, Angela and John Fisher walked in together. Sophie was both relieved and nervous as they sat on the next table, about a metre away. Sophie sat sideways so she could see them.

'What have you got for me this week?' she heard John ask.

'Quite a few names. Some new ones, and some prices,' Angela whispered.

'You're doing a great job,' John praised her, handing over the envelope. 'There's your cash – sure you don't prefer a cheque?'

Angela quickly put the envelope into her bag.

'No, that would show on my bank account when he checks it.'

'Why don't you go paperless?' John continued.

'It wouldn't work. This way he has no proof.'

'I see.'

'Someone's got to take him down, even if it means passing on customer info, I don't care.'

He's paying for information, Sophie thought to herself.

Sophie ate her sandwich, drank her coffee quickly and left, not looking around the pub, just in case she saw someone else she knew.

At home she went through the information.

Works for husband at Conway Engineering factory.

Copies customer information and gives it to Fisher Engineering company for payment.

Good for her, thought Sophie. Although what should she do now? She could just tell Peter that Angela is definitely not having an affair and end it there. Does she tell him she is giving customers' names to another factory? Does she tell him she knows he's having an affair?

Sophie drank her glass of red, the first she had bought for ages, and put away the Conway folder.

She could find out more about John Fisher.

Sophie turned on the computer again and clicked on Fisher Engineering. The company had only existed for a few years. Run by John. Divorced nine years, no children.

How did Angela know him? She only went to the book club. Looking at him, he certainly didn't need to go to a slimmers' club. She tried the book club. Clutching at straws, Sophie clicked on Packton book club, not expecting to find anything. But there it was, a photo of the members which must have been in the local paper previously. Sophie recognised John Fisher sitting next to Angela. *Great*, thought Sophie.

Now, who was Peter Conway's girlfriend?

The next evening, just before the factory finished, Sophie found herself, blonde hair, bobble hat, scarf and glasses, sitting in the car park of the factory. Five o'clock and the first workers, eager to leave, rushed out through the doors and the others followed, meandering out of the doors.

After an hour Peter appeared, made a phone call, and waited round a quiet corner of the factory. Five minutes later two women came out. They stood talking for a while. One woman walked to her mini and the other was picked up by a taxi.

Which one?

Sophie waited. Peter quickly walked to his car, looked across at the woman who was getting into her Mini, and they both drove off, followed by Sophie. He didn't drive towards his house but in the opposite direction, towards the coast road, the same one where Sophie had waited for Anthony when they had gone to London.

Five minutes later Peter's car and the woman's mini turned into a lane, and then after a short while turned into the drive of a row of three terraced houses. Sophie slowed down and looked through the gap in the thick hedge. She then drove away.

She made a mental description of the woman. Late thirties, short blonde cropped hair, slim. Short black skirt, white blouse, black jacket, and ultra-high heels.

Would Angela know her?

After a week of dance practice and working at the complex Sophie made another hair appointment.

Angela spoke first, saying she had now lost a stone in weight, and had managed to have a night out with some friends on Saturday night. Sophie congratulated her, saying she looked well and said that she had worked hard teaching art privately to pupils.

'Someone almost crashed into my car yesterday,' Sophie lied.'

'Oh no!' Angela gasped. 'Where?'

'I was just going past Timberry industrial estate, and a woman with blonde hair and driving a black mini pulled out quickly. She just blasted her horn at me. I sounded mine back and she gesticulated as I overtook her.'

'I expect that would be Fiona Andrews,' Angela said casually.

'How do you know?' Sophie tried to sound equally casual.

'Oh, she works there. She's Stuart Andrew's wife. Peter's partner. She works at the factory part-time. She's a very opiniated person. Peter can't stand the woman.'

'Oh, really?' Sophie hoped that Angela didn't catch sarcasm in her voice.

Interesting, thought Sophie.

She left it there, changing the subject to Christmas holidays, although it was only November.

Leaving Wavers hairdressers, Sophie treated herself to a coffee and cake in the local café and thought about what she had learned.

Peter was having an affair with Fiona, who was his business partner's wife. The house that she had followed them to certainly wasn't the house that someone with money would buy. Unless it was a second home.

Back home, Sophie looked up the terraced house where he had gone with Fiona. They were holiday lets – owned by Peter Conway. She wondered if Angela knew that he owned them.

Then Sophie looked for the owners of Peter's factory on the internet; there were only two. Stuart Andrews and Peter Conway.

She looked up Fiona Andrews. She wasn't on Facebook, but she found her name on the golf club website as the regular singer at the social club. Her picture certainly made her look very attractive.

Sophie thought she would love to go there on Saturday night. She couldn't go by herself. Perhaps Dave would go with her.

Dave agreed, as long as they could practise dancing at the same time.

Late on Saturday night at the golf club, after they had had an à la carte meal, Fiona sauntered on stage to welcoming warm applause. She wore a stunning short black animal print dress with matching shoes, and she sang and moved around with total confidence, the resident band backing her. The audience loved her.

Sophie looked around. There was no one there she knew, but then she saw Peter Conway sitting by himself on a stool at the bar. She hoped he wouldn't recognise her. Sophie did look a lot different from the last time he had seen her; she had a new hair style that Angela had persuaded her to have, and of course she was wearing different clothes.

Dave and Sophie danced to the music, managing to add a few rumba moves, and she was really surprised at how they were enjoying themselves. She couldn't remember the last time they had been this close. Dave was slightly showing off, but then he had had a few drinks, as he didn't have to drive because Sophie was driving him home. She was thankful that he had gone with her.

On Sunday afternoon Sophie had the day off from working at the charity shop and sat with her papers in front of her.

What should she do?

Should she tell Peter that Angela was giving information to another company?

Should she tell Peter that she knew he was having an affair?

Should she tell Angela who Peter was having an affair with?

There was only one man who could help her. She went to see Anthony.

Anthony met Sophie as the lift doors opened. He poured her a coffee and she sat down again in his plush leather chair and leaned against the large gold cushions.

She told him all that she had learned. He sat patiently, listening without interrupting.

'What do think you should do?' Anthony asked.

'Tell Peter that she isn't having an affair and that she is being paid for customer information from his factory.'

'What would you like to do?'

'Just tell him she isn't having an affair.'

'Why? Just because she's a woman with whom you have become friends?'

Had she become too involved? Sophie wondered.

'I will leave you to think about it more. Peter won't expect a result yet.'

Sophie left Anthony's disappointed, without the answer she had expected. She decided to walk down by the sea. The weather was cold, and the wind blew around her, but she enjoyed the cold wind on her face. She sat down on the bench on the promenade. There was no one around – no one else silly enough to brave the November elements.

Sophie closed her eyes. Suddenly she had an idea of what she could do. She walked quickly, almost running, back home.

She found Angela's mobile number, which Angela had given her, when Sophie had lied, telling her she couldn't get through to the salon to make an appointment.

She phoned Angela.

'I am going for a meal on Saturday with friends at the golf club. Would you like to go?'

Silence at the other end of the phone.

'Angela?'

'I don't know. Who's going?'

'There should be eight of us,' Sophie answered, hoping everyone would want to go.

'Can I think about it?'

'Yes, but I will have to book the table soon,' Sophie pushed.

Disappointed, Sophie ended the call.

Sophie didn't have to wait long. Angela called back after five minutes.

'What should I wear? Can I bring a friend?'

Ben and Emma, Mark and Julie all wanted to go, and Sophie asked Dave, who couldn't wait. So Sophie phoned the golf club and booked the table.

Saturday night arrived and, tickets collected, Sophie made an urgent phone call to Anthony, requesting his help.

Dave, looking smart but casual, arrived on time to pick Sophie up.

'Dave, I want you to do something for me tonight without questioning me.'

'Okay.'

'When we go out, I want you to say that we haven't been there before, and also, I don't want you to buy anyone drinks.'

'But...'

'Also, I don't want you to sit by or dance with Angela.'

'I don't even know the woman,' Dave said defensively.

'Just those three things for me.'

'Okay.'

Sophie wasn't sure he had taken it seriously. So, she added, 'It is really important.'

She hoped he would remember, but very much doubted it.

The group met by the fountain at the front of the golf club. Angela was quiet but was talking to her friend.

They were just walking into the building when Sophie's phone rang. Anthony couldn't have timed it better.

'I'm sorry everyone. My elderly neighbour has locked himself out, and I have to go and help him. I'll get back if I can.'

She dragged Dave to one side and said, 'Remember what I told you.'

She slid his wallet out of his pocket without him noticing.

She phoned a taxi and luckily one had just dropped someone at the golf club and was able to take her back. She sat in the taxi hoping her plan would work. She also hoped no one would mention her real name.

Sophie waited late at night for her mobile to ring.

Dave eventually phoned.

'Is it too late?'

'No, I was reading.' Sophie was so used to lying now.

'How is your neighbour?'

'Neighbour? Oh, he's okay. I stayed with him for a while to make sure. I am getting him a spare key. I can't keep getting through the kitchen window at my age.'

Dave laughed.

'How did the night go?' Sophie held her breath.

'It was a really good night. Good fun. Fiona the singer sang well, but she had to leave at the interval as she had a stomach complaint. I think Angela knew her, as there was some sort of confrontation at the bar about a photo Angela took when she went to get a drink. Then Fiona left with her partner. It was dark so I couldn't see too much. But the band carried on and we all had a good time. Angela left early too, but she said she had enjoyed herself. I think she was spending the night with her friend Tracey.

'Oh God, what have I done?' Sophie whispered.

'What did you say?'

'Nothing.'

'Did you take my wallet?'

'Yes, I've got your wallet. I'll see you tomorrow.'

'Okay, don't forget my wallet. I owe Ben money for the drinks and the taxi as I left the car there.'

Sophie ended the call.

Well, she hadn't said anything to anyone, had she? They found out for themselves. *Problem solved*, she thought.

After two days Sophie still hadn't heard from Angela.

Sophie dared herself to phone and make another appointment at Wavers.

'Sorry, Angela doesn't work here anymore. Becky has taken over her clients. What day and time would you like?'

Sophie thanked her and said she would phone later. Sophie phoned Angela and was pleased when she eventually answered.

'I've tried to make an appointment with you, and they say you have left Wavers.'

'Yes. I was going to phone you, but I have had a lot on my mind. When I went to the golf club, I was shocked to see Peter there. He was with Fiona Andrews, Stuart's wife, the partner of his company. It was her he had been seeing. She was singing. I didn't know she could sing, and in the interval, she went and sat by him. He bought her a drink and had his arm around her, and he actually kissed her. I took a photo of them.

'I couldn't help myself. I just walked to the bar, ordered a drink, and just stood in front of them and took the photo. You should have seen their faces. The look of shock. I didn't say anything, I just went back to the table and sat down. I didn't dream it was Fiona. He said he didn't like her. At least I have caught Peter out and I have just about come to terms with it.'

'What are you going to do now?' Sophie asked sympathetically.

'Well, after the divorce, I shall have half his share in the company; that will mean Stuart and I will have the controlling interest, so it won't be long before Peter will want out. Stuart has said he wants to buy my shares and I will use that money to go in with John Fisher, who wants us to be together. But he is a weak man and a bad businessman, and it won't take me long to work him out of the business.

'No man is going to make a fool of me again. I am going to take charge of my own life and make a lot of money.'

Sophie caught her breath.

'Don't trust any man, Jackie.'

Sophie ended the call, shocked.

'Or any woman,' Sophie said to herself, totally shocked.

Sophie found herself again in Anthony's armchair.

She expected a big lecture from him. He just turned to her and said, 'You have been your own teacher. Understand where you went wrong, and you certainly won't make the same mistake again.'

Sophie sipped her coffee.

'There never will be a next time,' she vowed.

'Oh, Peter Conway phoned, saying that the case had resolved itself and he has sent the relevant payment to the bank account,' Anthony continued. 'I will forward your payment to your bank.'

Sophie told Anthony that she had enjoyed working for him but didn't think she was suited to the detective agency. She walked to the lift and Anthony told her to take a break and he would be in touch. He watched her leave the complex, aware that she looked disheartened.

Job done, she thought, *but not very well.*

Dispirited, she phoned Dave and asked him out for dinner that evening.

Sitting opposite Dave in the Sea View restaurant, Sophie could feel her tension ease.

'How is the job at the complex going?' Dave asked, pouring Sophie a glass of red.

'Great,' Sophie replied, not wanting to think about Anthony tonight.

'Have you met any rich men?'

'No, why?' What had he heard?

'Nothing!'

'They are mostly women, who don't have much conversation.'

Dave looked at her. 'Are you okay?'

Should she tell him about the detective agency? Well, she no longer worked for them anymore.

'No. To tell the truth—'

'Why did you take my wallet last Saturday?' Dave interrupted.

'I'm sorry about that, but I knew you would pay for everything and Mark has never offered to pay for anything. He hasn't given me money for the tickets yet.'

Dave wasn't really listening. He was looking at his phone.

'Angela seemed a nice person. I said I would phone her.'

Sophie was shocked.

'When did she give you her phone number?' Sophie was genuinely worried and trying not to give the impression she was jealous.

'When I walked Angela and her friend to the car.'

'Please don't have anything to do with her,' Sophie now heard herself pleading.

'Okay. I won't. Why?'

'Let's just say she's poison.'

'Why?'

Sophie didn't answer.

Thankfully, Sophie watched as Dave reluctantly deleted Angela's number.

'I walked past your old shop yesterday. Nothing seems to have changed. There were some tables and chairs outside, but that was all.'

Sophie didn't really want to talk about it. It was still upsetting to think she would never go back again.

After an evening talking about Tom and dancing, and Sophie drinking more wine than she should have, Dave drove her home. She told him that she had enjoyed the evening and Dave told her to take care.

What if Dave had phoned Angela?

Fifty-One

Sophie was still enjoying her dancing lessons on Thursdays. There was a different vibe between her and Dave now and they were both eagerly looking forward to the next competition in two weeks. She hadn't heard from Anthony, and she didn't want to phone him.

Sophie was also working hard at the complex. She asked her pupils what they would like to learn and tried to incorporate it into the lessons. She had now included life portraits, which were popular. Sophie didn't have too much difficulty in persuading Phillipa, one of the cleaners, to sit for the group, for payment, offering her different style clothes that she had bought from the charity shop. Sophie was always surprised by the different ways in which the art group perceived the models.

Anthony made a detour from his usual route along the corridors to his penthouse. He walked past the workshop, hoping to see Sophie as he quickly glanced through the open door. He was pleased to hear her laughing with one of her pupils – he did miss her company.

Fifty-Two

Two weeks went quickly by and Sophie, Dave and their dance class found themselves again facing the judges. This competition was all about salsa. More people had joined the club over the past few weeks, and it was becoming popular. The number of dance schools joining the competition had also increased, which brought in more people to the Maple Leaf.

Dressed in suitable colourful dresses, the men looking very Latin in their trousers and shirts, the first group glided onto the dance floor.

Sophie admitted to herself that now she had one trophy she wasn't bothered about winning again. She just enjoyed dancing to the band. Sophie and Dave danced well and the couple from Texberry were there again, flamboyantly walking around each other, exaggerating every move. The judges must have loved them as they were awarded first prize, which they accepted by curtsying, holding up the trophy for the audience to see, and walking round the dance floor.

Sophie looked around for Anthony. He was there, sitting with his sister, and she felt sad that he didn't acknowledge her all afternoon.

The dancing ended and Dave took Sophie home. They agreed that it had been a brilliant afternoon, although Sophie was still a little hurt by Anthony not getting in touch with her.

Fifty-Three

Bit when he did phone the next day, Sophie was unprepared.
'I have another job for you.' Another client wanted her
help.

'If you come over to the complex, I'll tell you about it.'

Sophie hesitated. Could she do it? Did she want to take it
on? Could she face Anthony?

But she wanted to see Anthony again. She had made excuses
not to go to his suite for dancing lessons and had really missed
them, and of course, the money. Sophie said she would see him
after her art lessons.

She made her way again up to Anthony's suite. She was
surprised by how suddenly relieved and excited she felt that he
wanted her to take on another case.

As usual Anthony was waiting for her. She hadn't realised
how much she had missed seeing him.

He was talking on the phone when he opened the door, and
she sat down, waiting, looking out of the window, watching the
white seagulls circling in the dark sky. He invited her to make
some coffee while he talked to the client. She handed him a cup.

Sophie sat in her usual armchair and, after Anthony told her
he had enjoyed the dance competition, he asked her how she was
now feeling about her first detective case. Sophie told him she
wasn't worrying about it anymore. She had put it behind her and

was carrying on with her life. He told her he was pleased and that's what she must learn to do.

'This next case should be straightforward, Sophie. It isn't the kind of enquiry that we normally consider taking on, but sometimes I do take on cases without payment if I think the client needs our help. It will be something very different from your last case.'

Sophie listened.

'A worried grandmother phoned the agency, saying that she would like us to check on her grandson, as on Friday afternoons recently he hasn't come home from school at the usual time. He lives with her and she feels responsible for him. He gets back home about 10pm. When she asks him where he's been, he just says to a friend's house, and she is worried he may be taking drugs. She didn't know who else to turn to.'

'How old is he?'

'Fourteen.'

'Well perhaps he does go to his friend's house.'

'No. As I have said, when his grandmother has asked him which friend, he just shrugs his shoulders and goes to his room.'

Sophie thought that sounded normal for a boy his age.

'What's his name?' Sophie asked, totally disappointed by the case.

'Simon.'

'And his grandmother's?'

'Melinda Browning. Separated from her husband. Age late seventies.'

'Husband?'

'Doesn't keep in touch.'

Anthony glanced at Sophie's disinterested expression.

'His grandparents on his father's side are in Sidney.'

'Where do his mother and father live?'

'Somewhere in Shropshire. He has been living with his grandmother for two years, as there are no schools close to where they live, and he wanted to stay in this area.'

'Telephone and address?'

Anthony gave her the details. *Quite a nice part of Bilberry*, Sophie thought.

'She hasn't got a car at the moment, that's why she can't follow him.'

Anthony passed her the file with the details.

She picked it up from the table and walked to the door.

'Sophie, remember you can't judge a case from the first information received.'

Sophie realised that Anthony had noticed her apparent lack of interest.

She said she would keep in touch, took the lift, and walked out of the complex.

Anthony shook his head and smiled to himself. It was good to see her again.

Sophie decided to go to The Tavern pub. She sat at the corner table, opened the envelope, and looked at the information. Anthony had told her not to take any client information anywhere public, as she could leave her file behind. Sophie didn't think this file was that important. She stared blankly at the notes.

Simon attended Bilberry School, just off the main Bilberry road. The school photo of him, which his grandmother had given the agency, showed a happy fourteen-year-old, somewhat untidily dressed but with a nice genuine smile.

He was in the football club and interested in languages.

Not someone who would want to hurt his family. But she had learnt from past experience not to judge people too quickly.

She should recognise him by his purple school bag.

She finished her coffee and left The Tavern, checking that she had put all the information back in her file and hadn't left anything behind.

On Friday afternoon Sophie stood at the school gates, dressed in her Jackie disguise as she didn't want anyone to recognise her. She remembered waiting for Tom a few years ago, before he had insisted on walking home by himself, listening about how his day had gone. Sophie realised she would have worried if he had gone missing.

A few of the children were picked up in cars but most of them strolled out of the school gates, in no hurry to go home.

Sophie tried to look at every pupil walking out, realising that it wasn't going to be easy. Then she saw him, dressed in his football shirt and shorts, dragging his purple school bag along the ground.

He stopped and talked to his friends. They checked their phones and then Simon turned in the opposite direction and started to walk quickly down the road away from the school. Sophie followed him, thankful that she was wearing her trainers. He eventually walked down a quiet secluded alleyway and disappeared before she could catch up with him.

There were five gates. He must have gone through one of those. Sophie carefully stood on one of the bins that were left outside and looked over the wall, precariously clinging on to the part of the wall that wasn't broken. There was no sign of him. Annoyed, she got down and stood wondering what to do next.

She thought she could perhaps wait for him, but she didn't know when he would leave. She could be waiting until ten o'clock.

She decided to leave it until next week, when she would wait for him in the alley.

She walked back to the school and got into her car.

She could try finding out who lived in the five small houses that the alleyway backed onto. She could even knock on all the doors.

When Sophie arrived home, she looked on the internet.

There were five houses in Longton Lane, each with their small square fenced-in front gardens. They used to be railway cottages until the 1960s, when the trains stopped going past regularly.

The following day Sophie found herself walking down Longton Lane again. It was a very quiet area with a communal car park opposite the houses. No one was about. Sophie looked at each house for clues, but they all appeared the same and she thought there may have been a preservation order on them.

She went home, frustrated at having to wait until next Friday.

Sophie's dancing session with Anthony went well. They always lasted two hours, unless they forgot the time; then they would drink brandy and talk, Anthony asking her how her workshop was working out, and did she need anything else. She said it was going okay, although some of the women weren't very friendly. He told her they were probably on their guard with people they didn't know well and might be more talkative when they got to know her. Sophie very much doubted it.

*

Again, the week went by quickly, and on Friday afternoon Sophie found herself waiting by the alleyway in Longton Lane. The torrential rain poured down, her black fake hair hanging in wet ringlets, but her umbrella helped to hide her face while she pretended to be on her phone. This wasn't a job for her, Sophie thought. Simon's parents should be standing there getting drenched instead of handing over the responsibly to his grandmother.

She saw Simon stroll around the corner and walk up the alleyway and through the gate next to the bins marked Number 4. She heard voices and then a door close. She waited a while, but nothing happened. So she walked past the front of the house. The light was on as the heavy rain had made the afternoon dark. The net curtains shielded the two people who were in the front room and Sophie couldn't see properly through them. She knew that she couldn't wait there any longer. She was just about to head to her car, when Simon jumped over the front wall and ran down the road, carrying a brown carrier bag. Sophie had difficulty trying to run and close her umbrella at the same time, so by the time she had started running after him he was gone. She gave up the chase. What had he been carrying under his arm and why was he running? She wondered if he had stolen it. Should she knock on the door on the pretext that she was looking for her cat? She decided she would return the next day and knock on the door.

Walking back to the car she saw Simon talking to one of his school friends. Was he stealing to get drugs? He didn't have the bag with him. Simon turned around and headed back to Longton Lane. He disappeared up the alleyway again. Sophie drove away, annoyed.

Sophie was tempted to get in touch with his grandmother to keep her up to date, but decided, as yet, that she didn't really know anything, and she certainly didn't want her going to Longton Lane. Sophie had told his grandmother that she wouldn't be in touch until she had any news so she would wait until she had something to tell her.

On Saturday afternoon Sophie, wearing her running gear, headband and trainers, which she hadn't worn for years, parked her car out of sight. She splashed water on her face and knocked on the door of Number 4 Longton Lane. It was answered by a man in his mid-eighties.

'Sorry to bother you but I am in a running event. How far is Timberry from here?'

'I'm afraid you have another four miles to go. Do you want some more water?' He had noticed that her bottle was empty.

'Thank you. Can I use your bathroom?'

He hesitated. 'Wait a minute.'

He went inside and closed a door.

A neighbour called him into the back garden.

'I'll be back in a minute.'

Sophie took a chance and picked up his mobile phone from the hall table and searched his phone numbers. She quickly took a photo of them. The man returned, carrying a bag of apples, just as she had put down his phone.

He told her to go through to the downstairs cloakroom.

Just as she was leaving, she asked him, 'Do you live here by yourself? It's a lovely house,' Sophie added.

He didn't answer her question, but told her he hoped she would manage to finish the race.

At home Sophie phoned Simon's grandmother, asking if she could go and see her to ask her a few questions.

Sophie arrived at Melinda's house on Monday morning, when they knew Simon would be at school. Melinda was pleased to see her and asked her how she could help.

'Does Simon have a computer or tablet?'

'Yes. His parents bought it for him. I don't know anything about them as I am not interested. He offered to teach me, but I can't see the point of them. Wouldn't even know how to switch it on.'

'Do you think I can look at it?'

'Yes. It's in his room.'

Melinda led Sophie upstairs to Simon's bedroom.

'Sorry about the mess. I'm not allowed in here.'

'I understand. I have a son who went through the same phase.'

Sophie opened the computer. It wasn't locked. Sophie thought that it didn't need to be. There was nothing unusual. Sophie cleared her search history and closed the computer, carefully leaving it exactly where she had found it.

Melinda offered her tea and they sat talking about Simon.

'Does he have many calls on his mobile?'

'Yes. All the time, but he has had more recently.'

'Do you know who calls him?'

'Not really. He usually walks out of the room when he's talking.'

'Can I have his mobile number?'

Sophie made a note of it.

'Does he talk to you a lot?'

'Yes. We have a very close relationship. He is very helpful, and he says he loves living with me.'

Sophie just didn't know where to go with this case.

She thought quickly.

'Well, I'll have to go, as I have got to visit someone close to the railway cottages in Bilberry,' Sophie lied. 'I don't think I have ever been there before. Do you know that area?'

'Not at all. Now I can't afford a car I don't go anywhere where the buses don't go.'

They both looked through the kitchen window.

'Your garden is beautiful,' Sophie said, admiring the flowers and the large pond. There were also fruit trees hiding a garden shed. Even on a sunny winter's day it looked inviting.

'Yes. It is beautiful in the summer. I wish I could afford a garden bench so I could sit and listen to the birds. But looking after Simon takes a lot of my money, even with help from his parents – they also have four grown-up children to look after.'

Sophie agreed that it would be a lovely place to have a bench. She could even imagine herself sitting there, painting.

Sophie eventually said goodbye and told Melinda she would be in touch.

On Friday afternoon after school Sophie decided to visit Number 4 Longton Lane.

She had checked Simon's phone number and it matched the phone number of the man who lived at Number 4.

She knocked on the door, wondering what she would find. The man answered. She didn't think that he had recognised her, but Sophie had made him one of her chocolate cakes.

'Hello. I have brought you a thank-you present for your kindness when I was running past your house last week.

The man suddenly realised who she was and invited her in.

'How did your race go?'

'I managed to finish it eventually.'

'I didn't see any other runners.'

'No, you wouldn't. I took the wrong turning,' Sophie said, thinking quickly.

He thanked her and took the cake and put it in the kitchen at the back of the house.

'I'm Ron, by the way.'

'Sophie.'

It wasn't worth using her agency name.

Ron opened the kitchen door.

'Simon, do you want some cake?'

Simon appeared from outside, carrying a brown carrier bag full of wood shavings.

He put the bag down by the front door and shook the shavings from his jumper.

'For the neighbour's guinea pig,' Simon explained, with a cheeky smile. Sophie liked him straight away.

'This lady called in last week when she was running and lost her way.'

Simon smiled at Sophie as he wiped his hands on his trousers and took a large piece of cake.

'Simon, why don't you show Sophie the bench I am helping you to make for your grandmother's birthday next Tuesday?'

'Okay, Grandad.'

Sophie phoned Melinda to say she would have an answer for her next week and that she had no need to worry about Simon. Puzzled, Melinda was happy to accept her explanation.

The following Wednesday Sophie met up with Anthony.

'What did you think of that case?' Anthony asked Sophie, raising his eyebrows.

Sophie ignored his question.

'I wonder what Melinda thought of her bench,' reflected Sophie.

'She rang me yesterday to thank me, saying that you could visit her any time you wanted to.'

Sophie could imagine her sitting under the trees. Would Ron be sitting there occasionally?

Anthony closed the file and placed it on the shelf with the others.

Fifty-Four

After a busy week for Sophie, dancing with Dave and Anthony, as well as putting in extra hours in the complex workshop, Anthony phoned.

'Are you interested in a missing person inquiry?'

Sophie found herself sitting in her usual chair.

Sophie hesitated, still not sure if this was the kind of work she wanted to do. She asked about the case.

'Briefly, a woman called Janice has been in touch with us regarding her father, whom she is trying to contact. His name is Robert Morris. Apparently, they haven't spoken to each other for a while, which is sad.

'Janice told me that she had been working in Spain for eight years and when she returned home, she found her father and his partner, Barbara, living together. He had met Barbara at the local rambling club four years ago. Janice didn't know anything about her.

'Janice must have been totally shocked, and I suppose she made their life very difficult for them when she thought that all his inheritance wouldn't go to her. Eventually they just decided to move out when, I expect, Janice tried to interfere with their life.

'Robert couldn't update his address, as at first they never stayed long anywhere, just moving to wherever they wanted to, so the solicitor wrote to him at his house address, informing him that Barbara had died two weeks ago, leaving him all her money.

'I have been in touch with Barbara's niece, Donna, who explained to me that she had been living with her Aunt Barbara until they also fell out about her moving in with Robert. I suppose it was all about money as well.

'Two weeks ago, Barbara returned from the Isle of Wight for a few days to try and make it up with Donna, and Barbara died during the visit. Donna looked through her handbag and found the solicitor's card. She got in touch with them, and they wrote to Robert at his house address.

'His daughter Janice opened the letter and then got in touch with us. Janice told us that she and her father were never close, and she had no idea where he was.'

'What rambling club were they in?' Sophie asked.

'Bilberry Wanderers.'

Sophie had heard of them. She quite often saw the group striding along one of the roads whatever the weather.

'Did Robert know what she had written in her will?' Sophie thought out loud. She doubted it.

'I presume you have walking shoes?' Anthony questioned, eyebrows raised.

'Oh no,' Sophie sighed, sinking further into her comfortable chair.

Sophie phoned Bilberry Wanderers.

Could she join? Where were they meeting? What did she need to take and more importantly, how far was the walk?

Dressed ready for her eight-mile walk, wearing new walking boots that were already becoming stiff and uncomfortable, she arrived early and waited in the allotted car park for the rest of the group to arrive.

They were scheduled to walk along the lanes in Tillingworth, over fields, and then along the deserted beach, back to the car park, calling in at the Vintage pub halfway along the walk to have a drink and snacks sitting outside.

Sophie couldn't remember the last time she had walked more

than three miles. She had walked up and down the deserted promenade the night before, to get used to her boots, but hadn't got very far.

'Anthony had better pay me a good wage for this case,' Sophie moaned out loud to herself.

Everyone arrived at precisely nine o'clock, a strange assortment of about forty people, carrying backpacks, some with sticks. They chatted for a couple of minutes whilst putting on their walking boots and then headed off. The leader shouted information and instructions from the front, and a man stayed behind at the back of the group.

Sophie tagged along. She tried to make conversation with two or three walkers, but they weren't very sociable. A woman walking behind her caught up with Sophie.

'Nice to see someone new in the club. We don't get many.'

'I thought I might try and get fit by joining,' Sophie lied.

Nancy had been walking for twenty-seven years.

'Eight miles is a long walk for a beginner,' Nancy warned, looking at Sophie's brand-new walking boots.

Sophie didn't have to be told that. She was now in step with Nancy. Dancing kept her fit, but this was a different ball game, *or foot game*, she thought.

During the walk everyone stopped to take in the view of the sea between the cliffs. Some took photos, Sophie glad of the rest. After all, she had walked three miles. *Only another mile to go*, she thought, until she could sit down at the pub.

The group started walking again. Sophie waited impatiently until everyone had climbed over the broken gate – she managed to squeeze through the narrow gap by the side of it – and then reluctantly followed them around the edge of a huge field, stepping through stinging nettles and long grass. *How could people do this for pleasure?* she thought. She hoped there wasn't any hogweed which she would have to carefully battle through.

Sophie asked Nancy if she had known Robert Morris or Barbara.

'Not really,' Nancy replied. 'They were nice people.' She was quiet for the rest of the walk to the Vintage pub.

The ramblers piled into the pub garden, to the annoyance of the other customers who had anticipated a quiet meal in the countryside. Sophie sympathised with them.

Nancy was now drinking from her flask and talking to a group of ramblers who were eating biscuits. They looked over at Sophie, who was feeling out of place. She drank from her water bottle, disappointed that they weren't going inside, and was joined by one of the men who Nancy had been sitting with.

'My name's Fred. You were asking about Rob Morris?'

'Yes, my father used to know him. I was almost certain that he belonged to this club, but perhaps I was wrong,' Sophie answered, practising her lying skills again.

'I knew Rob. He was a good friend of mine. I introduced him to Barbara, his partner.'

'Where is he living now? My dad would love to know.'

'Since they left home, and also the walking club, I'm not sure. Rob and Barbara were always moving around, staying in mountain bothies, or living in caravans. That was the life they liked, not stopping anywhere for a long time, always on the move. Then they seemed to settle in the Isle of Wight and bought a caravan. They had a large dog which they had recently adopted. They were out walking, and it was wandering along a road and it had taken to them, following them everywhere. They were a lovely couple.'

'What type of dog is it?' Sophie wanting more clues.

'A golden retriever. I haven't been able to contact Rob as we don't know where he is now, and he hates phones.'

'Where was he staying last?'

'Barbara said they were still living at a caravan site in Brinton on the Isle of Wight. I tried to phone the caravan site, but there was no one there called Robert Morris. They must have moved on again.'

Sophie had to tell him that Barbara had died. It wasn't the ideal place to tell him, but he had to know.

'I did know. She wasn't well, but it was still a shock. It's Barbara that usually phones me, but as she has died, I doubt if I will hear from Rob again.'

'How did you know that she had died?'

'The solicitor got in touch, saying that she had left me all her gardening tools and a bird table which I admired when I visited her. We had many long happy conversations about our gardens.'

'How is her niece, after Barbara's death?' Sophie asked.

'Donna? Hard as nails that one.'

Sophie didn't say anything.

She could now feel her legs starting to ache and her boots felt too tight for her feet.

Sophie gave her phone number to Fred and he gave her his, just in case they had any news of Rob.

She took a long time to finish her snacks and told Fred that she might take a different walk back and told him not to worry if she wasn't in the group. She would phone him next week.

The walking group stood up, picked up their things, full of enthusiasm for the next four miles back home.

The pub garden became blissfully quiet again.

Sophie waited a while, took her phone from her pocket and called a taxi. She definitely wasn't going to walk the four miles back.

She collected her car and went home. She would sell her boots on the internet as she certainly wouldn't be wearing them again.

Sophie looked through her notes on her phone but didn't have much information.

She wrote the information onto the pad in her file.

Rob Morris. Could be living somewhere in Brinton, on the Isle of Wight, in a caravan. With a golden retriever.

Friend of Fred.

Daughter still living in family home.

Partner Barbara died two weeks ago.

Barbara's niece Donna fell out with her when she moved in with Robert.

Sophie's mind wandered. Had they had time to sort their differences out?

Does Robert know she has died? Does he know she has left him money?

Only one way to find out.

The next day Sophie was sitting on the ferry, watching the Isle of Wight appear through the sea mist.

After an hour, she drove her car down the ramp and headed for the Sand Dune Hotel where she was staying in Brinton.

The Sand Dune was a small family-run hotel on the side of a cliff. Sophie collected the key card. She would visit the caravan park the next day.

In the morning after breakfast, Sophie asked the hotel receptionist where she could find the Brinton park, and after a long conversation about the town she managed to escape. Sophie drove along the narrow roads until she came to the small white caravan sign which was almost hidden by the overhanging trees. She followed the other half-hidden signs up an even narrower track and turned right. The park was small and there were only a few cream and green caravans scattered on the mown grass. Washing on the lines was being dried by the strong sea breeze.

Sophie knocked on the door of a cream caravan which was the first one she came to. Eventually a woman, who was probably in her late sixties, opened the door. She took off her yellow washing-up gloves and walked down the steps to Sophie and looked around. The smell of chicken stew followed her. The woman's sleeves were rolled up and Sophie noticed a small black cat tattoo on her arm.

Sophie asked if a Robert Morris lived on the site.

'No, there's no one by that name living here,' she said, looking at Sophie suspiciously, while she waved at a woman who had just got off a bus and was struggling past carrying shopping bags.

'He has a golden retriever,' pushed Sophie.

'Oh, that's George,' the woman said. 'George Jones.'

'Which caravan is his?' Sophie asked.

'Why? Who are you?'

Just as Sophie was thinking about an answer, a golden retriever bounded out of a caravan and ran around the park, barking, followed by Robert Morris.

'This lady's looking for you, George.'

Robert looked at Sophie, puzzled.

'Can we have a private word?' Sophie said.

'Who are you?'

'A friend of Barbara's.'

'You had better come in.' Robert led the way to his caravan, which was tucked away in the corner of the park.

The woman she had been talking to edged her way towards Robert's caravan.

'I'll speak to you later, Nina,' Robert called.

Disappointed, the woman returned to her caravan, looking back at them inquisitively as she climbed the caravan steps.

'I'm from Oliver's Private Detective Agency in Timberry, and, unfortunately, I have bad news about Barbara.'

Sophie waited until Robert had sat down.

'She's died, hasn't she?'

'Yes. Barbara died while she was at her niece's home in Bilberry, two weeks ago.'

Robert looked down at the floor, shocked.

'I knew that she was very ill. I told her not to go as it would be too much for her, but she wanted to see Donna for the last time. She didn't want me to go with her, said I would be in the way.'

He rubbed his forehead.

'We don't have phones, so we don't keep in touch with anyone. There is a phone box at the entrance of the caravan park should we need it in an emergency.'

Sophie had noticed it and was surprised at how well-maintained it was.

'Could her niece have written to you?'

'Not really, we weren't that close to her. She didn't know where we were, either. That's why Barbara wanted to go and see her, to try and sort things out. Barbara used to write to her ages ago when we were living on another site, but she never had a letter back. So eventually she stopped phoning and writing.'

Sophie found herself boiling the kettle and making cups of tea.

'Why did you come all this way to see me?'

'Well, Barbara has left you all her money. The solicitor wrote you a letter, which went to your house, and Janice, your daughter, opened it and got in touch with us to track you down, as she didn't know where to find you.'

Sophie showed Robert the solicitor's letter.

'Oh,' was all Robert could say. He held tightly onto his teacup.

'Yes, we had a big falling out when Janice came back from working in Spain and found Barbara living with me. She made our lives hell, so we decided to leave her to it and just go walking. Anywhere. It was sad for me to have to choose but Janice had her own life. I also understand now why Donna wasn't happy. She must have thought I was after Barbara's money.

'So we eventually decided to buy a caravan on the Isle of Wight, without telling many people.'

'What about Barbara's funeral?'

'I will go back to Bilberry tomorrow and see what's going on. I doubt if her niece will organise it.'

'Would you like a lift there?' Sophie asked.

'No. That's kind of you, but I shall have to take Bounder, our dog, and I shall need to get around a lot.'

'Where will you stay?'

'I can book into a dog-friendly hotel. Don't worry about me.'

'I am sorry to bring you such bad news,' Sophie apologised. 'Do you want to get in touch with Fred at the walking club? I have his number.'

'Yes, I would love to speak to him. I did have it but must have lost it, with all the moving we have done. I will call him in the next few days when I am in Bilberry. I am so pleased you took the time to come and see me, or I might not have known

Barbara had died. I didn't worry too much as I was expecting her home in the next couple of days. I couldn't phone her niece as I didn't know her number. It's nice that Barbara has left me her money, but it won't replace all the different adventures we had together.'

Robert stood up shakily and looked through the window.

'Why did you change your name?' Sophie had to ask.

'We were having an adventure, and also because we wouldn't be bothered by Donna and Janice trying to end our relationship.'

Sophie finished her second cup of tea, while stroking Bounder. She gave Robert the number of the agency and also Fred's number and said if there was anything else they could do, let them know and then she left. Bounder followed her to the car.

Nina, the woman she had spoken to earlier, came down her caravan steps and made her way to Robert's caravan, carrying a casserole dish.

Fifty-Five

Two weeks after her trip to the Isle of Wight, and after receiving a letter of thanks from Robert Morris, Anthony was now convinced that Sophie was capable of taking on another case.

'The client is Sally Fenton,' Anthony said, looking at the notes in front of him.

'Briefly, while visiting Lillyton Art Exhibition last Thursday, Sally Fenton found herself walking past a portrait painting on display of a woman who Sally thought looked exactly like her mother. Her mother had recently died, so she was shocked. She took a photo of the portrait while the organisers were distracted, so that she could look at it in detail when she arrived home.

'Sally phoned the agency, to see if it was the type of case we would take on, although it's not exactly detective work. I told her we may be able to help, and she has sent us a photo of the portrait, as well as a photo of her mother. She would like to find out who the artist is and who is the woman in the canvas. I thought this might be a case that would interest you.'

Anthony took the two photographs out of the envelope and handed them to Sophie, knowing that, as an artist, she would be more than interested.

After admiring the technique of the painting Sophie compared photos. She was surprised by the likeness. No wonder

Sally Fenton was shocked to see the portrait. It must have been upsetting, too, for her to see the likeness so soon after her mother had died.

'Did she notice the name of the artist, and did she ask about it when she was at the exhibition?'

'No, she was too shocked and didn't want to draw attention to herself. Sally went back the next day to see if she could find out anything else, but the exhibition had ended. The canvas is just initialled on the front. You can just see it in the corner.'

Sophie looked but couldn't make out the initials. They were cleverly painted into the woman's skirt.

'What does she want us to do?' Sophie asked, forgetting that Anthony had already told her.

'Try and find out who the artist is and who was the woman painted on the canvas.'

'Did you ask the maiden name of Sally's mum?' Sophie asked.

'Of course.' Anthony looked slightly annoyed by her question. 'Bancroft.'

'And her mother's Christian name?'

'Isabella.'

Sophie thought aloud while she was drinking her coffee.

'I could phone the art club to see if I could talk to the artist, or try and join the club, but I know from experience some clubs are very exclusive. I really don't want to join another art club.'

'I will leave you to sort it out.'

Anthony took her coffee cup and put it on the table.

Sophie took the hint and left, taking the information with her.

On Monday morning Sophie phoned the art club, using her agency name, Jackie, again. She enquired about joining. She really didn't want to but couldn't see any other way.

'We have exhibitions, trips, and most of our members have been here a long time so they have years of experience and can help you. We do portraits and miniature paintings. We are all a talented bunch. We have exhibitions twice a year, November and June. If you want to come tonight you would be more than welcome, and you can show us what you can do. Bring a few of your drawings. By the way, my name is Irene.'

Sophie thanked Irene, not too sure again whether she really wanted to join a club like that, but she sorted out some of her worst paintings, which she had never finished, and collected all her things together.

At seven thirty, disguised with blonde hair and glasses, just in case anyone recognised her from her shop, Sophie, or as she was known tonight, Jackie, was sitting at a table in the small village hall, amongst twenty people, very much feeling the new girl. A few people talked to her, but they were all too busy, blowing pastel dust off paper, dipping paintbrushes, or rubbing out mistakes.

At 8.30pm everyone stopped for tea and biscuits. The artists, men and women, walked around looking at each other's work, commenting, admiring or criticising. They looked at Sophie's half-finished painting of Kenny, suggesting that perhaps the nose was too long, or the eyes were too small. Sophie thanked them for their comments, consoling herself that they couldn't be suspicious of her.

Sophie waited for the opportunity to ask questions and then, just as two or three people were around her table, she said, 'I came to the exhibition last week and walked around and there was a beautiful portrait of a woman in a blue dress with long hair. Who painted that? It was lovely.'

'That's Lizzie Bingham. She's our expert in portraits. Aren't you, Lizzie?'

Smiling, Lizzie walked over.

'Is someone talking about me?'

'Jackie was admiring your portrait at the exhibition.'

'Oh, it's of my mother. It didn't sell. It wasn't for sale. In fact, I am just finishing it off tonight. I realised I hadn't painted round the sides of the canvas properly.'

'Was it a life painting or did you copy it from a photograph?' Sophie questioned, now that she had Lizzie all to herself, as the others had walked on to the next table, giving their expert opinions.

'From a photograph,' Lizzie replied.

Now came the hard bit.

'I wish I could paint from a photo. Do you have the photo on you of your mother that you copied from? I would love to see the likeness and how you managed to copy it.'

'Yes. It's in my folder.'

They walked over to Lizzie's table.

Sophie had to think fast before the room went quiet again and everyone started painting.

Lizzie took out the small photo and apologised for it being marked with paint. She handed it to Sophie. It was a very good likeness.

'How do you manage to paint a large canvas from such a small photo?'

Not waiting for a reply, Sophie continued, 'She's beautiful. What's her name?'

'Felicity, Felicity Parsons.'

Sophie thought. How could she take a copy of the photo? Sophie thanked her, saying she would try painting a portrait soon. She pretended to slip the photo back into Lizzie's large art bag, whilst pushing it up her sleeve. Sophie quickly went into the cloakroom and took several photos of Lizzie's photo of her mother and walked out, pretending to dry her hands on a paper towel.

Everyone had started painting, concentrating again on their canvases. Sophie quietly walked up to Lizzie and asked her if she had a pencil sharpener, and while Lizzie was looking in her pencil case, Sophie dropped the photo back into the bag, which was on the floor. Sophie was pleased with her evening's work.

Artist's name. Lizzie Bingham. Maiden name Parsons.

Age about forty-five.

Hazel eyes, 5 ft 8 inches. Medium build. Hair quite curly, brown, with slight hint of blonde.

Mother's name Felicity Parsons.

Sophie decided she had enough information to start her investigation.

At home Sophie made up a new file and placed the information inside.

She now had two photos: one of Sally Fenton's mother, which she had been given by Sally, her client, and the other of Felicity Parsons, Lizzie Bingham's mother, which Sophie had secretly taken at the art club.

She placed the photos side by side and studied the photos of the two mothers.

The women appeared alike, as well as having similar hair styles.

Sophie sent the photos to her computer for face recognition, to check later. She would need photos of client Sally Fenton, and Lizzie Parsons from the art club. Sally's photo would be easy, but Lizzie would be a challenge, unless she was on Facebook.

That was easier than she thought. Lizzie was on Facebook. She went to college in Manchester, was a full-time professional artist and had her own website. Sophie stopped reading, she could do that later, and copied Lizzie's photo to her face recognition page. She now had Lizzie's, Lizzie's mother's, and Sally's mother's photo. All she needed now was a photo of Sally. She looked on Facebook. There was nothing, so she made a quick phone call. The photo was in Sophie's inbox within the hour.

After placing all photos on the computer, Sophie clicked on face recognition. Immediately the two mothers connected. There was no connection between Sally and Lizzie. Sophie tried reversing the images. Again, the mothers matched, but not daughters Lizzie and Sally. Sophie closed the page.

Sophie couldn't ask Lizzie from the art club many questions, as she didn't know her. Perhaps if she went back to the club and tried to make friends with Lizzie? But that would take a lot of effort.

Sophie went back to Lizzie's Facebook page. She was married to Daniel Bingham and had been working in Bristol and

Southampton for a while. She didn't have many photographs, but Sophie noticed there was one of Lizzie with her mother, sitting outside a small restaurant in Brockenbridge.

The next Monday night, art bag under her arm, Sophie found herself getting into her car and driving to the art club again. This job was interesting, and she hoped she would find out more tonight. She sat down at her table and, after everyone had settled in, Lizzie called her over to sit by her. Dan, who usually sat at the next table, wasn't there as he was going to the cinema.

Sophie didn't hesitate. She picked up her things and sat down next to Lizzie. She got out her drawing of a quickly sketched portrait of her mother, which she had done before she went out, making sure that she had made a few mistakes, and started painting. Lizzie looked over.

'That's not bad, I always have trouble with the skin tone as well.'

'Have you finished with your mother's portrait?' Sophie asked, trying to bring the subject around.

'Yes. She was really pleased with it.'

'Do you have any brothers or sisters you can paint?'

'No, there's only me.'

'Do you have any cousins?'

'No. Mum was adopted when she was born so there's only the two of us. Dad left years ago.'

'My grandmother was adopted,' Sophie lied, 'and she tried to find out who her parents were, but in those days, there was no information.'

'Mum wasn't exactly adopted. Her mother left her outside a farmhouse owned by the Jones family when she was six months old. They took her in and kept her, that's where she was brought up. But she had a lovely life living on a farm with horses and other children. Then, of course, she got married.'

So, Jones wasn't her proper surname.

Sophie carried on painting, not wanting to appear too eager to question Lizzie.

The first half of the evening went by quickly. Sophie hid the notes she had made in her handbag.

She was pleased she had gone the second time to the club. She felt as if she had got to know Lizzie quite well by the time she left, at 9.30pm.

Sophie walked to her car. Noticing that Lizzie was heading to the bus stop, she asked her if she wanted a lift.

Sophie felt as though she had made friends with both Lizzie and Sally, and now wondered how she should handle this.

To save time, Sophie ordered two birth certificates, one for Sally and one for Lizzie. They would arrive in two days if she paid extra. She didn't have time to wait a fortnight for them to be processed, or trawl through all the births on the internet.

Sophie spent the next two days at her art workshop, Anthony's sister covering when Sophie was busy. She knew that his sister didn't want the job full-time, so she was happy to let her help when she could.

The two birth certificates arrived on the day anticipated and Sophie opened them immediately.

Sally's mother's maiden name was Bancroft, which checked out with the information Sally had given her.

Lizzie's mother's maiden name was Jones. It must have been the adoptive surname. Sophie was getting more interested in the case now.

'So, Lizzie and Sally may or may not be cousins.' Sophie tried to work it out.

As Sophie knew that Lizzie's mum was given her new names when she went to live on the farm, it would be more difficult to trace her information. She looked online at the births registered under the name of Bancroft in the same area. There were two.

Sophie sent for both of them. Again, they came two days later.

Twins. Born in 1950 at an address in Bilberry. Their mother was Daisy Bancroft. Unmarried. Names Isabella and Sandra. That's why they looked alike.

Why were they separated at birth?

Lizzie's mum, Sandra, was left outside the farm at six months. Stayed living on the farm with the Jones family, who changed her name to Felicity as they didn't know her real name, and she lived with her adoptive brothers and sisters.

Sally's mum died recently. Where was her mum brought up? That was Sophie's next move.

Sophie got in touch with Sally again via the company email.

Sally had no idea that she had an aunt on her mother's side. She thought her mother didn't have any siblings. She asked Sophie if she could find out more.

'My mother lived with my grandmother all her life until she got married.'

'What was your grandmother's name?'

'Daisy Bancroft. I have a photo, I think. Do you want it?'

Sophie said she looked forward to receiving it via email.

Again, she received it by the evening and put it away until the next day.

The next morning, Sophie was awake at six o'clock, toast in one hand, papers in the other and photos on the table.

Refreshed, she went through it again.

Daisy Bancroft, born in 1932.

Had twins when she was eighteen.

Sandra (Twin 1).

Sandra's name was changed to Felicity Jones when she was given away to the farmer's wife at the farm where she grew up.

She became Felicity Parsons when she married.

Daughter – Lizzie, woman at art club. Married name Bingham.

Isabella (Twin 2).

Client's mother.

Carried on living with real mother Daisy Bancroft until Isabella married John Fenton.

They had Sally Fenton. Now aged 45.

Isabella died recently.

So Sally and Lizzie shared the same grandmother, who separated their mothers (the twins) at the age of six months.

Sally and Lizzie's mothers were sisters.

Sophie thought it was a lot clearer now. She wondered why Daisy, the grandmother, had kept just one of the twins.

How could she bring the two together?

She found herself again in Anthony's comfy chair, after having her usual dance time and brandy with him.

'Fascinating,' Anthony replied, after listening intently, and eventually understanding the family history line.

'You will have to take great care how you explain to the cousins how you worked this out. Leave it a few days to think about it before you speak to them. I don't think there is any need for you to attend the art class again, or you could just go once more and then say your workload is too much and that you are too busy to go again.'

Back at home Sophie shredded the photo of Lizzie's mother. She had confirmed the fact that they were twins and didn't want her to think that she had overstepped the mark, by getting the photo. She also deleted it from the computer. She wouldn't tell Sally that she had had the photo.

Sophie emailed Sally, telling her everything she knew on Lizzie's side of the family, sending copies of all the certificates.

A few days later Sally got in touch again, asking how she could get in touch with her cousin.

'As you know, she goes to the art club on Monday night; perhaps you could start there?'

There was silence over the phone.

'I suppose I could, but I can't draw, and also, she might not want to speak to me.'

'I am sure she will. Don't forget to take a photo of your mother just in case.'

Sophie couldn't help herself. Knowing that Sally, her client, had never met her, so she couldn't be recognised, she decided to go to the art club just one last time.

She arrived there early and sat in her normal place. Next came Lizzie. She had a quick chat with Sophie and then sat down, placing her artwork on the table. No sign of new girl Sally.

Sophie was just about to give up hope when Irene introduced Sally. They walked through the door at the same time. Sophie straight away noticed the likeness. The hair, shape of nose and eyes. Irene noticed it as well, laughing, saying that they must be long-lost twins. Sophie was surprised that they hadn't matched on face recognition.

The first half of the evening seemed to last forever. Then came the break. Sophie resisted the strong urge to introduce them, and just carried on sketching. When she had finished her tea, she looked up and saw Sally and Lizzie talking. She walked slowly past, and she saw that the pictures of their mothers were on the table.

Sophie placed her cup on the long table and walked back.

She stopped and said to Lizzie, 'Is that another portrait you're going to paint?'

'No, Sally and I think we may be related.'

Sophie left the club happy. Happy that she may have brought two cousins together and happy that she didn't have to go to the art club again.

Job done.

But disappointed, as she would have loved to have heard all about their lives and how it all ended.

A month later her agency received a thank-you letter with an invitation to a family reunion which was going to be held the following summer. Sophie couldn't wait.

Fifty-Six

Christmas was getting closer, with the excitement of a big dance night at the Maple Leaf. Gina had booked the large ballroom for the Christmas party in mid-December. After discussions, everyone decided to put up decorations and go in fancy dress. It would make a nice change from their usual dance costumes. The posters would be designed and distributed in a couple of days.

The Maple Leaf would hire the Bilberry Rockers, the same band who played on the competition afternoons, as Gina had become close friends with Nick, the bass player. Luckily, the band was free on that date.

Sophie wondered what to wear and searched the charity shop for something. Then she found it. A Mother Christmas outfit, which Sophie bought straight away, hoping it would fit her. After being washed and ironed, she tried it on. A little short, perhaps it had shrunk in the wash, but it was Christmas, after all, a fun time. She then put it away until the eighteenth of December. The outfit would look good with red tights and her high-heeled red shoes.

Dave and Sophie practised dancing a lot during the following weeks and they were looking forward to the Christmas party, somehow forgetting that they were divorced.

Dave asked Sophie what she was going to wear, and Sophie

said it was going to be a surprise. She asked Dave what he was going to wear, and he said that it was also going to be a surprise. They had to wait and see.

Sophie and Dave had now moved on to rock 'n' roll, trying some of the steps that Anthony had taught Sophie, which they were confident with, and they were looking forward to dancing to the band.

Sophie had settled back again into the life of dancing, working at the charity shop and the art workshop. Anthony hadn't given her any cases in the last two weeks, but she had seen him for their usual dance and brandy nights. She explained to him she didn't want any more work before Christmas and was pleased to be able to concentrate on enjoying the Christmas build-up.

December 18th arrived, and Sophie, dressed as Mother Christmas, was busy getting ready for the party. She made mince pies and sausage rolls as a part of her contribution to the party table. She took some Christmas crackers and balloons as well.

Sophie had told Dave she would meet him at the Maple Leaf as she was going in a taxi so that she could have a drink.

The taxi pulled into the drive early, and the driver waited patiently while she carried everything to the cab.

Sophie arrived at the club, where everyone was busy preparing the room amidst the buzz of excitement.

She still hadn't had time to take her coat off.

Dave walked through the door, late. His taxi never arrived on time. *Why hadn't he bothered to dress up*, thought Sophie, disappointed. Was that his surprise? He helped to finish decorating the tree which had been donated, and then he disappeared into the men's cloakroom.

Sophie, having finished putting food on the tables, went into the cloakroom to finish getting ready, while talking to the other women. She took off her coat, left the cloakroom and as she turned the corner of the corridor, she collided heavily with something red.

'Dave?' Sophie gasped, her red hat falling over her eyes.

'Sophie?' Dave, peering through his false white eyebrows and Father Christmas beard, stood in front of her, looking at her very short skirt and red tights.

'Why didn't you tell me what you would be wearing!' Sophie exclaimed.

'Why didn't you?' Dave said, still looking at her red legs.

They laughed and walked into the dance hall together.

The evening was a success, with everyone dancing to the band and enjoying the music. Party poppers popped and streamers floated through the air.

Sophie walked to the table to get some more food. When she turned around Dave was dancing with Emma. Did she feel slightly jealous?

Sophie was pleased that Anthony had also been invited, and he danced with his sister throughout the evening. Although he had shown her a few moves, Sophie hadn't realised that he could jive so well. They each acknowledged her, but no more than that. They were dressed as Bonnie and Clyde; Sophie admitted to herself that he really did look the part.

By the end of the night all the festive Christmas food displayed on the long table had been eaten, and empty bottles and glasses filled the small tables.

At 12.30am everyone left the club in festive mood, an hour later than planned as the dance club had decided to keep dancing after everyone else had left. The band had stopped playing but Mark was playing music on his phone and so the dancing began again.

Sophie and Dave decided to walk home. They were freezing, as their fancy dress costumes weren't keeping them warm in the cold frosty night, but they both agreed that they had had a fantastic time. Dave kissed Sophie goodnight. Sophie returned the kiss.

Fifty-Seven

The New Year had now turned into April and the months were beginning to fly by. Sophie was taking on more interesting detective cases and enjoying her work with confidence.

She received a call from Anthony one evening, just as she was setting out to her hot yoga class, which she had joined at the beginning of the year. Julie had persuaded her to go when Sophie had met her at The Tavern for a meal and, not wanting to disappoint her, she'd agreed, although she wasn't enthusiastic about it.

Anthony needed to see her straight away.

Glad of the excuse not to go the class, she phoned Julie to apologise, and made her way to Anthony's penthouse.

He met her at the main door just as he was going in.

He looked around, and they quickly walked along the hallways and up in the lift. No one saw them.

Although it was the beginning of April the weather was still cold. Sophie took off her scarf and coat and sat in her comfy armchair to hear what he had to say.

Anthony also took off his coat and hung it on the coat stand. He then picked up Sophie's coat and scarf from the chair where she had left them and hung them next to his.

He poured two brandies. He gave Sophie a glass and sat down.

'We are having some trouble at the complex,' Anthony began. He didn't have any papers to look through.

'Oh.'

'One of the residents has received an anonymous letter and, as you know, if this gets out it will draw unwanted attention to the complex, which wouldn't be good.'

Anthony reached over and picked up a black envelope from the table and passed it to Sophie.

Sophie opened the envelope and read the letter.

THIS IS A WORNING. £20,000 MUST BE
HANDED OVER NEXT WEEK OR I WILL
TELL EVERYONE YOUR LITTLE SECRET.
DATE TIME AND PLACE OF HANDOVER TO
BE CONFERMED

The note was written in capital letters.

Sophie noted the spelling mistakes. Were they intended or couldn't the sender spell?

'Who is the client?'

'William Saunders.' One of the residents.

'Did he phone you?'

'Yes. No one at the complex knows I work at the agency.'

'You want me to interview him here?'

'Yes. Probably best in the small private lounge.'

'What do you know about him?'

'Wealthy, of course, ex-lawyer. A quiet man, who's in our classic car club that meets every month.'

'Married?'

'Not too sure. Doesn't live here with anyone.'

Anthony was pleased that Sophie was taking an interest in this case, as it needed solving ultra-quickly, before rumours began spreading around the complex.

Anthony took her coat and scarf from the clothes stand.

'You only have a few days to solve this case, Sophie, otherwise someone will have to try and catch the blackmailers when William does the money drop, and I don't want to be involved in that.'

Sophie returned home, wondering why she hadn't just refused. She knew that Anthony would be breathing down her neck on this case. Surely this was a police matter?

She decided what disguise she would wear.

The next day, Sophie walked through the doors of the complex, dressed in a black trouser suit, white blouse with a tie neck and black high heels, complete with her new short blonde hair and briefcase. She put on her glasses. She looked through the glass door to the lounge, which now had a "Private Meeting" sign displayed. She had asked Anthony to arrange that.

William was waiting for her.

She took a deep breath and walked in confidently.

Unmarried. Aged 62. Retired lawyer.

Grey hair, very overweight. Walking stick. Wearing a brown suit and red and white tie. Heavy bags under his grey eyes.

'My name is Jackie Hunter, and I have been asked to speak to you about the anonymous letter,' Sophie said in a low voice.

She shook his hand.

'William.'

They sat down opposite each other.

Sophie took her notebook and pen from her folder.

'Is this the first letter you have received?'

'Yes. Two days ago.'

'Have you any idea who might have sent this? Do you know if you have any enemies?' Sophie asked.

'I was a lawyer!' William said, raising his arms.

'Of course,' Sophie answered.

'Do you have someone who is close to you?'

'You mean a woman? Good God, no. They would spend all my money.'

'What do you do when you leave the complex? Do you have any hobbies?'

'Yes. I play tennis.'

'Where do you play?' Sophie tried not to look too surprised.

'Do I look like a tennis player?' he laughed, and continued, 'I have set up an ex-offenders club to help out young kids who need guidance. Some of the time it's a waste of energy. Sometimes it makes a difference, and you can see the members moving on into normal life, which is good.'

'How friendly do you get with the kids?'

'Not too friendly, as they might become too attached, or they might take a dislike to you if you said the wrong thing.'

'Do you know anyone there that you may have upset?'

'No. I just tell them what I think. It's up to them to listen.'

'Do you ever tell them about your life?'

'I tell them that I was poor when I was young and now, through hard work, I live in an expensive place and own an Aston Martin, and there's no reason why they couldn't do the same.'

'Do they know your name?'

Sophie was thinking about his name being on the envelope.

'No. I don't allow anyone to use their proper names.'

Sophie changed the subject.

'How well do you get on with the people in the complex?'

'We all get on well.'

'What about cleaners or helpers?'

'I have my own cleaner. She has worked for me since I moved in. She does odd jobs for me. I have known her for years.'

'What's her name?'

'Phillipa.'

'Phillipa,' Sophie repeated to herself.

'Do you know her?'

He went to the bar and brought back two coffees, not waiting for an answer.

'I have to ask you this question,' Sophie continued, as they sipped their coffee.

'Okay…'

'You honestly don't know why you are being blackmailed? It would save a lot of time and your money if you think you might know.'

William shifted uncomfortably in his chair.

'No idea.'

Sophie was annoyed that he was holding information back from her.

'Well, let me know when you want to tell me more,' Sophie said, ending the meeting.

She watched him walk out of the lounge.

She had only a few days to solve this case before the money drop.

Sophie phoned Phillipa to see if she was available to do some more modelling for portraits the next day. Phillipa hesitated, until Sophie reminded her that she would be paid for it.

How could Sophie question her?

Sophie prepared some suitable clothes and hats that Phillipa could wear for her modelling.

The session went well. Phillipa was a good model, being able to stay quite still for a long time. Sophie thought she herself wouldn't be able to manage it.

After two hours everyone left for lunch and Sophie tidied up. Phillipa waited to be paid.

'Sorry, Phillipa, the complex hasn't paid us yet. I can bring it round to your house at two o'clock if that's okay.'

Phillipa looked worried, but Sophie knew that she would want the money.

'Can't I get paid now?'

'No. The office is running behind today. Let me have your address and I will get it to you by 2pm at the latest.'

'Cornfield Terrace. Number 3.'

'Okay. I will pop by later and pay you.'

Sophie disappeared out of the door quickly.

At 1.45pm Sophie sat outside No. 3. She was surprised by the houses. Large sprawling terraces with long gardens leading down to a narrow river. Why did she want the £50 so quickly?

Sophie knocked on the door and Phillipa answered. Sophie gave her the envelope with the money in. She asked Phillipa if she would sign the receipt that Sophie had invented; she might want to check the handwriting. She said she couldn't stop, as she was late for the dentist. She walked quickly down the path and got into her car, making out that she wasn't interested in Phillipa.

Would she blackmail William? If so, why?

She was his cleaner. Did she really need the cleaning job?

Could she question the neighbours without being seen?

The next day, Sophie asked Phillipa if she could sit, as some of the class had asked for her to sit again. Sophie was limited by time now, as William could well receive another, more detailed, letter soon. She asked Anthony if his sister could take the lesson. Anthony didn't question her.

Using a different car, which Anthony always kept available for the agency, Sophie parked on the drive of 3, Cornfield Terrace and walked towards Phillipa's door, Anthony's sister having confirmed by phone that she was now safely in the art room.

Sophie knocked on the door, holding a box of plants that she had dug up from her garden.

There was no answer, so she knocked at the house next door. A half-awake teenage boy, aged about sixteen, wearing earphones, opened the door a little.

'Hi, I have a box of flowers for Phillipa. Is she in?

'She lives next door.'

'Do you know when she will be in?'

'No idea, she's probably at work.' He shrugged, unhelpfully.

'Would there be anyone at her house that could accept them?'

'No, not unless Graham's there.'

'Who's Graham?' Sophie asked, knowing that the half-awake teenager wouldn't realise that she was interrogating him.

'Don't know, he's there quite often. I hear them talking and arguing in the garden.'

'What about?' Sophie said quickly, aware she was sounding too interested and was pushing her luck.

'Usually about money.'

'Can you accept the box, or shall I deliver it tonight?'

'Deliver it tonight as our families don't get on since he arrived.'

'Would your other next-door neighbour accept it?'

'The house is empty.'

'Thanks. Sorry to have woken you up.'

He closed the door, head down, more interested in looking at his phone.

Sophie doubted whether he would even remember talking to her.

She looked back at Phillipa's house and noticed the shadow of a man step back from the window. She was pleased she was in disguise. She reversed carefully, avoiding the car that was parked in the shared drive.

Sophie arrived home and replanted the plants in her garden.

She looked at her notes, which didn't tell her too much.

William living at the complex, being blackmailed by someone.

Has a cleaner called Phillipa, who does modelling for the art club.

She lives in an expensive house.

Why would she want to be paid urgently? Why would she have a job as a cleaner?

Who is the man who visits or lives with her? It must have been him looking through the curtains.

Sophie decided to go back and see William to ask him more questions.

They met again in the small lounge in the afternoon.

After talking socially for a while, she asked him what his relationship was with the cleaner. She wasn't going to pussyfoot around him any longer.

William picked up his stick, which was leaning against the chair, looked at it and then put it down again.

'She is a woman who I once worked with, many years ago. We were very close at one time, but she couldn't marry me as we were both starting our careers; she was also looking after her father, who was ill for a long time.'

William coughed and looked around.

'Looking after her father caused her to lose most of her money, as he was living in a nursing home for twelve years. So I bought her that house. I told her that she didn't owe me anything. She started work again and was on a good wage at the time, but since she retired, she has become short of money again, so she takes in lodgers occasionally. I think she has had the same one for a few months now. I pay her for cleaning my apartment and got her a job here as well.'

'What's the lodger's name?'

'Graham Davidson.'

'How does Phillipa get on with him?'

'Says he's become lazier in the last few weeks.'

'Could he be blackmailing you?'

'He may be.'

'Why?'

'I don't know. I can't say that I recognise the name.'

'He could have changed it.'

'Yes. That's possible.'

'I think I shall have to interview Phillipa.'

'If you must.'

'Can you arrange to call her?'

'Yes. I suppose so.'

Sophie arranged to have the call in William's apartment, which was on the ground floor, owing to his not being able to climb stairs, and not being too fond of lifts.

Phillipa agreed to the call, and William called her in the evening, when Graham wasn't in the house. Sophie listened to the case on speaker. He told her that he was being blackmailed and that he thought it might be Graham.

'How did he get in touch with you about the lodgings?' Sophie asked.

'He knocked on the door, asking if I wanted any gardening done. We started talking and he said he would manage the gardening and other jobs for cheap lodgings. He would be out most of the day as well as some nights. And to be honest, it was nice at first to have a man in the house, and there was something about him that I liked at first.'

'At first?'

'In the last month he has been asking me for money and threatening that he will expose William and my secret.'

'What secret?'

'I don't know what he knows.'

William got up and paced around his lounge. Sophie noticed that he wasn't using his stick but ignored the fact.

There was silence.

'How is your money situation now?' Sophie asked Phillipa.

'I have very little savings. He knows it. That's why, although I enjoy it, I have cleaning jobs. He is talking about taking the house from me. Before he does, I would imagine that he is now going to blackmail William.'

'What job does he have?'

'He doesn't. He lives in my house now and acts as though he owns it, and I can't do anything.'

'Don't worry, Phillipa, we are on the case now. If you can, try to act normally. By the way, does he have access to all the rooms in your house and your private papers?'

'Yes. I suppose so.'

'When he is not there, could you box up your papers and bring them to William's apartment?'

'Yes. I could do it now, as he is stopping over at his girlfriend's house.'

'He has a girlfriend?'

'Yes.'

'What's her name?'

'I don't know.'

They said goodbye and ended the call.

Sophie looked at William.

'Well?'

William shrugged.

Later in the evening Phillipa walked through the car park with a medium box of papers.

Sophie met her in disguise; a large hood covered her head. She took them from her, thanked her and disappeared into Anthony's lift.

An hour later, after explaining everything to Anthony, she sat looking through the papers. Nothing exciting, just bills, work information, house sales. And a birth certificate for a baby boy, dated 1983. Mother: Phillipa. Father: not known. Sophie printed a copy on Anthony's printer.

'Something interesting?'

'Maybe.'

She kept the copy of the certificate.

Sophie closed and sealed the box and took it to William's suite, so that he could give it back when Phillipa visited him next.

Sophie asked William if he had any children. He said no.

She had to ask Phillipa about her baby.

She would have to phone her. It wasn't the sort of thing she liked to do over the phone, but she couldn't do anything else.

She phoned Phillipa's number.

'Are you alone?'

'Yes.'

'I have finished with your box of information. Thank you for letting me look through it. I noticed there was a birth certificate for a baby born in 1983, named Darren.'

Sophie could feel Phillipa's emotions over the phone.

'Yes. It's William's baby. He doesn't know. He was an up and coming lawyer and, really, we were only just good friends. I got pregnant and I had to have the baby adopted. I was just starting my law career, and my parents were putting pressure on me to give him up for adoption.

'I always think of him, wondering what he is doing, especially on his birthday and at Christmas, but he would have had a better life than I could have offered him at the time.'

Could the blackmailer be her son? How would he know where she lived and how would he know that William was his father?

'I think William should be told about his son,' Sophie advised gently.

'I know. But it is too late now.'

'Think about it. It is better to solve this together. I will be in touch tomorrow.'

Sophie put down the phone. If it was her son, why was he blackmailing them?

Sophie made enquiries early the next morning and found that adoption records were freely available for him to search.

Sophie, fed up with people trying to make decisions and not telling her the truth, took it into her own hands.

When Phillipa was safely modelling at the art class, Sophie, in disguise, made another visit to Phillipa's house. She left the car further down the road and walked to the terraced cottage, through the side gate and around the back. She noticed the back door was open and walked in.

The man whom she presumed was Graham was standing at the sink, filling a glass with water.

Shocked, he told Sophie to get out, pointing to the door.

'Why should I? I'm a friend of Phillipa's and she told me to pop in any time.'

Graham stared at her. Sophie stared back. He backed away further towards the sink.

'I know you are blackmailing William, and your name will be given to the police if you don't own up to the letter you have written.'

'Why should I?'

'Because being her son, you should be ashamed, causing her so much stress.'

'Edward! You're joking, I am not a bit like him. I may be his stepbrother, but I am nothing like that stuck-up bloke.'

'Stepbrother!'

'Yes, you didn't expect that, did you? He was always treated better than me, just because he was clever and went to university. He had a good career, while I found it difficult to find a job, as I didn't have any qualifications, even though I am two years older than him. He had loads of money and I hardly had any.'

'How did you know where Phillipa lived?'

'That was easy. Edward has been looking for her for the last three years and was reluctant to call her in case she didn't want to know him. He had all the information and even who his father was. He showed it to me.'

'Why blackmail William?'

'Do you really think the posh lawyer bloke would want everyone knowing that he had abandoned his baby son?'

Sophie thought, *no, he wouldn't.*

How could this be solved? She noted the jealousy in his voice.

She would have to call another meeting.

'Where does her son live now?'

She knew he wouldn't say.

'Somewhere in London. He left a few months ago. Doesn't keep in touch now my parents have died, and he's too busy with his swanky job.'

'What posh job?'

'Lawyer.'

'Give me your telephone number and I will give you mine and perhaps we can sort this out before it goes too far.'

He calmed down and looked at her card.

'Detective Agency.' He looked worried.

'I will be in touch. I would honestly think again about blackmailing William. Take a look around you and appreciate what you could have. It will be too late when the police come for you.'

Sophie phoned Phillipa, telling her what she had learned.

'You must tell William before all this explodes,' Sophie advised.

Phillipa was silent.

'Could you tell him, Jackie?'

Sophie thought that it was really up to Phillipa, but agreed, as she wanted to close this case.

She knocked on William's door, preferring to tell him in private.

He invited her to sit down.

'I think I know who is blackmailing you,' she began.

'Before you begin, I know who is blackmailing me. I should

have told you about one of my cases which nearly caused me to lose my job.'

William was now getting worried.

'It doesn't have anything to do with any of your cases,' although she was annoyed he hadn't mentioned it before.

She saw William breathe a sigh of relief and visibly relax into his chair.

'I have something to say that Phillipa wanted me to tell you. She couldn't tell you herself, and it will probably come as a great shock, but hopefully it will turn out okay.'

Frowning, William listened.

'When you and Phillipa worked together and you were seeing each other, Phillipa became pregnant with your baby.'

William's jaw dropped.

'She had the baby, whom she called Darren.'

'Darren?'

'Yes. At the time you had lost touch with each other, and she couldn't afford to look after him. She was persuaded by her parents to have him adopted.

'The person who is blackmailing you is Darren's stepbrother.'

William suddenly looked sad.

'I did see her, just after she left her job, and thought she looked pregnant; I did wonder. But we were both young.'

'He has changed his name to Edward and he has become a lawyer.'

William's face lit up.

'A lawyer?'

'I think it is time that you and Phillipa got together for a long chat.'

Sophie picked up her papers and walked to the door.

William was on the phone.

Sophie asked Anthony's advice about Edward's stepbrother.

'Tell him it's either the police or an apology and tell him you recorded what he said to you,' Anthony advised.

'In a way he has brought William, Phillipa and Edward together so there is good that has come out of this.'

Sophie hadn't thought of that.

Out of interest, she phoned Phillipa and was pleased to hear that, although William was totally shocked, he was delighted they had a son, and he was now getting in touch with his lawyer friends in London to track him down.

Sophie asked about Graham.

'He has agreed to go to William's offenders group. I have said that he can still live here providing he gets a job. I think William is helping with that by buying him some gardening tools and a van.'

Sophie breathed a sigh of relief.

Job done.

Fifty-Eight

'Can you cope with another case so soon?'

'I think so.'

Anthony sat down at his desk and opened his computer.

'You will be pleased that this is another local assignment. A woman called Wendy Rochester has recently moved into Seaweed Cottage, which has been empty for years. The cottage is situated by itself, almost on the seafront.'

'Yes. I know it. I've always wanted to live there, but it needed too much work and it was also much too expensive.'

Sophie imagined herself walking out of her front door, across the narrow quiet road and straight onto the beach, sitting in the early morning sunshine, or at night, watching the sun go down with Kenny.

Anthony interrupted her thoughts.

'Are you listening, Sophie?'

Sophie apologised.

'Wendy Rochester is in the middle of renovating her cottage and while taking up the rotten floorboards to replace them, she found a bag in the rubble, which must have been there for some time.'

'What was in it?'

'She wasn't too specific. Quite a lot of money and clothes. With this case it's best if you go and see her at the cottage.'

Sophie didn't need asking twice and she didn't think there was any need to change her name to Jackie this time.

The next afternoon, after walking down the promenade, along the beach and carefully stepping through tall weeds, Sophie was knocking on the front door of Seaweed Cottage.

'Can you find your way round the back? The front door is stuck,' a woman's voice answered.

After defending herself against the stinging nettles and the out-of-control shrubs, Sophie walked round the cottage and was met by Wendy.

Dressed in old jeans, a blue T-shirt and black hair tied up in a loose untidy ponytail, Wendy invited her to sit down on one of the metal chairs. It was a square, medium-sized back garden, surrounded by a low broken-down wall, partially covered in ivy. The view from the back of the house was over an overgrown field, where two horses were grazing.

Wendy brought out a tray of drinks and apologised for the state of the cups, as she hadn't, as yet, finished opening her kitchen boxes. She passed Sophie a cup of coffee and placed a plate of biscuits on the table. Sophie thought how peaceful it was sitting there.

'I moved into the cottage a month ago. When I say moved in, I mean, I'm living and sleeping in the lounge, at the moment, as I have all my things in storage. There is so much dust and I'm trying to get it all done before winter.'

Sophie looked around the garden. It had been left to run riot, but some evening primroses had managed to survive, and would brighten up the corner of the garden in a couple of months' time, along with the delicate cornflowers which were also coming through. She could see so much potential. How she wished she could have afforded to buy it.

Sophie, realising that she was there for a reason, asked Wendy how she could help.

'Last week, I started taking up the floorboards in the hall, and I found a plastic carrier bag. I'll show you.'

She disappeared into the house and brought out a red plastic bag.

Sophie noticed that there wasn't very much dust on the bag – it couldn't have been there very long. She didn't say anything.

Inside were some items of men's clothes, trousers, striped shirt and pairs of socks. In another bag inside the carrier there was about five thousand pounds.

'I didn't want to go to the police as I haven't got time, and what could they do? Also, I'm fascinated to know who it belonged to.'

The clothes were clean, and the money was in neat bundles.

'Can I take these?' Sophie asked. 'I will give you a receipt.'

'Go ahead. There's nowhere safe I can put them anyway. I wouldn't want someone coming back for it.'

'Have you noticed anything else strange going on?' Sophie asked, looking around.

'No. Except on the day I moved in, there were towels hung over the wall of the front garden. But I think they had been left there by someone bathing in the sea.'

Sophie made a note.

'Do you want to look around?' Wendy waved her hand towards the cottage.

Sophie said yes immediately. She had hoped she would get a chance to see what it was like inside.

'Be careful. It's not very safe yet,' Wendy warned.

Sophie noticed the gaps in the floorboards; the stairs hardly existed. The room at the front was the only one that could be lived in and the cold downstairs bathroom was just about usable.

She still wasn't disappointed. Although the cottage was in a mess Sophie could visualise what she would have done with it.

After being kept talking by Wendy for about three hours Sophie started to leave, carrier bag placed inside another shopping bag.

'Go out through the back door, as I still have to fix the new door at the front. It won't open properly. The new back door, thankfully, fits perfectly.'

Sophie thanked Wendy and promised she would report back

to her soon. Would she prefer her to phone any information or call and see her?

'Call around,' Wendy said quickly. 'It will be great to have some company. I have only just moved into the area after recently being divorced, so I haven't had time to meet people yet.'

Sophie was pleased with her answer and looked forward to her next visit to the cottage.

At home Sophie looked again at the items in the bag. Clean clothes and money. She tipped them onto the floor. She looked inside. A forgotten receipt was tucked neatly into the fold of the bottom of the bag, a receipt from the local small supermarket. It was dated two months ago.

She looked at the size of the shirts, which were medium; the trousers were slim fit.

Sophie got ready for her usual dance night with Anthony. After the allotted two hours they sat talking. He told her that she was progressing well with the case. She could always try the local pub. See if people in there knew anything.

The next day Sophie was eating a sandwich lunch at the Sandcastle pub, which was the nearest pub to the cottage. She hoped someone might know about it. She asked the barmaid.

'It's been empty eight years. Geoff, the owner, had to go into the Seagull Care Home. Nice old bloke, slightly eccentric, but always friendly. Although he did like his own company. Some sort of writer. He died this year and had no relatives, so the cottage went up for sale. Even before he stopped living there the cottage was in disrepair. I think a woman lives there now. She can't mind living in the mess. There's always a car outside when I walk to work.'

Sophie thought she could remember seeing the man who owned it years ago, when she walked past; he used to sit outside in the front garden, wearing a cowboy hat, and had two dogs that wandered around.

Someone must have been living in the cottage when it was empty, she decided. If it had been vacant for eight years, and if it had only been put on the market recently, during the day the mystery man must have hidden his possessions under the floorboards until he returned, so no one would see them. The cottage had thick old curtains so a dim light wouldn't have attracted any attention.

Sophie wondered where the intruder was now. He must have returned last month to find that the door had been changed. She thought he must be short of money now, but he hadn't tried to break in.

Sophie's phone buzzed. A message from Dave. Did she want a dance practice? She said she was too busy, but they could go to lunch.

He met her at the café by the beach and, after talking and eating, they went for a long walk on the sand, passing Seaweed Cottage.

'Someone must have bought it,' Dave exclaimed, stopping for a moment after noticing the sign was lying on the ground.

Sophie hoped she wouldn't see Wendy.

'I would have loved to live there. Close to the sea,' Sophie sighed.

'You live close to the sea now.'

'Yes. But not actually that close. There is something about the cottage.'

'I haven't heard from Tom recently. Have you?' Dave now changed the subject, not listening to what she was saying.

'Yes. He phoned last week. He's still enjoying himself and promised me he's studying hard.'

'And your mum and sister?'

'Yes, they're really settled in Sydney now.'

They turned around, the gentle warm wind blowing in their faces, Dave picking up pebbles and throwing them into the water.

At home again, Sophie's mind was in work mode.

Where could the mystery man be, and who was he?

Should she put something on the internet? But she doubted he would be online. She could wait on the beach to see if he showed any interest in the cottage. She could put up notices in shops and boards saying a striped shirt had been found in a plastic bag on the beach. She needn't say anything about the money. She could walk round the shops, seeing if it looked as though there was anyone who was sleeping rough. Or she could go on the beach at night and see if there was anyone sleeping there. All the ideas sounded ridiculous.

She decided the shirt in the plastic bag was the best option.

Sophie made a notice and put it on the board in the supermarket where the receipt and bag had come from:

RED PLASTIC BAG FOUND NEAR BEACH CONTAINING VALUABLE ITEMS

Sophie put the phone number of her spare mobile.

In the afternoon she had her first phone call, from a woman asking what was in the bag, as it could be hers. When Sophie asked her what she thought was in the bag the woman put the phone down.

Sophie had a few more false calls. She had almost given up hope on the notice.

But four days later she had a call from a man saying that the bag probably was his.

'What is in the bag?' Sophie asked.

'I don't really want to discuss it over the phone.'

Sophie realised that he was worried about the money.

She agreed to meet him at the beach café.

Three hours later she sat waiting, drinking coffee, carrier bag at her side.

In walked Wayne, breathing heavily. *He's put on a bit of weight since wearing the clothes in the bag*, thought Sophie.

'Wayne?'

'Sophie? You have my carrier bag?'

Before Sophie could answer he reached over, grabbed it and was through the door before she could react.

'I'll catch him.' The teenager on the next table had been listening and was now running to the door.

'No, don't do that. There was nothing important in there. Just some clothes from the charity shop.'

Sophie thanked him for offering. He looked disappointed.

Walking back home along the promenade, Sophie noticed the carrier bag with its contents scattered on the ground. She picked them up and put them into the recycling box, pleased that she had left the original bag with the money at home.

A week went past. She was slightly worried about having £5,000 in her house and handed it over to Anthony to put in his safe.

Sophie went back to her normal routine. She enjoyed dancing with Dave, which continued to surprise her. The Maple Leaf publicity had attracted even more people. A fishing club had also started up and the social dancing on Saturday nights, which Dave and Sophie went to when they weren't busy, was a success. For a couple that hadn't got on when they were married and who had divorced, Sophie thought they were getting on quite well.

Sophie had almost forgotten about the carrier bag incident, so when her spare mobile phone rang, she was jolted into the investigation again.

The man phoning seemed quite pleasant.

After he had described the shirt and trousers Sophie knew that he was the owner. He never mentioned the money. She didn't either.

Sophie arranged to meet him at the beach café. It wouldn't be busy at 10am the next day.

His name was Jonathan.

She sat and waited for him. There was only one other person in the café, a girl, and she had headphones on, busy listening to music on her phone.

In he strolled, Sophie thought his age was fortyish; dark, slim and athletic. He bought a coffee, looked round and came to sit by her.

'Sophie?'

'Jonathan?'

'Where did you find it?'

'Why was it there?'

Jonathan hesitated, knowing that it had been found in the cottage.

'I was sleeping in the cottage for a while as I was new to the area and, to be perfectly honest, I loved it there. I didn't break in. The door at the back of the cottage was broken and I just walked in. It was great, all by myself, recently divorced, it was just what I needed. After work I would shower at the swimming baths and come back with a takeaway and a beer and enjoy the sound of the waves. Sometimes, I would go to the pub for a meal or cook on my homemade barbecue. There was a water pump which worked. I slept in my sleeping bag that I kept in my sports bag, which I took to work.'

Sophie thought it sounded heaven.

'Then one day when I returned from work there was a sold sign and a new door fitted. I couldn't get in unless I broke in. I wouldn't have done that. I couldn't ring the doorbell and ask for my bag. I didn't know it was on the market.'

'Where are you living now?'

'I am staying with a friend from work, but I shall have to leave soon, as his girlfriend is coming back from China so I will be in the way.'

'Where do you work?'

'I am a builder, but I can do most plumbing, electric and painting jobs. At Dentons Builders.'

'How did you see the advert?' Sophie asked, interested.

'I was in the supermarket doing some shopping and I was also looking for somewhere to stay.'

Sophie continued, 'The lady in the cottage found the bag while she was renovating and, not having time, she asked me to find out who it belonged to.'

'Was the money still in the bag?'

'Yes. Of course.'

Jonathan sighed with relief.

'I would like to go and see her and thank her.'

Sophie thought for a while.

'I can always ask.'

After toasted teacakes and another coffee, they left the café and Sophie said she would be in touch with him.

'Thank you, Sophie. I really hope I hear from you again.'

They swapped phone numbers.

Sophie shook his hand and he disappeared, clutching his plastic bag.

The next day Sophie strolled down the beach to Seaweed Cottage, hoping Wendy would be there. She picked up shells, small stones and sticks which she could use in her art workshop. She also picked up the usual plastic bottles left there and put them in the bin.

Sophie walked around to the back garden through the jungle of branches which had been cut down, hoping she wouldn't scare Wendy.

She was painting an old cupboard outside and was pleased to see Sophie.

Sophie was surprised by the amount of work that Wendy had done since her last visit, and she explained what had happened and about Jonathan wanting to come and thank her.

'At the moment, he is working for Dentons Builders and is living with a work mate. He seems a really nice person.'

Wendy said she would be happy to see him.

'Tell him to come around any time in the evening or weekends. I have started working at the local garden centre for a few hours a day as this allows me time to finish work on the cottage.'

Sophie stayed longer than she had intended. She helped weed the patio, swept the yard and cleared the side passageway with secateurs and shears, wishing again that it was her garden. After tea and more cakes, she returned home.

The following weekend, as she walked past the cottage, she was hoping she would see Wendy in the front garden and that she would be invited in again.

As Sophie approached, she noticed Jonathan's van parked in

Wendy's drive. Sophie turned around and headed home. The van was also there a few days later when Sophie walked past.

Of course, he was a builder. Sophie smiled.

Job done.

Fifty-Nine

A nthony got in touch again.

'I have a case that would really interest you.'

Sophie was slightly annoyed, as she wanted to go clothes shopping.

She found herself settling into his cosy chair and listened.

'I have been contacted by Jerome Mitchell.'

'The singer?' Sophie questioned.

'Yes. He's now living at the Morton Hotel in Bilberry.'

'That's a fantastic hotel,' Sophie replied.

'He wants to know if someone can go and see him to discuss his case.'

'And you want me to go?' Sophie was more than interested in meeting the 1960s pop star.

This was better than going shopping.

'Well, you could go and talk to him and see what you think about taking on the case, and then you can discuss it with me. You will have to be discreet and use the exit doors at the back of the hotel.'

Sophie agreed to see Jerome, and after googling him – famous in the '60s, controversial, many hit records, song writer, known for his outrageous clothes and behaviour, cautioned for impersonating a police officer, married four times, divorced four times, left England to live in California – she found herself walking through the emergency exit of the hotel, being met by the pop star.

She followed him quickly up the side stairs to his suite, which was the only room on the floor. It was not as modern or as extensive as Anthony's, but it was still very large, old-fashioned and certainly lived in. Huge Victorian windows, high ceilings and with an assortment of sofas and guitars around the room. Sophie and Jerome sat on chairs in the alcove of the large bay window, which was framed by heavy dark red curtains. Jerome pushed back his long grey hair, which still showed signs of the black it had been when he was younger. His smile, through his greying moustache and beard, was kind and humorous, exposing a perfect set of white teeth.

'I hope I can rely on total confidentiality,' he drawled in an English-American accent.

'Of course,' Sophie replied, mesmerised by his deep brown eyes, which never left her. They weren't darting like Anthony's.

'I have been living in the hotel for five years, as I find it much easier than living in my old house. It was a huge place and although it was great for all the parties I used to have, and entertaining, I find it more convenient living here, as I can concentrate on writing, and when I sometimes go on tour, I know that everything is safe here. Well, it used to be, and that is the reason I got in touch with you.'

Sophie was listening with great interest.

'Some things have gone missing. It started off with small items disappearing and then larger things were taken. Recently, my Gibson guitar disappeared, and also some sheet music I was writing. I left them on the sofa when I did a gig in the ballroom downstairs and when I returned, they weren't there.'

Sophie made notes.

'I could call the police, but that would draw a huge amount of attention to myself, both here at the hotel and in the press. I also have large amounts of money hidden away, which I don't want anybody knowing about, tax-wise. I haven't even told the manager of the hotel about the thefts, for the same reason.'

Sophie listened. She liked the thought of working on this case and could listen to his voice all day.

'Who else has a key card?'

'No one. We still have ordinary keys.' Sophie had noticed this when he had let her into his suite. 'I have the only key to my apartment. I made that clear when I moved in here.'

'When does your room get cleaned?'

'I have the same cleaner who used to clean my house. I don't want anyone else looking around. It's not exactly tidy, is it?'

Sophie liked the room. It had an atmosphere of comfy chaos. You could put your feet up on one of the many sofas, which were covered with throws, and no one would care. She wouldn't dare do that in Anthony's suite. But then she wondered how Jerome could find anything. It quickly went through her mind that perhaps he had mislaid the things he thought were stolen.

'Does your cleaner have a key?'

'Yes, she has my spare one.'

'Has she ever lost it?' Sophie asked.

'Not that I know of.'

'Do any of the people working here know who you are?'

'Yes, some do, but no one bothers me. I don't think they are particularly interested.'

Sophie asked if he went out a lot and he replied most days, at all hours; he didn't have a routine, sometimes he was out all night.

'Can you make me a list of everything that has gone missing and an estimated value, and also, where you kept them?'

Sophie looked at another Gibson which was on the wall.

'Do you play?' Jerome noticed her looking at it.

'I used to a long time ago.'

'Next time you come I will show you more of my guitars. I have twelve of them.'

Jerome quickly wrote the missing items on some music paper from his table and Sophie said she would be in touch again.

He stroked his moustache slowly, and again asked her not to speak to anyone about his case. She assured him that he could rely on her.

Back at Anthony's, Sophie explained what had happened during her visit and Anthony listened. While waiting for a reply she compared Jerome's suite to Anthony's. So different but both spectacular.

'You might be able to get a job at the hotel,' Anthony broke into her thoughts.

'I thought that,' Sophie answered. 'I might look online, and see if there are any jobs going or I could phone or call in.'

At home, Sophie looked online. There were no jobs advertised, so she decided to go to the hotel again. She hadn't seen anyone when she visited Jerome so she felt quite sure that they wouldn't connect her with him.

The next morning, Sophie was in the reception of the hotel asking for the manager. He wasn't very helpful and told her he would send the housekeeper to see her. After about half an hour, Nisha, wearing a green uniform, appeared and offered her a job if she could produce references. One of the cleaners had just walked out without notice. Sophie phoned Anthony and he said he could fix it.

Two days later, references accepted, Sophie found herself wearing her uniform, cleaning washbasins and toilets in the downstairs cloakroom. There were four cleaners. She had quickly made friends with Sarah, who had worked at the hotel for nine years. Sarah showed Sophie what to do. They finished their shift at 2.30pm, for which Sophie was thankful, as vacuuming the hall and miles of corridors and cleaning toilets wasn't the kind of work she was used to or really wanted to do. Sophie and Sarah sat in the small staff room, talking.

She learned that Nisha, her boss, was a nice person and easy to work for most of the time, except when there was an influx of guests, and then they had to work extra hard. Sarah said that as a place to work there was a family atmosphere.

'You were lucky to get the job, as people don't usually leave. Anika had to leave quickly because of a family tragedy.'

'How many bedrooms are there?' Sophie asked.

'Thirty. But they are all quite easy to clean. We are hardly ever fully booked. Most guests don't want to be interrupted to have them cleaned. You just hand them milk and whatever they want and leave them to it. When they leave, we might have to work quickly before the next guests arrive.'

'What about the manager?' Sophie asked. 'Do you see a lot of him?'

'Brian? No. He walks around the hotel nodding to people and sorting problems out. He's only been here about a year. He seems very laid back as well. He doesn't say much.'

Lunch and work finished, Sophie walked around the hotel and up the two flights of stairs and then walked up the third flight to Jerome's suite. Nothing unusual was happening and she walked back down the stairs.

Just as she was walking along the second landing, she saw Nisha heading towards her. Luckily, Sophie noticed a folded hotel brochure on the floor, and she picked it up.

'That's what I like to see, someone who is on duty all the time and not just on paid time.' Nisha asked her how her first day had gone and Sophie said she had enjoyed it.

'Oh, Sophie, I forgot to say. There is no need to go to the third floor, as that is a private floor.'

'Okay,' Sophie said, disinterested.

'Yes. And if you see a man with a beard wearing hippy clothes, just say hello and don't question him.'

'Okay,' Sophie said again.

'I expect you will recognise him. He's Jerome Mitchell.'

'Who?' Sophie tried to sound uninterested.

'Jerome Mitchell; he was big in the '60s and he is still performing.'

'Oh, yes?' said Sophie, still trying to sound unimpressed.

'His personal visitors use the emergency exit, so you may see people in the area.'

'Okay.'

'I'm around most of the day, as we are short of people working at night in the bar, now that the university students have gone back.'

265

'I might be able to come back and do a few hours,' Sophie heard herself saying.

'Well, see how you do this week and then we can talk about it again. You would have to ask the manager.'

'Okay. Thank you.'

They had now reached reception and, having said goodbye, Sophie was pleased to make her way to the car. How did she get herself into these situations?

She looked up at Jerome's window. The curtains were still closed. *He must have had a late night*, she thought.

Back in Anthony's suite, she told Anthony about her day and that it would be quite difficult to access Jerome's suite without being seen.

'That's for you to figure out,' Anthony said, with a twinkle in his eye. 'I have arranged for my sister to take over the art workshop for a month. That will give you more time to concentrate on Jerome.'

Sophie thanked him.

'Oh, yes, I almost forgot. Jerome has sent you a spare key to his suite. He must like you.'

Sophie carefully put it in her bag.

Relieved, Sophie returned home, looking forward to taking on the case. She fed Kenny and packed her suitcase.

Should she give Dave the number of Oliver's Antiques, just in case anything went wrong? After all, no one else would bother if she went missing for a few days. Even Anthony wouldn't be too worried. No one else knew she was working for him. She had this strange uneasy feeling that something was going to go wrong.

She phoned Dave and gave him the number of Oliver's Antiques.

Sophie told him she would phone him every night at 11.30pm, and if she didn't phone him at that time, to ring the number she had given him, informing them. She told him she was going to London for a month to work in a night club which belonged to her old friend Nicky, but she wasn't looking forward to it as it was in the back streets.

Dave asked where it was and said he would go with her, but she said he would be bored and ignored the address bit.

'What about the dance competition?' Dave suddenly remembered.

'Take someone else,' Sophie said, irritated. 'Carole's never got a partner.'

'Yes, but she's—'

'It's better than not dancing.'

After Sophie had finished the phone call, Dave, not used to being told what to do, also made a phone call.

'Oliver's Antiques.'

Slightly worried, he ended the call and made a note to call that number should he not hear from Sophie.

He then phoned Carole. She was more than delighted. He wasn't.

Sophie phoned the hotel.

'I would like to book a room for a week, preferably on the second floor. South facing.'

'Yes, we have one available with a balcony. Are you sure you want one south facing, as it looks over the car park? We have nicer ones available.'

'Yes. Thanks. I shall be out most of the day.'

'Can I have your name? Is that bed and breakfast and evening meal?'

'Jackie Hunter. Just evening meal, as I don't eat breakfast.'

'Thank you, Jackie. Look forward to seeing you.'

Must remember to take cash, Sophie thought. *Different name on bank card.*

It would be relatively easy to walk up the stairs after work to her room, but what about her car? She couldn't leave it at home. She decided to park it in the public car park down the road, just in case she needed it, and hoped no one would see it.

Sophie, disguised with black hair, glasses and hat, left the car in the local car park and walked to the hotel.

She checked in. She didn't recognise the man on reception. The manager walked past her, nodded, his head held high.

Sophie made her way up the stairs, down the long corridor and opened the door to her hotel room, pleased she hadn't been recognised, and placed the "Do Not Disturb" notice on the outside of the door.

Her window did overlook the car park, which meant she could watch people come and go. She hoped it would be lit up at night.

Sophie could have breakfast in the staff room, which they allowed her to do if she got there early, before she started cleaning, and she would have her evening meal in the restaurant. She had brought sandwiches for lunchtime.

At six o'clock Sophie walked down to the restaurant, where she ordered her meal and looked around. She didn't see anyone she knew. Nisha hadn't arrived for her second shift. The manager was sitting at one of the tables, talking to some of the staff. He blankly glanced over occasionally then left, making a phone call.

Sophie enjoyed her meal and then walked slowly around the hotel, surprised that there weren't many staff on duty. She would say she was lost if anyone questioned her. She went up and down the stairs, checking there were no cameras.

She walked up to Jerome's suite and quietly knocked on the door. No answer. She turned the key and entered his room, calling out to him, but everything was still except for a music programme, which was quietly showing on the television which had been left on.

She looked around, noting where everything was. She walked into his bedroom (after all, she had been given permission to look around). She noted the ultra-large bed, over which throws were arranged. The bed took up almost the whole of the wall. She looked at the large assortment of clothes which were hanging in the wardrobe (the wardrobe conveniently having been left open). Again, she looked for cameras, but there were none that she could see. The heavy curtains were still closed.

Having established that he was a bohemian sort of character, she quietly locked his door and made her way down the stairs, breathing a sigh of relief when she reached the corner of the landing without being seen.

In the morning Sophie dressed for work and, making sure she placed the "Do Not Disturb" notice on the door, went down to work, using Jerome's enclosed inside fire escape stairs. She walked around the grounds to reception and through into the staff room and took her coat off, made herself some toast and tea and waited for Sarah and Nisha.

Nisha gave Sophie the keys to the rooms she was to clean and get ready for the next guests who were arriving.

Sophie changed the beds, cleaned and vacuumed, leaving milk and water in the fridge. She was pleased with what she had done and surprised that she was enjoying it.

After a few days Brian, the manager, called her into his office. She was slightly worried by what he was going to say.

Would she like a job behind the bar at night, 8pm until 11pm? And had she had any experience? Sophie explained that she had worked in a bar in Birmingham years ago and she was willing to learn. The bar times suited her as she would still be able to go into the restaurant for dinner.

She started the same night. There was only one other person working in the bar: Jack, a young lad, his head always bent using his phone. He would never be aware of anything else. It was only Brian she had to worry about.

The till was reasonably easy and there weren't too many guests. Sophie knew she was being watched by Brian, who was sitting in the bar drinking orange juice, shuffling papers.

At the end of an interesting day, Sophie made her way to her room, out through reception again, and around the hotel and back through the fire escape door and up the stairs. She walked up the next flight of stairs knowing that there wasn't anyone on duty who would see her. Seeing a light on in Jerome's room she knocked on the door. No one answered.

'It's Sophie,' Sophie said in a hushed voice.

She heard the floorboard creak – the one by the door which had creaked when she had walked over it previously. The faint strip of light which showed under the door went out. Sophie waited; someone must be in there. She tiptoed back down the stairs and quickly went into her room and looked through the window.

She waited eight minutes and then a figure appeared from the direction of Jerome's private stairs. Sophie presumed it was a male figure as it was quite tall, heavy and took large steps. He was dressed in black, carrying some sort of briefcase. He walked through the gates and down the road. Sophie thought that he must have left his car in the same car park as her.

Sophie found herself again outside Jerome's door and quietly let herself in. There was nothing disturbed. She looked around and was just about to leave when she saw that his book of music notes was missing, unless Jerome had taken them with him. She locked the door and went to her room.

Well at least she had one clue; the suspect was a man, and he must have a key.

The morning cleaning went smoothly, and Sophie was enjoying being sociable with her work friends and guests, almost forgetting why she was there.

Brian was sitting in the bar as usual for most of the evening. Sophie chatted to the guests when she served them drinks. When everyone had left to go to their rooms Sophie cleaned the bar and glasses. Brian said goodnight. Just as Sophie was leaving the bar, she noticed that his keys must have fallen out of his pocket and they were left in his armchair. She walked out of the bar and checked that he was in his office. She watched him close the door. She quickly picked up the keys and disappeared into the cloakroom, where, with trembling fingers, she checked the keys on his keyring, one by one, with that of Jerome's, disappointed that none matched. She put Jerome's key back in the hidden zipped pocket in her trousers. What had she done?

Back in the bar she slipped the keys back on Brian's chair and pulled a cushion over, slightly covering them.

Heading towards Brian's office she saw him making his way back to the bar. He nodded to her and she said goodnight as she walked to the main entrance.

Sophie had remembered to phone Dave every night at 11.30pm. She told him she was having a good time in London, serving in the bar and going out during the day. Dave had been practising dancing with Carole, not enjoying it, but it was the competition again the following week, so he woudn't have to dance with her for long. Sophie checked that he had been feeding Kenny. Dave said that the cat was missing her. Sophie thought perhaps she could sneak back to the house but realised someone might see her.

After her evening meal, and forgetting she was in disguise, she knocked on Jerome's door. He opened it, looking puzzled, asking what she wanted. Sophie, suddenly realising that she was in disguise, took her glasses off and removed her black hair.

'Sophie, I didn't realise it was you. How are you doing? Anthony has been in touch, saying that you may have seen the person who stole my notes.'

'Well, someone was in your room and left through the car park, carrying a briefcase.'

'The notes, I just left them there on the table for fun. The original ones are locked away. I would like to see his face when he realises that the music notes he took were just rubbish.'

'What night are you going out again?' Sophie asked.

'Tuesday. I always meet the gang about 10pm and may stop overnight. Depends how much we drink and when we wake up.' Sophie noticed the bottle of rum on the table. They sold it in the bar, and it was the most expensive bottle.

Sophie said she would keep watch on that night.

'Don't forget we'll have to get together and play the guitar,' Jerome promised, his deep brown eyes penetrating her gaze yet again.

Sophie put on her glasses and her black hair and left him.

Every night before 11.30pm Sophie patrolled Jerome's landing.

On Monday night she made the usual patrol.

'Sophie, what are you doing on this floor?' Brian's voice boomed behind her.

Sophie's heart stopped beating for a second.

'Mr. Mitchell has asked for a bottle of rum,' Sophie lied, thankful for her well-prepared answer and the bottle of rum in the large pocket in her jacket.

'I will take it to him,' Brian replied, annoyed.

Sophie handed over the bottle of rum and walked slowly along the landing, stopping for a moment, listening. Brian knocked on the door. Jerome answered.

'I have brought the bottle of rum you wanted, Jerome.'

'Great. Thanks.'

Jerome closed the door.

Sophie breathed a sigh of relief.

What was Brian doing on that floor? Did he have Jerome's spare key hidden somewhere else?

Sophie flew down the stairs, along the corridor, through the entrance doors and sat on the wall outside, trying to get her heart rate to calm down.

Brian strolled past her, long coat flapping, got into his car and drove away, leaving only dozy Ted on night duty.

On Tuesday morning Sophie made her usual route to the staff room and started working. Brian came up to her and told her that under no circumstances should she ever go on Jerome Mitchell's floor. If he phoned down for anything at all she should tell him. Sophie apologised and said no one had told her.

'Who is he?' Sophie asked.

'Google him,' snapped Brian and walked away.

On Tuesday evening she had her evening meal as usual, went back to her room, changed and headed down to the bar. It was quite busy and hectic as some of Jerome's friends were there before they headed to his suite. Then they all left noisily in a stretch limo. Jerome walked past her and smiled slightly.

Sophie was now beginning to feel nervous. She had to make sure that Brian had gone before she could even think of going to Jerome's suite. She was sure Brian could sense her eyes looking at him for any signs of leaving. He seemed to be looking at her more than usual.

Luckily someone had spilt a pint of beer in the bar and she took her time cleaning up.

At 11.30pm Brian came out of his office, talking on his phone; he broke off his conversation.

'See you tomorrow,' he nodded and left the hotel. Sophie, relieved, watched him drive out of the hotel car park.

She looked at her watch; she would phone Dave in a minute when she had put the mini screwdriver, spare phone, and a snack bar in the secret pocket in her trousers, just in case she needed them, together with Jerome's key.

Sophie quietly left her room and made her way up the stairs to Jerome's suite. She hurried. as there was nowhere to hide along the landing. She quickly opened and locked his door, and she looked for a safe hiding space. She could easily hide under one of his throws, but she wouldn't be able to see anything. That's if anyone came tonight. She decided to hide behind the thick curtains in his bedroom. They were always closed untidily and the chairs placed in front of them with throws scattered were also untidy, so she wouldn't be seen there.

She had just made that decision when she heard a key being put in the lock and the door opening. She quickly hid behind the curtains, trying to get her heart to beat quieter. She heard someone call, 'Jerome?' in a low gruff voice. Whoever it was, was now searching the lounge. Sophie heard cupboards being opened and closed. There was silence and then footsteps came into the bedroom. Sophie hoped that the mustiness of the curtains wouldn't suffocate her. There was the sound of drawers being opened and closed again. The man coughed, sneezed and she could hear him breathing quite heavily nearby, and it was now frightening her. The tall figure opened the curtains slightly, looked through the window and then closed them again. She caught sight of the sleeve of his jacket; leather with silver zip rings. He left the bedroom and moved into the lounge again. She heard him pour a drink and sit down heavily on the sofa, coughing again.

Sophie quietly slid from behind the curtains and walked

carefully to the door of the lounge, hoping the ancient uneven floorboards wouldn't give her away.

'Come in,' the gruff voice invited.

Sophie froze for a moment and then walked shakily into the lounge.

'Sit down. Have a drink.'

Sophie sat down.

He poured her a rum, which she drank quickly.

'My name is Jake Mitchell. I'm Jerome's brother.'

Sophie relaxed a little. She could see the resemblance. Beard, brown eyes, moustache, same laidback vibe.

'Why are you here?' Sophie asked, now feeling more composed.

'Why are you here?' he quizzed playfully.

'How did you get in?

'With a key. How did you?'

Sophie ignored him.

'Where from?'

'I had it cut while Jerome was still out stone cold in the morning after the party we had been to one night.

'We had all met up at the Bridge Hotel in Brighton. He was bragging about how much money he'd made, what great songs he had written and was still writing, living in a luxurious hotel. And then I suddenly realised it was me who had written most of his songs, and had played in his band, and I haven't received a penny. I didn't mind in those days as I was making a load of money for myself, but now I am almost broke, and he is living the life of a king on my money.'

Sophie listened.

'So, it is you who has been stealing from him?'

'Not stealing; it was my guitar in the first place, and I only took what was mine. I was looking for the lyrics that I had written that were never used, so I could use them to make some money. The music I took the other night was nursery rhymes – he knew someone would take those. I bet he had a right laugh.'

'Have you spoken to him about all this?'

'No. He wouldn't give me back the things that are mine. He has moved on now. It was Tommy, one of the other members of the band, who invited me to the party. Jerome hardly spoke to me.'

'You realise I will have to tell him about you, as he has asked me to investigate who was stealing from Jake?'

Sophie almost felt sorry for him.

'If you must. I have too much on him for him to press charges against me.'

Sophie wondered what to do.

'Give me your phone number and I will be in touch,' she said.

Jake wrote his number down on a piece of paper which was on Jerome's desk.

Jake got up casually from his chair, and was about to leave empty-handed when Sophie said, 'How did you know I was behind the curtains?'

'Don't wear perfume, girl, if you want to play hide and seek on your next case. I am allergic to perfume. And I know Jerome don't wear it.'

He laughed, shook her hand, gave her the key to Jerome's suite and left.

Sophie, realising she hadn't phoned Dave yet, made a phone call from her spare phone just in time, before he called Oliver's Antiques.

Dave told her he had come second in the competition but didn't enjoy dancing without her. Carole had tried to persuade him to take her out to celebrate.

'You should have gone,' Sophie teased.

'But she's a cougar.'

The next day Sophie went to see Anthony, after informing the hotel that she was leaving the job; she also cancelled her room.

As usual Anthony was waiting for her in his suite, and she told him everything that had happened.

Anthony advised her to go and see Jerome and explain everything. She had to give the keys back anyway.

Looking forward to legitimately being able to go up to Jerome's suite without being stopped, she walked through the hotel and up the stairs to see Jerome. She knocked on the door.

'It's open.'

She walked in to find Jerome and Jake, laughing and drinking rum together. She looked at them questioningly.

'We're brothers, after all,' Jerome explained.

Sophie didn't know what Jake held over him, but it had worked.

She told them she was there to hand the keys back.

'Thanks, Sophie, you have done a good job. Don't forget, anytime you want to play guitar…'

She smiled and placed the keys on the table.

Job done.

She left them arguing over who had owned the most expensive car.

Anthony was pleased with her work and offered her a higher than usual payment.

Sophie thought that that was definitely her favourite case.

Sixty

Sophie settled back into a routine with her dancing and took over from Anthony's sister at the art workroom. She thought it felt refreshing not having too much to think about and Dave was relieved that he was no longer dancing with Carole.

Early the following spring, Sophie found herself on the beach, walking past Seaweed Cottage, and decided to call in as she wasn't at work until the afternoon. What a difference Wendy had made since Sophie's last visit there at Christmas. She hadn't modernised it on the outside, just repaired it in a sympathetic way, but the garden had been made into a cottage garden. It was then Sophie noticed the small "Sold" notice in the front window.

Sophie was shocked. Why was she leaving? Sophie walked into the garden and knocked on the door. Jonathan answered.

'Hello, Sophie, Wendy's shopping.'

'I can't believe she is leaving,' Sophie said, almost in tears.

'I have got a job in Bournemouth and we have bought a cottage in the New Forest. We tried to get in touch with you, but we've changed phones and didn't have your phone number, so we called your agency and they said they would get in touch with you, as they couldn't give out private numbers. We were really surprised you hadn't been in touch.'

'Who's bought it?' Sophie asked, realising she was now getting too involved.

'Oh, a man was walking past, came to look at it and offered to buy it straight away. We didn't have to advertise it.'

Sophie asked Jonathan when they were leaving Timberry.

'Hopefully before summer.'

He invited her in to wait for Wendy, but she declined, saying she had to get back to work.

'Thank you for everything, Sophie.'

'I am really pleased it has turned out well for you and Wendy. Tell her I hope to see her before you leave.'

She completely forgot to ask Jonathan for his new phone number.

Sophie left and walked heavily home, not noticing the Aston Martin sweep into the drive of Seaweed Cottage.

Totally annoyed with Anthony for not telling her about the phone call from Wendy, Sophie made excuses not to see him and declined his calls. She couldn't face him at the moment.

Dave phoned her, inviting her out for a meal in the evening and Sophie was pleased to go, as she had become bored with her own miserable company.

They went for a drive along the lanes and ended up at a small restaurant on the cliffs. The air was fresh and as Sophie breathed it in, she was beginning to feel a lot less stressed and irritated.

Dave asked her if she was okay, and she told him about the cottage and how annoyed she was. He listened and reminded her that she couldn't afford it. He didn't know that now she could, as she was earning very good money.

Bored with the subject, he asked Sophie if she wanted to go to the Saturday dance, which was now proving very popular, and she agreed to go with him. It would be good to go out and meet the others.

Saturday turned out to be a good night and it was great to be out with friends again. Dave and Sophie danced together most of the night, as though they were a couple.

Sophie noticed Anthony sitting at the back of the room with his sister. He never spoke to her or looked at her. Sophie found herself wondering why he never danced with his sister in his ballroom.

When Dave dropped her home that night, she was pleased that he had suggested going out. Were she and Dave becoming closer again?

Anthony phoned her the next day, saying Wendy wanted Sophie to check that they had taken everything from the cottage; they had had to leave much earlier than intended and had left in a hurry. She had left a key with him.

This meant that Sophie had to see Anthony. He was waiting for her with her usual coffee. She immediately found her annoyance evaporate.

'Are you avoiding me?' His normally twinkling grey eyes showed concern.

'No. I have been busy,' Sophie said quickly, not looking at him.

'Here's the key to the cottage. Jonathan had to leave for his new job months earlier than he had anticipated. If you would just check around this morning, then I will be able to return the key to them. Wendy has left you her number so you can keep in touch.'

Sophie took the key reluctantly and put Wendy's number in her phone.

'I have a new case for you next week. I'll speak to you when you return the key. Don't forget our usual dancing session.'

Sophie said that, if she had time, she would see him later that evening.

Anthony opened the lift door for her and shook his head as he watched her leave through the complex entrance.

She walked slowly down the promenade, along the sand and into Seaweed Cottage drive. She sat outside for a while in the quiet back garden, looking at the plants and flowers that Wendy had patiently planted. Sophie hoped the next person who bought the cottage would love it as much as she did. The broken wall fixed by Jonathan and a small barbecue stood in the corner. How could Wendy leave after all the work she had done? Sophie stood up and let herself into the cottage. She looked around the kitchen and then walked into the lounge.

'Dave! What are you doing here?'

Dave was sitting on one of three packing boxes by the window. On another box in front of him was a box of her favourite chocolates, a bottle of red wine and two large wine glasses.

Sophie was totally confused.

'I am thinking of buying the cottage.'

'What? Why?'

'When Wendy knew she was moving, she tried to get in touch with you to see if you were interested in buying, as she knew you loved it so much. She had lost your number, so she phoned Anthony at the agency and he phoned me. He knew you wouldn't make your mind up easily.'

'You know about Anthony? How did he have your number?'

'Apparently, Anthony had my number from when I phoned Oliver's Antiques, and also from the telephone list at the dancing club. He said you would explain to me if you wanted to.'

Sophie shuffled uncomfortably. She should have known that Dave wouldn't do as he was told, and that Anthony would make a note of Dave's number. But then that was his detective training.

She told Dave that she was working for Anthony at the agency. She said she was also working at the complex as an art teacher. That part he knew. She owed it to Anthony not to tell anyone about his dancing arrangement with her. Sophie left that bit out.

Dave listened, totally transfixed by her secret life. Did she see a fleeting expression of admiration on his face?

'Well, you kept that quiet.'

'Why are you thinking about buying the cottage?' Sophie asked again.

'Because Anthony told me how much you liked it and I agreed with him that you were always talking about it.'

Sophie then realised that he did listen to what she said.

'How can you afford it?'

Sophie had now eaten four chocolates and Dave was handing her another glass of wine.

'Well, Anthony bought it straight away as there was someone else who wanted it. He knew it wasn't fair to keep Wendy waiting and he knew that you wouldn't make up your mind quickly. Should you decide you want to buy, he will sell it to us.'

'Us?'

'Well, we have been getting on well, dancing together, haven't we, and we don't argue so much now. We don't have to get married again.'

'Married?'

Sophie's mind was reeling.

Buy Seaweed Cottage?

Leave her home?

Would Kenny like it?

What about the agency and dancing with Anthony?

What about buying an art shop again? Could she sell her art in the front garden of the cottage and sell refreshments?

Live with Dave?

Dave was looking at her.

Sophie stared out of the window towards the sea.

A familiar grey Aston Martin sped along the narrow road in front of the cottage.

Sophie took another sip of wine.

Dave would have to wait a long time for an answer.